THE WAY IT USED TO BE

The gravel road was dusty, and as they came out from under the dappled shade of trees on either side, they came into golden sunlight and paused at the sight of a fenced pasture.

"I don't remember this . . ." she whispered.

"Well, you didn't live in this exact area," he said.

"I mean, any of this," she said, looking up at him. "I don't remember you! Apparently, I used to kiss you on back roads and agreed to marry you during a buggy ride. Those are the kinds of memories that are supposed to matter!"

"They meant something to me," he said, and there was a thickness to his tone that betrayed deeper feeling.

"I'm sorry," she added. "I'm not saying that those things didn't matter, I'm just saying I don't remember them, and I'm upset about that. I . . . I *want* to remember it."

She wanted to remember feeling something, loving someone, being excited, even. She couldn't remember anything but confusion and mild fear since she'd woken up in that hospital. And here was a man Elizabeth and Bethany assured her she'd been in love with, and she couldn't remember any of it. Frustrated tears prickled at her eyes, and she blinked them back.

"You used to hold my hand," he said quietly. "When we walked together."

He held his hand out, palm upward, and she looked down at it. His hand was calloused from work, and some of the lines in his hands were stained black.

"Maybe it will help jog a few memories," he said softly.

She hesitated a moment,
his . . .

Books by Patricia Johns

THE BISHOP'S DAUGHTER

THURSDAY'S BRIDE

JEB'S WIFE

THE PREACHER'S SON

THE PREACHER'S DAUGHTER

LOVING LOVINA

Published by Kensington Publishing Corp.

Loving Lovina

The Infamous Amish

PATRICIA JOHNS

ZEBRA BOOKS
KENSINGTON PUBLISHING CORP.
www.kensingtonbooks.com

ZEBRA BOOKS are published by

Kensington Publishing Corp.
119 West 40th Street
New York, NY 10018

All Kensington titles, imprints, and distributed lines are available at special quantity discounts for bulk purchases for sales promotion, premiums, fund-raising, educational, or institutional use.

Special book excerpts or customized printings can also be created to fit specific needs. For details, write or phone the office of the Kensington Sales Manager: Attn.: Sales Department. Kensington Publishing Corp., 119 West 40th Street, New York, NY 10018. Phone: 1-800-221-2647.

Zebra and the Z logo Reg. U.S. Pat. & TM Off.
BOUQUET Reg. U.S. Pat. & TM Off.

First Printing: April 2022
ISBN-13: 978-1-4201-5238-8
ISBN-13: 978-1-4201-5241-8 (eBook)

10 9 8 7 6 5 4 3 2 1

Printed in the United States of America

Prologue

The hospital bed was rumpled, and she got out of it to pull the sheets smooth again. She hated rumpled sheets. They irritated her; somehow they always came loose. She wore a hospital gown and bathrobe—there wasn't anything else to wear. Her clothes had been torn in the accident, and they'd been thrown out. Someone had gotten her a pair of socks, which helped keep her feet warm.

A TV hung suspended from a metal arm across the room, and a gardening channel was playing—a woman with a bright smile was pulling plants out of little plastic pots and putting them into the ground, lovingly patting them down. It was soothing.

"How are you today?" A nurse came into the room holding a clipboard.

"I'm fine," she replied. "How are you?"

The nurse didn't answer that, but she did hold out a little plastic cup of pudding with a spoon.

"I brought you something," the nurse said. "I thought you could use a treat."

She smiled and accepted the gift, then sat on the edge of the bed, peeling back the cover and taking a bite. It was tapioca. She liked this flavor. She also liked this nurse. She was always kind, and tended to bring little treats for her when she checked in to see how she was doing. Once she brought some magazines, and another time she brought her a donut. Sometimes she'd sit and chat with her about whatever was on TV, or about some of the crazy styles in the magazines. It felt good to laugh.

"Do you know what year it is?" the nurse asked.

"No." She licked the spoon clean, enjoying the tapioca pudding.

"Do you know who the president is?"

"Sorry." She took another bite and looked up, waiting on the familiar list of questions. They'd done this every day for the last week.

"Where do you live?"

She shook her head.

"What's your name?"

"Still no idea," she replied. "Trust me, I'd be very glad to have a name at this point. It's rather tiring not having one."

"If someone were to shout to get your attention, what would they say? Someone shouts, you turn, and they say—"

"Hey?" she said with a shrug. "I still don't remember."

The nurse jotted something down on the chart. "Okay, here's a different one for a change—what's your favorite food?"

And for the first time that week, she had an answer. It jumped into her brain with absolute clarity. She could see it—she could almost smell it.

"Cannelloni," she replied.

The nurse blinked. "You remember that?"

"I do . . ." She felt a flood of relief. "I do remember it! With the big tube noodles stuffed with this cheese and spinach, and the tomato sauce on top—it's amazing! I love it!"

A smile spread over the nurse's face. "My Italian grandmother made the most amazing cannelloni!"

The nurse started writing in the chart again, her pen moving excitedly across the page.

"What's wrong with me?" she asked. "Why can't I remember the things that matter?"

"The accident jarred your brain," the nurse said. "That's in layman's terms. And there are some bruises in there. As they heal, your memory will come back."

"Do you promise?" she asked.

"I'm not allowed to promise anything," the nurse said with an apologetic smile. "That's one of the things with working in medicine. But I can tell you that ninety-seven percent of the time with cases just like yours, that is how it works."

"Those are good odds," she murmured.

"Now, I need to ask you something, and I want you to just relax and say the first thing that comes to mind," the nurse said.

"Okay?"

"Is there any chance that you're Amish?"

She scraped the last of the pudding cup and licked off the spoon.

"Why?" she asked.

"Because there is an Amish man out there who saw your picture at the police station, and he claims to be your father."

Her heart hammered hard in her throat and the little

plastic container slipped from her fingers and bounced across the linoleum floor.

"What did he say my name was?"

"Lovina Yoder." The nurse looked at her hopefully. "Does any of that feel familiar?"

Chapter One

Lovina lay in her bed in the little Amish house, a crisp white sheet and a light blue and white quilt on top of her. A ray of sunlight slanted across her legs, and she poked a foot out from under the covers to feel the warmth against her skin. From down the hallway she could hear the clank of a pot against the woodstove.

Waking up in this one-story house was so different from waking up in the hospital. A week ago, everything hurt and she was frightened and confused. There were always different nurses and clinical doctors clicking their pens and pursing their lips as they asked her the same questions over and over again.

Do you know what year this is?

Who's the president right now?

Where do you live?

The hospital staff had been considerate and did their best to make her feel comfortable. She'd enjoyed the company of the one nurse who always brought her treats, too. But when this Amish family had arrived at the hospital, she'd learned another thing about herself: she could speak and understand Pennsylvania Dutch. And they seemed to have convinced the hospital staff that she belonged with them, because they'd dressed her in a simple Amish dress, complete with *kapp* and apron, and she'd gone home with these strangers in a bouncing, rocking buggy, listening to them go on about how happy they were to find her and how worried they'd been.

Apparently, she was loved. And Amish.

But she couldn't verify any of that from memory.

The bedroom was getting hot, and Lovina pushed back the light covers and sat up. Her hair was tangled, and she looked around the room to find a comb waiting for her on the dresser. Elizabeth—the woman who said she was her sister—had shared this room with her last night, but no one had woken her up this morning. She combed her golden hair, and when she ambled over to the closet, she found several dresses hanging there in an array of colors—blue, pink, purple, teal . . . A couple of them were smaller—her size—so they were her clothes, presumably. Lovina chose one and looked at the dress and the box of pins on the dresser.

"Do I know how to do this?" she murmured.

She took off the cotton nightgown and slipped into the dress. The pinholes at the waist were at the right place, and her fingers seemed to know the work of pinning the fabric in place. From somewhere else in the house she heard a baby's wail and a woman's soothing tones.

The bedroom door opened and Elizabeth poked her head in.

"You're up!" she said with a smile. "How does it feel to be back in your own clothes?"

"So this is my dress?" Lovina asked. "It seemed like it would fit."

"*Yah*, it's your dress," Elizabeth replied. "Did you sleep well?"

"I think so."

"Has anything come back to you?" Elizabeth's expression froze as she spoke.

"No, sorry."

"Don't apologize," she replied. "That's not your fault. But you must be hungry, and we've been keeping some breakfast warm for you. It's oatmeal with fresh blueberries—your favorite."

Was it her favorite breakfast? Somehow, she had a memory of something different—an English muffin with sausage, scrambled egg, and a slice of processed cheese inside. Did that sound right? She couldn't think of a name for it—but she knew the scent. In her mind there was a little packet of catsup that went with it . . . a brown napkin on the side. And it was on a plastic tray. Fast food?

"Are you okay?" Elizabeth asked.

"I'm fine." Lovina forced a smile. "I am hungry, though."

"Good—an appetite is an excellent sign!" Elizabeth replied. "Come on, then—"

An excellent sign of what? Everyone had been congratulating her every time she ate, as if it were a lifesaving occupation, but she had a feeling these people were just choosing optimism. Because she still couldn't remember anything that would identify who she was or where she belonged. All she'd done so far was wake up and get dressed, but she did feel better for being in some clothes.

"Are you going to put your hair up?" Elizabeth asked.

She looked at herself in the mirror—her blonde hair

was hanging loose around her shoulders. She liked it down. It was pretty. It was also shorter than Elizabeth's hair. She'd noticed that last night when Elizabeth had let her hair down to comb it. Elizabeth's hair went all the way down to her waist, while Lovina's was just past her shoulders.

"Do I do that?" Lovina asked.

"*Yah*, we all put our hair up," Elizabeth said, giving her a funny look. "It's modesty. Our hair is for our husbands."

"Oh . . ." Lovina ran her fingers through her hair and then gathered it at the back of her head.

"Let me help you," Elizabeth said, and she picked up the comb and took over in twisting her hair up into a small bun at the back of her head. "It'll be easier when it grows longer."

"But why isn't my hair longer?" Lovina asked.

"You cut it." Elizabeth passed her a fresh *kapp*, and Lovina put it on.

That was a simple enough explanation, but she sensed some reticence in her sister's reply. She was holding something back. Lovina looked at their reflection, their faces side by side in the mirror. She couldn't see a family resemblance. Elizabeth was tall and lithe. Lovina was short and slim. Elizabeth had rich brown hair in contrast with Lovina's pale, fair tresses.

"Come on," Elizabeth said. "Let's get some breakfast into you."

Lovina followed Elizabeth down the hallway toward the kitchen. She could smell the aroma of cooking—the yeasty scent of rising bread and the lingering smell of oatmeal and eggs.

"You're up!" Bethany said as they came into the room. She had a baby on her hip, and she smiled at the sight of Lovina. "You look like you had a good sleep. Did it help?"

"Not really," Lovina replied. Because she knew what Bethany was asking—it was the same thing Elizabeth had asked.

Bethany's gaze flickered toward Elizabeth, and they exchanged a look.

"Well, have a seat," Bethany said. "And would you hold Mo?"

Without waiting for any reply, Bethany tipped the baby into Lovina's arms, and she looked down at the surprised face of the tiny boy. He blinked at her, and she couldn't help but smile.

"You're cute, aren't you?" Lovina said, and she adjusted him in her arms, then she looked over to Bethany, who had returned to the stove to dish up oatmeal. "What's 'Mo' short for?"

"Moses," she replied. "Isaiah and I thought he needed a strong name . . . he'll need it."

Bethany turned away again, and Lovina looked down at the baby in her arms. He was very sweet, but she didn't feel any tickle of recognition when she looked at him.

"Why?" Lovina asked.

"Why what?" Bethany asked.

"Why does he need a strong name?" Lovina asked.

Bethany regarded her for a moment, then pink tinged her cheeks.

"We don't talk about that," Elizabeth said quickly.

"Oh—" Lovina let out a breath. Would she remember all of this later?

"It's because Isaiah isn't Mo's *daet*," Bethany said

after a beat of silence, and she cast Elizabeth a helpless look. "Lizzie, she's family." Then she turned back to Lovina, her cheeks blooming pinker. "I was pregnant already when your brother and I started courting. I had been engaged before, and my fiancé left our faith. He's . . . out there somewhere." She gestured vaguely toward the window. "Mo's father's name is Micah. He comes to visit from time to time, so things will be complicated for Mo as he grows up. Isaiah will be the *daet* who raises him, but everyone will know the truth."

"I'm sorry . . ." Lovina felt her face heat. "That's . . . awful."

"It's life," Bethany replied, meeting her gaze evenly.

"It shows what grief comes of leaving the faith," Elizabeth added. "Our family has learned that lesson the hard way."

"And it also shows you what kind of man your brother is," Bethany said quickly, and she shot Elizabeth a warning look. "I thank Gott every day that he's my husband."

Lovina dropped her gaze to the baby in her arms, uncomfortable. Why did she feel like she was being preached at here? Mo shoved a fist into his mouth and blinked up at her with wide brown eyes, and Lovina touched his nose with the tip of her finger. He smiled.

"Speaking of husbands," Bethany said, changing the subject brightly, "Elizabeth, we should work on your wedding quilt today. We'll have to sew fast to get it done in time, but if we get enough women working on it, I think we'll manage it!"

Bethany brought a bowl of oatmeal to the table. A dish of fresh blueberries sat within reach, and a pitcher of thick, creamy milk was next to it.

"Oh, and sugar—" Elizabeth brought a bowl of brown sugar to the table and then held out her hands for the baby. "Come here, *bobily*."

Lovina handed the baby over and sat down at the sturdy wooden table. She licked her lips and glanced up hesitantly.

"I can't believe it's happening!" Elizabeth said, sliding into another chair at the table. "I'm marrying him!"

"And you'll be happy," Bethany said. "That man loves you."

Lovina watched the two women silently.

"Why don't you say grace, Lovina?" Bethany suggested.

Lovina was about to refuse. She hadn't said any prayers over food since she woke up in the hospital, but the casual way the request was made seemed to loosen some words that floated to the surface inside of her. She bowed her head, her eyes open.

"For this food You have blessed us with, we thank you, Lord," Lovina said.

"Amen," Elizabeth said, and her eyes misted. "Oh, Lovina, I've missed you."

The way Elizabeth said it, it was like she'd been gone for years. It had only been a week or so . . . hadn't it?

"How long was I gone?" Lovina reached for the blueberries and sugar, adding them to the top of her oatmeal.

"Oh . . . it felt like forever," Elizabeth said. "That's all."

They'd missed her, and there was a certain comfort in knowing that while she didn't remember them, they not only remembered her but they'd missed her.

"If I remember how to pray, it must be coming back," Lovina said.

"*Yah*, I would say so," Elizabeth agreed, and she smiled brightly. "Gott is answering our prayers."

Once Lovina started eating, her appetite came back in full force. The blueberries mingled with creamy milk, and Lovina accepted a fresh piece of buttered toast that Bethany brought to the table.

Elizabeth and Bethany both sat down.

"You should help us with the quilt," Bethany said, and she reached for her baby boy, pulling him into her arms and kissing his plump cheek. "They say that sometimes familiar activities can help to bring back memories. And we'll need all the hands we can get to finish it on time."

"Do I know how?" Lovina asked, swallowing.

"We all know how," Elizabeth replied with a rueful smile. "And this one is special. It will be on the bed I share with Solomon after we're married. It wouldn't feel right to start my home without a wedding quilt."

Lovina smiled faintly. "Congratulations. I should have said that before."

"Thank you."

"It sounds like you'll be very happy," Lovina said. Elizabeth looked happy, at least. She had a dewy, glowing look about her.

"Do you remember being engaged?" Elizabeth asked, leaning forward.

Lovina slowed in her chewing, her pulse speeding up. She met her sister's gaze.

"Me?" she asked past the food in her mouth.

"Do you?" Elizabeth pressed.

Lovina searched inside of herself for a memory of a man. She shook her head.

"You've got a man who loves you," Elizabeth said. "And you were planning on marrying him."

Lovina swallowed with difficulty, and her eyes flicked between the two women. They were both looking at her with such hope in their eyes that she felt a wave of guilt at disappointing them, but she had to be honest.

"I don't remember him," she said.

"His name is Johannes Miller, and he's a good man," Elizabeth said. "He's handsome, and sweet, and he just thinks the world of you."

This new information swirled around in Lovina's mind, looking for a place to land, but there was none. It didn't feel right. But then, none of this felt right! It was beautiful and appealing, and she wanted to believe that this was her life, but there was something about all of it that felt like it was being draped on top of her. Like a sheet. Like a lie.

"The man from last night," Lovina said. "The one who came to see me. Is that him?"

He hadn't said much, and his chin had trembled when he took her hand in a brief handshake.

"*Yah*, that's him," Bethany replied. "He's a good man. He farms with his *daet*, and he's very respected in our community. He's honest, hardworking, kind, faithful— he's a *good* man, Lovina."

Good or not, he was a stranger.

"I'm supposed to marry someone I don't remember?" Lovina asked, her voice choked.

"No!" Elizabeth shook her head. "Of course not! In fact, I think we can assume the wedding is off until you do remember. That wouldn't be fair to either of you. Marriage is too serious for that. I just thought you might like to know that you have a life here—a really beautiful life."

"And you'll remember it, eventually," Bethany said

"That's what the doctor said," Elizabeth added.

These two women in their neat Amish clothes both looked a little too hopeful, a little too eager, finishing each other's thoughts and hovering around her as if they were afraid she'd run off.

Were they afraid she'd run off? Lovina glanced toward the door, and she felt a momentary urge to do just that—to stand up and walk out that door, and put all of this safety, security, and sweetness behind her.

But this is my family, she told herself. *These are the people I came from.*

She just didn't remember any of them.

Johannes rinsed the last of the breakfast dishes and put them in a rack to drip-dry. He was used to doing the kitchen work—he and his father traded off on house chores, since their home ordinarily didn't have any women in it.

Except for right now, when their home seemed to be brimming with femininity . . . although it was only temporarily. Sovilla Miller was out in the garden pulling up the tomato and pea plants that had already given their last produce for the year and tossing them into a wheelbarrow. She was from a different branch of Millers, no blood relation to Johannes's family. It was a very popular Amish last name. She wore a pair of gardening gloves, and her work apron was already streaked with dirt. Her

two young daughters, Becca, who was four, and Iris, who
was two, were sitting in the dirt next to their mother,
"helping." The three of them had been here for two
weeks now, and the girls filled the house with laughter
and joking, and Sovilla's cooking and cheerfulness had
brightened up their ordinarily quiet house like a ray of
sunlight.

Sovilla was an attractive woman—slim, with a pretty
face and sympathetic eyes. He liked her eyes, and she
had a low way of talking that was soothing, too. The
community wasn't wrong when they said that she'd make
him an excellent wife. Unfortunately, Johannes had
ruined the possibility of an arranged marriage between
them because he'd been unable to hide his tangled, messy
feelings for Lovina Yoder. That hadn't been smart on his
part.

Johannes glanced over to the table where his nephew,
Daniel, sat munching on some bread and sweetened
peanut butter. At the opposite end of the table, his father,
Bernard, was re-lacing a boot.

"Are you done with that plate?" Johannes asked.

Daniel shoved the last of the bread into his mouth and
brought the plate over to the sink. Johannes dunked it in
the water and washed it off.

Sovilla had been the one to call the engagement off,
and he didn't blame her. What woman wanted to marry
a man who was hopelessly in love with someone else?
Outside the window, Sovilla pushed herself to her feet
and brushed off her hands. She said something to her
older daughter, who ran over to grab a bucket.

Johannes had never been book smart, but he'd

comforted himself with the thought that he was good on his feet. Right now, looking at the ready-made family he was giving up, he had to question even that. Because even after breaking it off, Sovilla was still managing to be a bright spot in their home. She was a good woman, and he wasn't trying to convince her to stay.

Later on this afternoon, Sovilla was going to spend some time with an elderly couple, and when that happened, the Miller farm would be back to being an exclusively male domain. Daniel's *mamm*—Johannes's sister—had said she wanted Daniel to have some male influence. At least around here, male influence was hard to miss.

"So what are we doing today?" Daniel asked.

Bernard paused to measure the laces he was threading into his boot, then continued pushing the laces through the eyes.

"We're going to the south field," Bernard said. "There's some new calves that need to be taken to the barn."

"Oh." Daniel leaned his elbows on the table. "Seems mean to take them away from their mothers so soon."

"That's how you keep a cow producing milk," Bernard replied. "We're a dairy. Milk is what we do."

"Still . . ." Daniel's gaze moved over to Johannes. "Are you going to see your old fiancée, Uncle Johannes?"

"*Yah*, that's the plan," Johannes replied. Keeping secrets from this boy wasn't easy, either. And the whole situation with Lovina and her lost memory had captured the boy's imagination.

"Do you think she'll remember you yet?" Daniel asked.

"Nope. I don't think she will." Johannes wrung out the cloth and hung it to dry. He wasn't getting his hopes up.

The way she'd looked at him—like he was a perfect stranger . . .

"That might not be so bad," Daniel said. "My *mamm* was talking about what happened when your fiancée left last year. I know that she ran off when her *daet* was put in jail, and she wouldn't even send a letter to say she was okay. And then all those other young people from around here who did the same thing—jumped the fence because of the preacher who broke the law. Mamm thinks she's no good. She comes from a bad family, and she jumped the fence, so—"

Johannes shot his nephew a baleful glare, and the thirteen-year-old fell silent.

"Daniel, why don't you go out and get the eggs," Bernard said quickly. "I'll be ready by the time you come back."

Daniel hesitated, his gaze locked on Johannes. Johannes pulled out some bread to make sandwiches for his father and nephew. They'd need lunch out there in the fields today. He'd be back as soon as he could to help them.

"Uncle Johannes, I didn't mean to—" Daniel swallowed. "My *mamm* thought you were over her, is all, and—" He shrugged weakly.

"It's okay," Johannes said. "Go on out and get the eggs."

Daniel grabbed the egg basket and headed for the door. Bernard didn't speak again until they heard Daniel's boots on the last step.

"I keep forgetting he's lived with women only," Johannes said, giving his *daet* a small smile. "I think I scared him."

"He looks up to you," Bernard said.

"They sure talk about me a lot over there," Johannes muttered.

"That's family," Bernard replied. "A couple of weeks ago, your sisters were all talking about your cousin Solomon." Bernard cast Johannes a smile. "The point is, now it's about you and Lovina . . . If you're family, they talk. And now with sending Sovilla away, there will be plenty more people discussing you, I'm sure. Your life is just more interesting than anyone else's right now."

There would be more gossip. His father was right. All Johannes had wanted was a quiet, respectable life. But that was getting harder and harder to achieve.

"Linda wants Daniel to learn from us," his father went on. "We're the men in his family, and he's going to see from us how a man's responsibilities work. That's a heavy duty."

Johannes looked out the window toward the chicken coop. The door was open, and a hen came wandering outside the fenced area.

"He's losing the chickens," Johannes said.

Bernard pulled open the side door and called, "Daniel, mind the birds!"

Johannes smiled as Daniel came running out after the runaway hen, catching it in a flutter of feathers before carrying it back inside. Bernard came back to the table and sat down with his boot once more.

"Lovina really didn't remember anything?" his father asked quietly.

"She shook my hand like I was a complete stranger," Johannes replied. "She didn't know any of us. It was like . . . It was like she was a shell. That wasn't the Lovina I knew."

"Maybe she'll remember more today," his father said.

Maybe. That was the hope, wasn't it? Except that if she remembered, then he'd want answers, and that wasn't what her family wanted from him, either. He was supposed to be the tender, caring fiancé, bringing her back into the Amish fold. He wasn't supposed to have any demands of his own. But Lovina did owe him that much, even if no one else wanted him to ask for the explanations he deserved.

Everyone wanted something from Johannes these days. The Yoders wanted him to help Lovina return to the community for good. The bishop wanted Johannes to marry Sovilla. His sister Linda wanted him to show his nephew how to be a man.

But what about what Johannes needed? It wasn't much, actually—just some respect in the community and a chance to heal. Some explanations from Lovina might help with getting over her at long last. If he was going to be realistic, he had to accept that Lovina had left him once already, and when her memory returned, she'd remember why. He *needed* to move on from Lovina . . .

Later that morning, as Johannes reined in his horses in front of the Yoder stable, his stomach was in knots. He scanned the house, looking for Lovina. Would she be any better today?

The side door opened and Bethany Yoder poked her head out, the baby on her hip.

"Hello, Johannes!" she called.

"*Yah*! Hi!" he called back.

Bethany gave him a smile, then disappeared back into the house. Everyone seemed rather excited to get Johannes and Lovina back into each other's company again, as if it would all be the same. But how could it?

Johannes got down from his buggy, heading around to start unhitching the horses.

Isaiah and Bethany Yoder lived on a small acreage, and Elizabeth was living with her brother and his wife until her marriage to Sol. Johannes glanced toward the fenced field next to the stables. Three quarter horses were already out there, heads down as they grazed. He led his horses by the bridles toward the gate and slapped their sides as they passed him, not really needing any encouragement to go graze. He locked the gate after them and then turned back to look at the house.

Lovina was waiting for him. More precisely, Lovina's family was waiting for him. And he was supposed to pretend to be the seasoned, steady Amish fiancé still—to tamp down all that old hurt and betrayal and give Lovina something beautiful to remember.

Gott, I don't know how long I can do this . . . he prayed.

The side door to the house opened again, and Elizabeth appeared this time and waved. She had that same hopeful look on her face that her sister-in-law had had.

"Come on inside, Johannes!" she called. "We've got coffee!"

As if this were some simple, friendly visit and his arrival was some pleasant surprise.

"*Yah*! Coming!" he called back, and headed in her direction.

The goal was to help Lovina remember her Amish life here in Bountiful, Pennsylvania, and then his obligation would be fulfilled and he'd be free.

Chapter Two

Lovina sat at the kitchen table, reams of fabric piled on one end of it and a quilt pattern cut from newspaper spread out in front of her. She might not remember who she was, but this made sense. She could see how the pattern pieces would work together to create a pattern of flying birds. She could see how the pattern needed to be flipped and the fabric folded before they cut. It made sense in her head . . .

Elizabeth had told her that this was to be her wedding quilt. Lovina should feel something—shouldn't she? She should be happy for Elizabeth. She should feel *some*thing . . .

"Is he coming in?" Bethany asked. She had pulled down a plastic tub of cookies and was arranging them on a tray.

"*Yah*, he's coming," Elizabeth said.

Lovina pinned down another piece of the pattern to the fabric, and she looked up at the women uncertainly. Her fiancé was coming inside in a minute, and none of this made complete sense to her. Something was off . . .

"Do I have a wedding quilt started?" Lovina asked.

"Since I was supposed to marry this Johannes. Did we work on one for me?"

"You were picking your pattern still," Elizabeth said.

"Oh . . ." Was this why quilting patterns seemed so familiar? She looked down at the pattern again, searching for something more deeply familiar than just the shape of quilting pieces and how they related to each other.

The side door opened then, and Johannes came inside. Lovina looked up at him, holding her breath. He nodded at Elizabeth and Bethany, then turned to Lovina, his expression strained.

"Hello," Lovina said.

"You're quilting?"

"Apparently, we do this when someone gets married," Lovina replied.

Johannes froze.

"Me!" Elizabeth said quickly. "It's my wedding! And we're working on a quilt."

"Right." Johannes chuckled, but it was forced.

For a man who supposedly loved her so much, he seemed less than enthusiastic about a wedding. She watched him as he shifted his weight from one foot to the other. He glanced up at a plate of cookies that Bethany put down on the table.

"Oh, those look good," he said, and he took one, biting into it. Then he pulled out a chair and sat down. Lovina pinned down another paper pattern piece, and she smiled hesitantly.

"I remember this much," Lovina said. "I can see how a quilting pattern works. I can remember making stitches and cutting fabric. It's so strange not to remember more important things, but a task like this—"

"It might help bring more back," Johannes said, his voice quiet.

"What will I remember?" she asked, glancing up at him.

Johannes smiled, and his faced pinked slightly. "A home. A family. A way of life."

"What will I remember about us?" she asked.

Johannes cleared his throat, and he glanced toward Elizabeth. Bethany scooped up her son from where he was playing on the kitchen floor.

"Why don't you two take a walk?" Elizabeth said. "Bethany and I will start cutting the fabric. And I'm sure you two have more to talk about than you care to have us overhearing."

Lovina didn't actually care terribly who overheard what. But Johannes seemed to relax.

"*Yah*. That's a good idea," he said. "We could walk up the road a bit. It's a nice morning."

Lovina looked over at Bethany and Elizabeth.

"Go on," Elizabeth said. "Maybe it will spark something."

Lovina pushed back her chair and stood up. Johannes did the same, and for a moment, they just looked at each other.

"Shall we?" Johannes asked, a smile curving up one side of his lips. There was something almost familiar in that lopsided smile, something that felt safe.

"*Yah,*" she said. "Let's go."

Elizabeth accepted the box of pins from Lovina and gave her an encouraging smile as she headed toward the door. Johannes opened it for her, and she stepped outside into the cool morning. She sucked in a deep breath and glanced back as Johannes pulled the door shut after them.

They were alone, and she eyed him, wondering what he would do.

"You seem uncomfortable," she said.

"You don't remember me," he replied. "That's an uncomfortable thing."

"I'm trying to remember," she said.

"It's okay," he replied. "It's not your fault. Besides, Elizabeth and Bethany are looming."

Lovina chuckled. "They are, aren't they? Are they always like this?"

"They're just trying to help," he replied.

They headed down the stairs, and Johannes fell into step beside her as they headed up the drive. He was taller than her, and there was something warm and nice about having him next to her like this. Overhead, a few leaves were starting to turn yellow on the trees—just one here or there, a promise of the autumn that was on the way.

"So what will I remember about us?" she asked, glancing up at him. "You didn't want to answer that inside."

"It's a hard question to answer," he replied. "I might remember one thing as being important, and you might not. I might remember a kiss . . . you might remember something I said to make you laugh."

"Are you funny?" she asked.

"Not really." He smiled wryly. "Maybe you were laughing to make me feel better."

"And you don't think I'd remember a kiss?" she asked. What were his kisses like? She found herself suddenly wondering what it might be like to have his face bend over her as he pulled her close . . .

"I'm just saying I don't know what will come back for you first," Johannes said. "I don't know how this works."

Neither did she. But she knew what she'd seen in that kitchen, and it was near panic at the thought of her working on a wedding quilt.

"You don't want to marry me, do you?" she asked.

Johannes stopped and caught her hand, pulling her back to where he stood. His dark eyes caught hers. "Lovina, you don't remember me." His voice was low and insistent.

"I know."

"And I don't think I can expect a woman who doesn't remember me to joyfully tie herself to me for the rest of her life," he said.

"True." She let out a long breath.

"But that doesn't mean that . . . I don't feel anything." He pressed his lips together. "Okay?"

"Okay . . ." What was he trying to say? Was there more that he was hiding under all the awkward discomfort from earlier?

Johannes started walking again and she caught up to him. When they got to the road, he put his hand on the small of her back, nudging her toward the right. He dropped his hand as quickly as he'd touched her, but the place tingled all the same. He took the spot closest to the road, and she looked up at him cautiously.

"How did we meet?" she asked.

"We've known each other since we were *kinner*," he said. "There was no meeting that I can recall."

So they'd been childhood friends. That was a rather sweet thought.

"Then how did we become . . . involved?" she asked.

"I took you home from singing," he said.

"Oh." That didn't mean much to her. "What does that mean?"

"That's how we do it here," he said. "That's how we start courting. A boy takes a girl home from singing, and they get a chance to talk in the buggy ride home."

"And why me?" she asked. "Why not some other girl? There must have been others."

"I'd developed quite a crush over the years," he said. "You were so pretty, and so full of life and humor. Plus, you laughed at my bad jokes."

Lovina smiled at that. "It all sounds very proper."

"Not all of it," he said, and there was something in his gravelly tone that made her breath catch.

"No?" she asked.

"Do you want to know this?" he asked. "Or will it scandalize you?"

"If I did it, I should know," she said.

"Sometimes, we'd sneak off together on Service Sunday," he said, "and we'd walk the back roads, and I'd kiss you."

Were those the kisses he'd hinted at earlier? The thought of him tugging her close, his lips over hers—she felt her cheeks heat.

"More kisses," she murmured.

"Of course, more kisses," he replied matter-of-factly. "We were in love, Lovina! And you kissed me as often as I kissed you."

Her pulse sped up at that, and she allowed herself to sneak a peek at him from the corner of her eye. He didn't seem ruffled by the topic.

"When did we decide to get married?" she asked. That might be safer territory.

"I'd been thinking about proposing for a while," he said. "I was ready to get married, and I was in love with you . . . I took you on a buggy ride after singing one Saturday night, and it came up rather naturally. We were talking about what we wanted, and I said I had to save a bit more if I was going to be able to buy a new buggy and all that to be ready to propose to you, and you said—"

Johannes looked over at her, and she stared back at him, her breath bated.

"What did I say?" she whispered.

"You said you didn't need a new buggy. You just wanted me." Johannes laughed softly, shaking his head. "And I couldn't believe I could be that fortunate to find a girl who thought that living with me was better than waiting for all the proper comforts first—being properly financially ready."

"That seems very forward," Lovina said. "Doesn't it?"

"You *are* very forward," Johannes replied, and he turned front again, his pace slow and easy.

She was the kind of woman who told a man what she wanted. That was good to know. It didn't seem like that would be the norm in a place like this.

"And that's it?" she asked. "That's the story of us?"

He paused for just a hair's breadth longer than necessary, then he said, "More or less."

The gravel road was dusty, and as they came out from under the dappled shade of trees on either side, they came into golden sunlight and paused at the sight of a fenced pasture, spotted with grazing cattle. Some tiny birds balanced on the barbed wire, chattering at each other.

"I don't remember this . . ." she whispered.

"Well, you didn't live in this exact area," he said. "Your brother and sister-in-law moved into that house recently, so—"

"I mean, any of this," she said, looking up at him. "I don't remember you!"

"It's okay." He shook his head. "I'm not offended."

"So why can't I remember you?" she demanded. "Apparently, I used to kiss you on back roads and agreed to marry you during a buggy ride. Those are the kinds of memories that are supposed to matter!"

She hadn't meant her words to be sharp, but Johannes winced all the same.

"They meant something to me," he said, and there was a thickness to his tone that betrayed deeper feeling.

"I'm sorry," she added. "I'm not saying that those things didn't matter, I'm just saying I don't remember them, and I'm upset about that. I . . . I *want* to remember it."

She wanted to remember feeling something, loving someone, being excited, even. She couldn't remember anything but confusion and mild fear since she'd woken up in that hospital. And here was a man Elizabeth and Bethany assured her she'd been in love with, and she couldn't remember any of it. Frustrated tears prickled at her eyes, and she blinked them back. She didn't want to cry—that was no help. She just wanted to punch through this fog in her head.

"You used to hold my hand," he said quietly.

"What?" she asked feebly.

"When we walked together," he said. "And when no

one else would catch us, of course. But we used to walk the back roads so that you could hold my hand."

He held his hand out, palm upward, and she looked down at it. His hand was calloused from work, and some of the lines in his hands were stained black.

"Maybe it will help jog a few memories," he said softly.

She hesitated a moment, and then put her hand in his. His strong fingers closed down around hers and he swallowed hard.

"And then we'd walk," he said, his voice gruff.

They started walking again, and she adjusted her hand in his grip. He ran his thumb gently over the back of her hand, and he smiled down at her.

"That's better," he said.

Did this help her to remember? Not really, but it did feel nice. Holding his hand this way kept her closer against his muscular body, and the musky scent of him filled her.

Once upon a time, a time locked away in her own head where she couldn't reach it, she'd belonged with this man, and it seemed like it would have been wonderful.

As they walked down the road together, her hand clasped in his, Johannes knew he was making a mistake. He wasn't supposed to let his heart get entangled again. She was going to remember why she left him, one of these days, and she'd also remember just how long she'd been gone. And then what? How was he supposed to explain himself? Except she'd already started sensing the distance between them, and he had the choice between fessing up now and telling her the truth about everything, or holding her hand . . .

And it felt so much better than he'd even imagined to have her hand in his again.

"Maybe you could tell me about you," Lovina said.

There had been no introductions necessary before. They'd known each other for as long as they could remember. Two weeks ago, the community had tried to arrange a marriage for him, and he had been faced with a very nice stranger. Ironically enough, this was the same for Lovina—he was a stranger in her eyes, no matter how well he knew her.

"Okay . . ." He cleared his throat. "My *daet* is a dairy farmer. My *mamm* died when I was a teenager, and my sisters are all married, so now it's just me and Daet at home. We have my nephew staying with us right now."

And Sovilla . . . but he couldn't mention her.

"And what does your family think of me?" she asked.

"They love you," he replied. Or they had . . . before all the drama unfolded.

"That's good, I suppose."

A few were angry now—including his sister Linda, it seemed. Lovina had fallen in their eyes, and this entire year he'd felt the obligation to protect her good name to them. But his *daet* bore Lovina no ill will. In fact, he spoke of her fondly—he'd always liked Lovina.

"You and I went to school together," Johannes added. "I'm older than you, by the way."

"*Yah*?" She looked up at him. "Were we friends in school?"

"Not really," he admitted. "The older boys played sports,

and the younger girls played . . . I don't know . . . girls' games, I suppose."

"What were you like?" she asked.

Why had he brought this up? He felt the old tug of insecurity from those early days.

"I wasn't very good at school," he admitted. "Neither was my cousin Sol. We were both a trial to our poor teacher. I think she was glad to be rid of us." He looked down at her. "You were smart, though."

"*Yah?*"

"Very. You were working a grade ahead, and I remember you reciting your Christmas verses. You did better than I ever could, and I was a few years older."

School had never been easy for Johannes, and he'd been just as relieved as the teacher had been when he was done with it. But he'd also watched the *kinner* like Lovina who seemed to catch on to things so much more quickly than he did, and he wondered what it was like to have reading come easily, because it never had for him. He'd felt stupid in the classroom, and he only ever felt like he was competent out there in the fields where he didn't have to read or spell, where his instincts mattered more than some memorized verse. And Lovina had seen that side of him—the competent side. He'd liked that.

Johannes slowed to a stop. He was opening up more than he'd intended, and that wasn't really part of his plan.

"We should head back," Johannes said.

"*Yah*, they want my help with that quilt," she said.

That quilt . . . She'd been agonizing over her own wedding quilt, trying to pick a pattern, when her *daet* had been arrested. She hadn't mentioned the quilt again after that. Not even once, and he'd started to suspect that she'd lost interest in their wedding.

They turned and headed back down the road. He spotted a buggy on the crest of a hill and he released her hand.

"Am I familiar at all?" he asked quietly, and he glanced down at her.

Did she remember those towering emotions, the windswept kisses, the earnest promises . . . or were those emotions only towering for him?

She shrugged faintly and gave him an apologetic smile. "I'm trying."

"It's okay," he said, forcing some brightness to his tone. "You can get to know me again. I'm not that complicated."

Except this time around, she might not see quite the same things she had before. And even if she did, he knew how it ended. She wasn't the only one who left the Amish life when her daet was put in jail. Other young people left, too. Lovina might fit into his arms just perfectly. She might fill his heart to overflowing. She could love him back with a passion he truly believed in. But she was also capable of walking away and never looking back.

And no fresh start could change that.

That afternoon, as Johannes drove his buggy home again, he watched the passing countryside and listened to the slow clopping of his horses' hooves. In some ways, it was tempting to pretend that the last year had never happened. How many times had he taken Lovina for a walk and driven his buggy home again just like this?

But it was different now. This time, instead of driving

home and dreaming of the day she'd finally be his wife, he was kicking himself for having held her hand.

Because she *would* remember him. She'd eventually remember all of it! She'd know why she left, and why she'd not bothered contacting him even once since her disappearance. How often had he tried to figure it out in the last year—sifting through things she'd said, things she might have thought . . . It had driven him crazy trying to figure it out, but whatever her reasons, she had left. Getting himself emotionally entangled with her all over again was a terrible idea. How was he supposed to heal and move on if he kept holding her hand and pulling her close against him like that?

He had to stop it . . . somehow. But how was he supposed to keep his emotions separate while pretending that the last year hadn't happened? And what guarantee was there that she'd remember a happy Amish life? All of their reasons for this plan seemed rather flimsy right now, but what was he supposed to do, tell Isaiah and Elizabeth that he was out of their plan to help Lovina remember *now*?

A neighbor, Ben Albrecht, passed him in a buggy going the opposite direction, and he nodded at Johannes and gave him a smile.

"Good day, Johannes!" Ben called.

"Hello!" Johannes called back. "Beautiful weather!"

"*Yah*—good for the ripening wheat," Ben replied, and their buggies slid past each other.

Ben was a friend, and he'd gotten married the same fall that Johannes and Lovina had been supposed to get married, too. Ben's wife, Vannetta, was already large in her first pregnancy. Johannes liked to chat with him on

Service Sundays. Ben tended to be diplomatic, and he didn't mention Lovina—something Johannes appreciated more than Ben might know. Other men seemed to fall in love with appropriate women. Johannes wasn't quite so fortunate there. If it were possible to take his heart back, he would.

He reined the horses as they approached his drive, and the horses turned in.

Lord, show me how to handle this, he prayed. *Lovina is vulnerable right now, and I need to be the man who helps her, not takes advantage.*

Johannes had prayed for her to come back. Gott had answered . . . but in His own way. She *was* back, but she wasn't whole.

He reined in his buggy next to the farmhouse. He could see his father and nephew in front of the barn, hoisting bales of hay up into the back of a wagon. Iris and Becca came around the corner from the garden, both dressed in clean new dresses with small kapps pinned to the backs of their heads. Becca waved shyly at him.

"Hi, girls," he said with a smile, and he tied off the reins and jumped down from the buggy. "Where is your *mamm*?"

He spotted a suitcase on the step, and the side door opened to reveal Sovilla. She was dressed in what looked like her Service Sunday best, her apron starched and neat.

"You're back, then?" Sovilla said. "I've cleaned up the kitchen. You've got some carrots and lettuce that we brought in, and I made some muffins to tide you all over."

"Sovilla, you are better than we deserve," he said. "I mean that."

"Oh . . ." She shrugged faintly. "I've just taken care of some of the women's work for you, that's all. Are you wanting to take me to the Kauffmans now?"

"If you're ready," he said.

"*Yah*, we're ready." She beckoned to her daughters. "Come on, girls. Time to go. Thank Johannes for being so kind to us while we were here."

"Thank you, Johannes," Becca said. Iris just stared up at him mutely, her blonde curls falling in front of her eyes. He cleared his throat uncomfortably. They'd been told that he'd be their new *daet*. And now he was sending them away. Did they hate him just a little bit? Or were they relieved that they wouldn't have to deal with him?

"We'll all stay friends, won't we?" Johannes said, forcing a smile. "You're very nice girls, and I'm glad we got to meet."

The girls didn't answer, and he didn't really expect them to. There was no polite way to make this moment more comfortable.

"Let me get your bag," Johannes said, and he grabbed Sovilla's suitcase and hoisted it into the back of the buggy. She went inside and brought out one more bag, and she carried it down the steps before he took that one from her hands, too. The least he could do was carry her bags to her new home.

He opened up the back of the buggy and put her bags inside. There was a bench seat along one side, and when he stepped back, Sovilla lifted Becca up into the back. Johannes followed her lead and scooped up the smaller child and deposited her next to her sister.

"Now, you sit still. I want your dresses clean when we

arrive, you hear me?" she said sternly to her daughters.
"No fooling around. You sit nicely."

Becca nodded, and Iris smiled sweetly. Somehow,
Johannes doubted that the girls would be completely
spotless by the time they arrived. He'd seen enough of
their ability to play and get dirty over the last couple of
weeks.

"Waneta Kauffman seemed very pleasant," Sovilla
said as she hoisted herself up into the buggy. Johannes
followed her and picked up the reins.

"*Yah*, they're a very nice couple," Johannes agreed,
perhaps more enthusiastically than necessary.

Johannes got the buggy turned around, and they headed
back up the drive. People would talk—even though the
wedding hadn't been announced, people in the community
were already aware of the plan to get Johannes safely
married. This arranged marriage had been as much for
him as it had been for Sovilla and her daughters.

"What will you do now?" Johannes asked, glancing
over at the woman by his side. She sat straight in the seat,
and she looked back at her daughters in the back of the
buggy before answering.

"I'm going to get a job," she said.

"I'm sure the bishop could find another man—" he
began.

"No," she interjected, then licked her lips. "I thought I
could marry a man for reasonable, unromantic reasons. I
think we both learned that it's not quite so simple, is it?"

Johannes glanced over at her uncomfortably. "I suppose not."

"So no more of that. I'll get a job."

"And the girls?" he asked. "Who will watch them?"

"I don't know," she replied, her voice low. "I'll figure something out."

Would she find someone to watch her children for her? He'd never seen her away from them yet, and he wondered how much she'd hated the idea of marrying him to make her willing to be separated from her little girls.

"If I see anyone hiring, I'll let you know," he said.

"Thank you." She looked over at him. "And it's okay, Johannes. I came to Bountiful to try to make a match. It didn't work. These things happen, you know. I'm not angry or hurt or offended."

"Okay . . ." He smiled hesitantly. "Because I really am sorry."

"Oh, you'll be much happier with Lovina," she said, but her smile seemed forced.

Johannes reined the horses in at a four-way stop and waited while two cars went ahead of him. Then he flicked the reins and they carried on through.

"I might not end up with Lovina," he said after a few beats of silence.

"After all of this?" she asked. "After loving her and losing her, and having her return—"

"She left for a reason," he said. "And she'll remember it soon enough. She didn't come home to me. She was brought home because of the accident."

"So you're giving up?" she asked.

"I'm—" He shrugged. "I'm just trying to help her while she gets her memory back. That's all."

"Fair enough." She didn't seem to be ruffled by this at

all, and she reached back into the buggy. "Iris, put that down. Brush off your hands—not your apron!" She sighed. "It's dirty now."

"No one will mind," Johannes said.

"I'm trying to look our best." Sovilla straightened her back again. "But sometimes we have to rely on personality."

She shot Johannes a joking smile, and he laughed at her humor.

"Oh—" She reached back again and fiddled for a moment, then pulled out a small tin and handed it to Johannes. He took it with one hand and looked at it.

"What's this?" he asked.

"It's for Daniel," she replied. "He asked if I'd leave him some needles and thread, and I forgot to put it on the table for him."

"What for?" he asked with a frown.

"Mending his clothes?" she replied, then shrugged. "I'm only guessing. Daniel is a sweet boy, and he's pragmatic, too. Maybe he knows that without a woman around, someone has to mend the tears."

Pragmatic, and used to being in a house filled with women. Was his nephew nervous at the thought of just the men fending for themselves?

"I'll give it to him," Johannes said.

"Thank you."

She'd made such a difference in their home these last couple of weeks that Johannes had to admit that he'd miss her, too. A man could get used to some good cooking and a good-natured laugh around the house.

"I hope we can stay friends," Johannes said. "I do mean that."

"There is a certain bond that forms when the community tries to make you marry someone, isn't there?" she asked with a rueful smile.

"I suppose," he replied. "I just think you're a good person, and you're a good cook. You're a great *mamm*, too. You'll find a man who will be glad to call you his."

"I want more than that," she replied softly.

"Oh?"

"I want a man that *I* love." Her smile dropped.

And that had not been Johannes, either. He felt a little tug of sympathy at that. Although loving someone wasn't always the easier path—it certainly wasn't proving to be for him.

He shouldn't have agreed to the arranged marriage to begin with, but the fact that his community—the bishop and elders—had thought of him as a strong, reliable potential husband for Sovilla had tugged at that old yearning for respect. He'd never been a good student, a good reader, or even a brilliant dairy farmer. But he was a lot like his grandfather the deacon, Menno Miller, and he did have moral fiber, and in this situation, that had counted.

And he'd liked that feeling . . .

"And, Johannes?" Sovilla said, interrupting his thoughts. "*Yah?*"

"Be gentle with Daniel. He's a good boy, but he's sensitive."

Yes, Linda had sent Daniel to spend time with men, and it seemed that she'd noticed how sensitive he was, too. He was different from the other boys, and while Johannes and his family all loved this young man dearly, being too different wouldn't give him the good, Amish life they wanted for him. He had to learn to be a man, and what better place to learn that right here?

Chapter Three

That evening, Lovina watched as the sitting room was transformed. All of the kitchen chairs were pulled into the other room and were placed around a large quilting frame. The stove in the kitchen was stoked up and four irons were heating on the stove top. An ironing board had been set up next to it. There were plates of cookies, muffins, pastries, and sliced, fresh peaches on the table. Kerosene lamps hissed softly from their hooks overhead, casting warm, golden light over the room. The neighbor women had come to help complete a wedding quilt in record time.

Of the fourteen women who arrived to help, every single one of them had to have Lovina's situation explained.

She doesn't remember anything . . . Please don't ask her questions. We're trying to give her a rest so that she can heal . . .

And then there were some more explanations murmured, lower so that Lovina couldn't hear, and she watched their expressions change—curiosity, disbelief, worry. What were they saying?

But not all the conversation was about Lovina. She'd overheard a few snippets of discussion about Elizabeth's choice in husband. Apparently, Solomon Lantz had a history of his own that worried everyone just as much as Lovina's situation.

"The Yoder family has gone through so much," one woman had said. "To choose to make things harder by marrying a man like that . . ."

Like what, though? Another couple of women had murmured close enough for Lovina to hear, and they'd been saying that Solomon was dangerous, that he scared them. But then they moved on into the other room and joined their work with the others. As much as they disliked the idea of Elizabeth's upcoming wedding, it didn't seem they were going to say anything about it openly.

Lovina sat at the kitchen table with a quilt block in front of her. The women's gossip moved on. There was news about a girl who'd married a boy in another community and was now pregnant with twins. There was concern over an older man who was refusing to follow doctor's orders about something to do with his diet— she couldn't quite make that one out. There were some teenagers who were spending too much time with *English* friends.

They talked, and they shared, and they commiserated, and they sewed. Lovina had nothing to add, and right now the relative quiet in the kitchen was a relief. A portly woman stood at the stove with the irons, pressing down her quilt block with firm, practiced strokes.

"It's a miracle that Lovina's back . . ." someone said from the other room, the voice carrying.

The conversation in the sitting room had turned toward Lovina again, apparently.

"Gott does work in mysterious ways," someone else agreed. "Maybe this is His way of changing her heart."

Lovina froze. Changing her heart away from what? There was a murmur of remonstrance, and whoever had been speaking stopped. Lovina's gaze flickered toward the middle-aged woman who stood with an iron suspended above the board, and their eyes met. The woman's cheeks, already pink from the heat of the stove, deepened in color.

"We're glad you're back," the woman said quickly.

"Thank you," Lovina said weakly. "Do I know you?"

"I'm Dorcas," she replied. "You used to play with my daughters when you were little."

"Oh!" Lovina cast about in her mind—this was the first time anyone had mentioned her childhood.

"And of course Elizabeth played with my girls, too," Dorcas said. "You and your sister were inseparable. All of you girls would plant your own garden with little stones, and then you'd set your dolls up and you'd feed them salad made of grass."

Lovina smiled. "That sounds . . . sweet."

"You were very sweet. Do you remember any of that?"

Lovina shook her head.

"You haven't remembered your sister yet?" Dorcas asked cautiously.

Lovina shook her head again.

"I think you will soon," Dorcas said gently. "You two were always close."

"I overheard some women saying something about her fiancé?" Lovina said. "What's his story?"

"Solomon Lantz." The woman nodded. "*Yah*, he's got history. He left our community during his Rumspringa and he didn't come back. While he was out there in the world, he got caught up with some bad Englishers. They were really bad—involved in crime and the like. Anyway, he was with them when they were robbing some store, and exactly how involved he was in that robbery is the question, isn't it? Anyway, they claimed he knew everything, and he claimed that they'd just asked him to pick them up at a certain time in a car. He ended up spending a full year in jail."

Lovina's heart pounded to a stop. "Jail?"

"*Yah*. It was serious. He got out, and he came back to Bountiful, looking to start over. That's when he and Elizabeth started getting to know each other again, and . . . well, here we are, working on the wedding quilt."

There they were . . . but no one had told her anything about this. How much were they holding back?

"My sister is marrying an ex-con?" Lovina asked.

"Well, I mean . . . of all people, Elizabeth would understand him. And we've all known Sol since he was a baby. He's got a good heart, but he had a rough time after his *daet* passed away, and his *mamm* really did her best, but Sol was the kind of boy who had to learn his lessons the hard way. Every time."

"And you think he's learned?" Lovina asked.

"He's working hard, he's attending worship services, he's been baptized . . . If Gott could change Saul from the Bible on the road to Damascus, then we have to believe that Gott can change anyone. And whether or not he has been converted into a new creation or not . . . that is Elizabeth's chance to take."

It seemed like a rather risky chance to take to Lovina, and she looked over her shoulder toward the sitting room again.

"And you all . . . support the wedding?" Lovina asked at last. "I mean, you won't warn her off of it?"

"The bishop supports the match," Dorcas said. "And we all pray for the best."

Another woman came into the kitchen and headed for the ironing board, and Dorcas fell silent.

Why would Elizabeth understand Sol best? But more things than just that felt confusing, and right now, she was clinging to that description of her childhood play with the other girls. She could remember something foggy— something to do with grass clippings, but she wasn't pretending they were food, she was forming them into . . . a bird's nest? Was that right?

But she couldn't remember where she was, or how old she was, or even if she'd been alone. That layer of mist over her mind was so frustratingly dense!

"I think I remember playing with grass clippings," Lovina said, and Dorcas and the younger woman both turned toward her. "Except I remember trying to make a bird's nest, I think."

"Do you remember that?" the younger woman asked with a smile. "That was at recess at school when we were *kinner*. We spent weeks making huge bird's nests out of grass clippings. And then it rained and our nests were all soggy and smelly, and we had to stop."

Except Lovina wasn't remembering a big pile of grass. She remembered her hands cupping a small woven nest, and she was holding it out for someone to look at . . . But maybe there were more memories she could rustle out of the slog of her mind.

"Did I play with you?" Lovina asked.

"*Yah*—all us girls were playing," she said.

"What's your name?" Lovina asked.

"Sarah Helmuth."

She couldn't place that name, either. Was she expecting too much from herself? The doctor had said it would take some time . . .

"Were we friends?" Lovina asked hopefully.

She seemed like a nice young woman.

"*Yah* . . ." But there was something in Sarah's tone that sounded off. They likely hadn't been friends—not good ones, at least. But it would be impolite to say so.

But there was a memory returned—it was coming back. Even if she couldn't quite place the memory into a time and place, at least she'd started to remember *something*. And she didn't have the emotional energy right now to tell these women that her sussed-up memory wasn't one connected to them.

Lovina picked up her needle and thread again, and she started stitching the next piece of fabric into the pattern. Her fingers moved deftly on their own, and her stitches were neat and small. She seemed to not only know this work, but to be good at it.

Dorcas and Sarah finished ironing their squares and then headed back to the sitting room. For a couple of minutes, Lovina was alone in the kitchen, stitching. It was a soothing task, and as her fingers moved, she could let her mind rest.

"How's it going, Lovina?"

Lovina looked up to see her sister. Elizabeth came to

the table and picked up a cookie. She looked over Lovina's shoulder.

"You always could stitch better than me," Elizabeth said.

"*Yah?*" Lovina looked up at Elizabeth.

"*Yah.* You've always been a good seamstress." She pulled up a chair next to her. "Sarah said you remembered a game from our school years."

"Not really," Lovina admitted quietly. "I remember weaving a bird's nest and putting grass clippings inside, but I don't remember the game she was talking about. I just didn't want to disappoint her."

"Oh . . ." Elizabeth nodded. "What do you remember?"

"Just that—weaving a small nest and padding it with grass clippings. I was holding it out to show to someone."

"Who?" Elizabeth asked.

"I don't know."

They fell silent, and Lovina sighed. This should be a victory, but it felt small. So she said, "I heard a little bit about Solomon."

"What did they say?" Elizabeth asked, and her tone turned tired.

"That he's been to jail, but you both still seem to have the community support to get married," Lovina said. "And Dorcas thinks that you're someone who would understand him. *You*, particularly."

Elizabeth was silent.

"Why?" Lovina pressed. "Why you?"

"Because I love him enough to look deeper," Elizabeth replied. "And you should know that you and Johannes had the community's support, too. You made a lovely couple."

They *had* the support. They *made* a lovely couple.

"That sounds like it happened in the past," Lovina replied.

"You *make* a lovely couple," Elizabeth said. "I'm sorry. I misspoke. Do you remember anything about him yet?"

"Not unless I was showing him a bird's nest," Lovina said with a small smile. "I'm not working with much at the moment."

Elizabeth smiled at Lovina's humor, and for just a moment, Lovina felt a rush of warmth and comfort. This was what it was like to have a family, wasn't it? She might not remember it, but this was a lovely life that she was leading—a brother and sister who loved her, a sister-in-law and a baby nephew who truly seemed to like her company . . . and there was this community of people who made her feel safe. Even with no memory, she felt like she could trust them. If she needed help, these people would never turn her away—she could feel that on a heart level.

I have a beautiful life, Lord, she prayed in her heart. *Thank you for this . . .*

That was the first time she had prayed since the accident, and perhaps that was a returning memory, too. She'd done it instinctively, and the warmth of comfort grew inside of her. She had been a woman of faith—she was suddenly very sure of that.

Outside the kitchen window, the evening sky was dark and inviting.

"I think I'll go outside for a few minutes," she said. "I want some fresh air."

"*Yah*, sure," Elizabeth said. "I'd best get back to my quilt—I can't do less work than the others, can I?"

Lovina cast her sister a smile. "That would be terrible."

When her sister rose to her feet, so did Lovina. She went to the door, already propped open to get a breeze inside, and she sucked in a lungful of late-summer air. She could smell autumn on the way—that crisp undertone that promised colder weather to come.

She pushed open the screen and stepped outside, feeling the welcome embrace of cool evening breeze with a hint of wood fire, the scent of cut grass that tugged at a new memory in her mind. This one seemed to float to the surface more freely.

Lovina could remember sitting in a bedroom, a window open to let in air that smelled very much like this. She was sitting on a bed, propped up with pillows, and she had a laptop computer on her lap . . . There was a movie playing on the screen. It was about a girl and horse, or something, and she remembered pulling a hand through her hair—and no *kapp* getting in the way of it. She'd been wearing blue jeans. Her heart skipped a beat, and for a moment, she held her breath.

She remembered it clearly. There was a lamp on the bedside table—an electric one, and a clock with glowing numbers. There was a cell phone beside her on the bed, too. In her memory, it pinged, and she picked it up to check a text. It was someone saying, "You want popcorn?"

That was all . . . But it was clear and she felt completely

certain of it. That *was* a memory . . . and it wasn't Amish at all.

She looked over her shoulder toward the light coming from the kerosene lamps hanging in the kitchen. The women's voices were low and friendly. Someone laughed, and then someone else joined in.

Her heart hammered hard in her throat, and a faint breeze drew goose bumps up on her arms, despite the warmth. She looked back toward the screen door. Her memory of the bird's nest—that didn't have to be Amish, did it?

Who was she? Was she Amish . . . or was she *English*?

Johannes flipped through the *Budget* newspaper, scanning the articles and little bits of news. There were some weddings that had taken place, a farm that had come up for sale in the next church district over, and a new buggy maker who was coming onto the scene. He sighed and looked up at his father, who stood by the window, sipping his coffee.

"It was nice having a woman here for a while," Bernard said.

"You didn't like my cooking tonight?" Johannes joked.

"It was decent," Bernard said, a twinkle in his eye. "But Sovilla's cooking was better."

Johannes shrugged. "You could get married again, too, Daet."

Bernard laughed softly. "That wasn't kind to point out, son. But tell me about Lovina. What happened?"

Johannes felt a tug of guilt, and he looked down at the newspaper again. "Not much."

"Are any memories surfacing for her yet?" Bernard pressed.

Johannes sighed. "No. But . . . Daet, this is wrong. I don't like lying."

Bernard nodded. "I see the complication. But there are times when we hold back information from our *kinner*, for example, because it's for their own good. We might not tell them about a distant relative whose spouse left them, because we don't want to sour our *kinner* toward marriage. Or we might not tell them about something happening in the *Englisher* world, because it will only upset them. And I'm not suggesting that you treat Lovina like a child, but she has been severely injured and needs some gentleness while she recovers. The whole story will come out, but maybe some of those details could wait."

But Johannes held her hand today. He'd walked with her slowly down that road, and he'd held her hand the way he used to when they were still happily planning a life together. He'd tugged her close against his side and felt the warmth of her arm pressed against his.

And he'd melted a little.

He wasn't supposed to . . . He was supposed to keep his emotions in check. This wasn't real, and she'd remember that eventually. When she did, if he'd acted the part of doting boyfriend a little too well, he'd have some explaining to do.

"I'm supposed to act like her fiancé," Johannes said.

"*Yah.* But . . . a very, very well-behaved fiancé," his father pointed out.

Johannes smiled faintly. "I held her hand."

"That's all, though?" Bernard asked.

"*Yah*, that's all. I still feel guilty about it. I want to help her, and I want her to heal and get her memory back, but I don't want to take advantage of her, either."

"You said you'd do this for a few weeks, and then tell her the truth if she hasn't remembered yet, right?" Bernard asked.

"That's what I said."

"I think you're doing okay," Bernard said. "And if it makes you feel any better, I'll let you know the minute it seems like you're overstepping."

"Thanks, Daet," Johannes said. "That does help."

Because if his father could be counted upon for one thing, it was his honesty.

"And everything was fine with Sovilla when you dropped her off with Iddo and Waneta?" his father asked.

"*Yah* . . ." Johannes leaned back in his chair. "Sovilla has been incredibly gracious through all of this. She holds no ill will toward me, and she says she really does wish me happiness."

Bernard nodded. "I know it will sound like pressure, but she would have been a delight to have around the home, son."

"I wouldn't have made her happy," Johannes said. "And she knew it. She seems to think that I might win Lovina over after all."

"You might," Bernard agreed.

Johannes shot his father a rueful smile. "I don't need false hope, Daet. I need you to give me that honest truth you're so known for."

"I am giving you my honest opinion," his father replied.

"You and Lovina had a connection, and if she could see her way to come back home, I don't see why she couldn't see her way to come back to you, too."

But Johannes wasn't so sure about that. For the older generation, it was about the Amish life versus the *English* one. But it was more complicated than that. Lovina had already found it in her heart to walk away from him once, so it would seem obvious that he hadn't been enough.

"You're overthinking things," his father said.

"Hmm?" Johannes looked over at his father.

"I can tell. You're overthinking it. Just . . . help her remember, and leave the rest to Gott."

But Gott's ways were not their ways, and Gott's thoughts were not their thoughts. Maybe Gott didn't want a future for them together.

The side door opened and Daniel came inside. He pulled off his straw hat and hung it up, and then turned to the sink to wash up. It was late.

"How is the newest calf doing with the bottle?" Bernard asked.

"Good," Daniel said, drying his hands and coming into the kitchen. "He's draining a bottle and a half every feed."

"Is he listless?" Bernard asked.

"No, he's up and looking for attention," Daniel replied. "I know calves, Dawdie. We have plenty of them at home."

"*Yah*, I know," Bernard said with a smile. "But I have to check. You're doing well. You have a good sense for how animals are doing, how comfortable they are, how well adjusted. Not every boy your age has that ability."

Daniel smiled sheepishly. "I like the baby animals. They're really cute."

"I'm glad you're here to help us out, Daniel," Bernard said with a nod.

"Can I get a snack?" the boy asked.

"You don't have to ask permission to eat," Bernard said with a smile. "As long as you clean up after yourself, you eat whatever you want."

Daniel headed to the cupboard, and Bernard nodded toward the stairs.

"I'm going to head on up for a shower," Bernard said. "The morning comes early enough."

"Good night, Daet," Johannes said.

"Good night, Dawdie," Daniel added.

His father headed for the stairs and made his way up, and Johannes watched as his nephew piled a few muffins on his plate and pulled out a tub of sweetened Amish peanut butter.

"You want some?" Daniel asked.

"No, thanks," Johannes said. "I'm fine."

Daniel came back to the table and sat down. He had a butter knife, and he cut the blueberry muffins in half and spread them with the peanut butter. It didn't look appealing to Johannes, but he remembered being that age and being constantly hungry. It was part of fast growth.

"How was your *mamm* doing when you left?" Johannes asked.

"Fine, I guess," Daniel said as he chewed. "There was a man coming around."

"A man?" Johannes frowned. His sister was widowed, and an attractive woman, but he still felt a protectiveness for her. "Who was he?"

"A new farmer in our area," Daniel said, swallowing. "He wanted to court Mamm."

"And you think she's interested?" Johannes asked.

Daniel shook his head. "No, she didn't like him. He's too gruff. He's always finding fault with anything I do. He's old, like Dawdie."

"Does your *mamm* let him find fault with you?" Johannes asked.

"She stands up for me, but I heard him say that if they get closer, she'll have to let him run things." Daniel looked up and met Johannes's gaze. "And if she marries him, I'll run away."

"Where to?" Johannes asked.

"Anywhere."

"That isn't a thought-out plan," Johannes said. "There are always more options than two, if you look for them. And if you ever need somewhere to go, you come here."

"*Yah*?" Daniel swallowed a bite. "You wouldn't send me home?"

Not for some gruff farmer to pick on him. Johannes felt a welling of protectiveness for the boy.

"We'd help you sort it out," Johannes said. "You aren't on your own, Daniel."

But this did cast a new light on his sister sending her son to them. Did she want to get to know this farmer a little better? Johannes wasn't sure. But looking at the earnest gaze of his nephew, Johannes's heart went out to the boy. Life was complicated enough without having to consider his own *mamm* remarrying.

"Sovilla said to say goodbye to you," Johannes said.

"*Yah*? Did she . . . ?" Some color touched Daniel's cheeks. "She's so nice."

"*Yah*, we all agree about that," Johannes said. "My *daet* is going to miss her cooking, too."

"It's not just her cooking . . ." Daniel took another jaw-cracking bite and then chewed a moment before adding, "She's nice. And her little girls are fun."

Daniel was used to having girls around. He might miss it.

"I'm sure we'll see her around," Johannes said. "And we'll just have to fend for ourselves in the kitchen. It's not a bad thing for a man to know how to cook for himself, you know. Even after you marry, if your wife falls ill, you'd need to be able to cook some basics."

"Did Sovilla leave anything for me?" Daniel asked hopefully.

"*Yah*, she did," Johannes said. He stood up and went over to the windowsill where he'd left the little sewing box. He brought it back to the table and handed it over to Daniel.

Daniel put down his muffin and pried open the lid. He pulled out some spools of thread and several needles that he inspected closely.

"Tell her thank you from me when you see her next," Daniel said, closing the lid, and the box disappeared under the table.

Johannes looked down at the newspaper again as his nephew continued to eat, and then he glanced up at the boy.

"What are you doing with that sewing kit?" Johannes asked.

Daniel's chewing slowed, and then he swallowed. "Nothing."

"But you wanted it?" Johannes said.

"*Yah* . . ." But he sounded less sure of himself. Somehow, Johannes didn't believe that this boy was overly worried about split seams or mending tears in his shirts. If Johannes knew boys, it was about something different.

"Why?" Johannes asked. "Is there a girl you want to give it to?"

Daniel's cheeks flushed crimson and he put the sewing kit up onto the table again.

"Take it," the boy said. "I don't want it."

"No, it's fine," Johannes said, lowering his tone. It certainly wasn't a crime for a boy to make a kind gesture to a girl he admired. "I don't mean to ruin it for you. I just remember being your age. I know you see some old man when you look at me"—Johannes smiled, hoping to coax his nephew into a better mood with a joke—"but I'm not as old as that, you know. Not too long ago, I was a teenage boy, and I had a crush on a girl."

"What girl?" Daniel asked.

"Lovina." He felt his own smile slip. "It doesn't matter."

"And you gave her presents?" Daniel asked with a frown.

"*Yah*. I gave her presents," Johannes said. A polished stone. A package of ribbon. A dried leaf. "It's perfectly natural to have a crush."

Daniel licked his lips. "Okay. Whatever. But I don't have a girl."

"Just between us?" Johannes asked. "I wouldn't tell your *mamm*."

Daniel eyed him for a moment. "I wouldn't want to lie to you, Uncle Johannes."

The frankness of those words gave Johannes a jolt.

"Oh." Johannes had actually expected his nephew to tell him.

Daniel took the sewing kit again, and it disappeared under the table once more.

It felt too pushy to ask anything more about it, and Johannes picked up the *Budget* again and pretended to be much more absorbed in the contents than he really was. His nephew finished eating and brought his plate to the sink. He turned on the water and washed it off.

"I think I'll go to bed, too," Daniel said.

"Sure. Good night," Johannes said.

His nephew's footsteps creaked up the staircase, and Johannes heard the bathroom door open as his father came out.

They were a house full of men, and each one of them seemed to be missing the female touch around a home. Women were the heart of a home, the comfort, the sunlight. And when men were left alone to be men, to take care of the land, and to shoulder the responsibilities, their minds kept going back to the gentler gender—even if those women couldn't be their answers to everything. And Johannes could take comfort in the fact that, at the very least, he wasn't alone in that.

Chapter Four

The next morning, Johannes and Bernard hoisted the three large milk tins up onto the back of the wagon in the predawn twilight. A few birds had started to stir and sing. The second tin clanged against the first as they pushed it back into the wagon. This was the milk that they sold to the cheese factory just outside of Bountiful. That factory kept a lot of young Amish people employed, and the local dairies made ready money from their raw milk, too.

"I'm glad Sol has this job now," Bernard said through gritted teeth as they slid the last tin onto the wagon bed.

"*Yah*, it's good for him," Johannes agreed. Solomon was now collecting the milk from the local dairies for the cheese factory. It was a good job to have, and he'd managed to take over for a retiring older man who used to do the job before him.

"I never thought I'd see him married before you," Bernard said. "Truth be told, I never thought he'd come back."

"*Yah*—" Johannes jumped up into the back of the wagon to strap the jugs into place so they wouldn't spill on his drive up to the road, where Sol would meet him. "I was more shocked to see him baptized than I will be to see him married."

Bernard chuckled. "I might have to agree with you there. You got this?"

"*Yah*, I'm fine," Johannes said.

Bernard headed back into the barn, and Johannes finished strapping the milk jugs into place, then he climbed up over the seat and settled into place. He untied the reins and gave them a flick.

Sol was indeed back, and while Johannes was happy for his cousin, there was a little bit of resentment that he hadn't quite purged from his heart. Sol—the cousin he'd had a little too much in common with—was also the one who'd never understood Johannes's desire to do better. Johannes's grandfather, and Sol's great-uncle, had been a deacon for this area, and he'd been known for his quiet wisdom. While Johannes had been struggling to read after school in the evenings, it was Dawdie Menno who'd pointed out, "Johannes, it doesn't matter how easy it is for others. All that matters is what you have to do to get your results. Who cares if Sol doesn't try? Who cares if younger *kinner* than you are breezing through it? Maturity means that you put your head down and do what you have to do. That's how a man gets ahead."

So while Sol fooled around in class and drove their teacher to distraction, and while Sol went to *English* parties with drinking and girls, while he defied authority and eventually jumped the fence, Johannes had worked twice as hard as anyone else. He'd put in the work. And the entire time, he'd silently hoped that one day he'd be like his grandfather—deeply respected by anyone who knew him. That would be more than enough for Johannes.

So it was ironic that Sol could jump the fence, get in trouble with the law, go to jail, and then come back and get engaged in a blink. It would seem that Sol had finally started to try, and it was still harder for Johannes to achieve the same things than it ever seemed to be for his cousin. What would his grandfather have to say about that?

Johannes reined in the horse at the top of the drive. He could see his cousin's wagon coming down the road, the clop of his quarter horses' hooves echoing through the quiet morning.

Sol would be married, and he'd start on that houseful of *kinner*, and somehow the community would forgive him. And Johannes? He was stuck in love with the wrong girl. If Johannes were smart at all, he would have just married Sovilla.

"Good morning!" Sol called as he pulled up. The back of his wagon was filled with about a dozen milk containers already.

"Good morning, Sol." Johannes tied off his reins and hopped down from the wagon. "How are you liking the new job?"

"It was easier than I thought to get used to getting up so early," Sol said. He tied off his reins as well and hopped down to the gravel on the side of the road. "Remember I thought I'd sleep too late?"

"Glad it's working out," Johannes said.

"How are things with Lovina?" Sol asked.

"Fine." Johannes heard the clipped sound in his own voice. He didn't feel like discussing her with Sol.

Johannes was going to see her today after the morning work was done.

"Okay . . ." Sol eyed him for a moment, then reached up to a satchel on the seat of his wagon. "Before I forget, I have to give you your receipt for last week's milk. Going forward, they're going to be using email only for these things."

"Email?" Johannes squinted at him. "We're Amish."

"And they're saving money," Sol said with a shrug. "According to the letter here, it has to do with the way they're doing their bookkeeping. There's some instructions. Basically, you just set up an email account, and they'll send you copies of everything there. It'll all be strictly online going forward."

"Saving money . . ." Johannes muttered. "How much could it save?"

"I have a feeling it has a bit to do with me, too," Sol said. "I've been to jail. They don't want me delivering checks or financial documents."

Johannes froze. He hadn't thought of that. "Right. Sorry, I—" He shrugged. "I would be fine with you delivering all that, you know."

"Yeah, I know," Solomon replied. "I mean, not everyone would feel that way, but . . . thanks."

They were silent for a moment, the awkwardness hanging between them. Solomon's time in jail had changed a lot for him, and not everything would come back to normal. That kind of history couldn't be erased.

Solomon handed him the envelope. "Anyway, the information is in there."

"I don't have an email account," Johannes said. He

accepted the envelope from Sol. "I don't even know where to start with that stuff. Do you?"

"I probably know a little more than you, but I'm not great with it," Solomon replied. "There isn't a public library here, either. In the city, there were libraries where you could get help with this stuff. You'll have to start with a cell phone that has Internet access."

Johannes shook his head in disgust. "We're Amish dairies! Whatever happened to sending this stuff in the mail? What's the cost of a postage stamp?"

"I don't know," Sol replied. "Look, I'm sorry. I'm just the messenger. I drive a wagon, and I'm not going to be trusted with a whole lot more than that."

And Johannes knew that was the case.

"How much are cell phones, anyway?" Johannes asked.

Sol sighed. "When I had one, it was like . . . a couple hundred bucks."

"For a glorified mailbox!" Johannes said, slapping the tin mailbox next to him. "I know there's one cell phone in the district for emergencies. Your *mamm* has it now, right? Do we all use that one? Will the bishop even authorize all us farmers getting cell phones?"

Sol shrugged again. "I guess you'll have to talk to the bishop to see what's allowed."

Johannes let out a frustrated breath. "Right. I'll do that."

And he wouldn't be the only one. Sol having a job to help provide for his family was going to make life more difficult for all of them. Because Sol was probably right about why things were suddenly changing. The cheese factory wasn't going to take any chances with more fraud risk, and the online option was probably safest for the company, even if it made everything more difficult for the Amish.

"So, work aside," Solomon said, "you're coming to help me with the eck for the wedding, right?"

The wedding—the biggest source of gossip for the season up until Lovina had come back.

"Of course," Johannes said.

Solomon relaxed and nodded, shooting him a grin. "You're the only one standing with me, you know. You can't let me down."

"I won't. You know I'm there for you." They were family, after all.

"Give me a hand?" Sol asked.

Johannes jumped up onto the bed of his wagon and started unfastening the belts that held the milk tins in place. His grandfather always said that Gott gave them community for a reason, and right now, it was his job to be there for his cousin. Every man went through difficult times. Every man had successes and victories. Every man got old and couldn't pitch in like he used to . . . and it was their responsibility to remember that they'd experience all three in their lifetimes.

He released the straps and pulled the first tall tin of milk toward the edge of the wagon. They'd do what their fathers and grandfathers had done as they faithfully followed the Amish life—find a way.

Lovina stood outside with a large bucket and a sturdy wooden ladder. She planted the legs of the ladder under the apple tree, then started up the rungs into the leafy depths of the branches. The apples were ripe, and she reached for a round, red one, popping it off the stem. There was another behind that one, and she put the first apple into a sling at her waist and reached for the next one. This was a bountiful apple crop, and she continued working until she couldn't reach any more apples and the sling was bulky and uncomfortably heavy. Then she backed down the ladder again and carefully emptied the apples into the larger container.

She hadn't had any new memories since last night, but the one she did have had fleshed out and gotten clearer. Along with the movie she'd been watching, the jeans she'd been wearing at the time, and the comfortable feeling of a cell phone in her hand, she remembered her toenails having been painted purple, and that she'd liked it.

She looked down at her own bare feet, and there was something she'd noticed that morning . . . Her toenails had just the tiniest hint of red around the edges, as if they'd been painted and then the polish was removed. That was not Amish. Not in any possible way . . .

She went back up the ladder, this time climbing a little higher than she'd gone before, and she stretched toward the apples within reach. This family claimed to be hers. They said she was Amish, and everyone here seemed to know her. She spoke the language! But she didn't remember anyone, and the strongest clues in her brain that had started to resurface pointed to a different life altogether.

Was she going crazy, remembering things she'd

imagined? Or was there more to her past that they weren't filling her in about?

Am I even Lovina Yoder? she wondered. Because she could be anyone, and she'd be none the wiser right now.

The rattle of a buggy on the drive drew her eye, and she turned to see Johannes reining in his horses by the house. He shaded his eyes and waved at her.

"My fiancé," she murmured. Or was he?

She climbed back down the ladder and emptied the apples into the bucket, making sure they tumbled gently so as not to bruise.

It was rather nice to think of this simple life being hers—the loving family, the soothing scenery, the handsome fiancé—but *was* it hers? So far, she didn't exactly feel at home here. It felt like a vacation, a sweet little pocket of rest in the midst of some other life she couldn't quite recall.

Was that ruggedly handsome man really someone she'd loved? She paused in her work, watching as Johannes got down from the buggy. He patted the side of one of his horses as he walked past it and ambled in her direction.

Bethany poked her head out the door, but she disappeared inside again without saying anything, and Lovina could only assume that they wanted to give her time alone with Johannes. He came to a stop a couple of feet away from her, and he glanced down at the bucket of apples, then shot her a smile.

"You look busy," Johannes said.

"Just picking apples," she said.

"Are you going to bake anything with them?" he asked.

Lovina shrugged. "You'd have to ask Bethany or Elizabeth. I don't know the plan."

"You used to make a really delicious apple pie," he said. "The crust was flaky and perfect, and you had this apple filling that was both sweet and tangy, and . . ." He chuckled. "I wonder if you remember how to do that."

"I don't know," she admitted. "I haven't tried."

"*Yah* . . ."

"Did I *really* bake such a good pie?" she asked, eyeing him, watching for his reaction. "Is that true?"

"*Yah*, you did. Why?" He looked calm enough, just meeting her gaze.

"I don't remember it," she said.

"You don't remember a lot," he said with a short laugh. "It'll come back. Unless—" His smile slipped. "Do you remember something more?"

For a second, she was tempted to tell him exactly what had come back to her, and she dropped her gaze down to her bare feet and the faint edging of red around her toenails. But she didn't know what that memory was, hanging alone in her head like an apple from a tree branch. There was zero context.

"No, nothing," she said.

Johannes dropped his gaze for a moment, then glanced back up at her. "Are you hungry?"

"A little," she said.

"Do you want to come into town with me and have a meal out?" he asked.

So far, all the meals she'd eaten, she'd had a hand in preparing, and it did sound rather nice to have a meal that didn't involve work for her. She glanced toward the house again, and she saw Elizabeth at the side door this time with a laundry hamper full of wet laundry balanced on one hip.

"Hello, Johannes!" she called. "Beautiful day!"

"*Yah*, very nice out," Johannes called back. Then he turned back to Lovina.

"Well?" he asked. "My treat, of course."

"I'll see what Elizabeth thinks," Lovina said, and she turned her steps in the other woman's direction, leaving Johannes by the apple tree.

Elizabeth took a man's shirt out of the hamper of wet clothes and shook it out with a snap. Then she reached into a bag of clothespins and began to pin the shirt to the line.

"You should spend some time with Johannes," Elizabeth said, securing the shirt and then reaching for another wet item.

"The apples need picking, though," she said.

"The apples can wait." Elizabeth shot her a smile. "I'll even help you with them later."

"He wants to take me to town to eat," Lovina said.

"That sounds nice," Elizabeth replied. "I'm a little jealous."

"You could come, too," Lovina said.

"No, no, I'm only joking," Elizabeth said. "Go on and have a good time, Lovina. It might help. I can't help but think that relaxing might be just what you need. The doctor did mention rest for you."

Maybe Elizabeth was right. She licked her lips, then glanced back to where Johannes stood, his thumbs hooked in his suspenders.

"I'll go, then," she said. "Thanks, Elizabeth."

"You love him," Elizabeth said with an encouraging nod. "You'll remember that. I know it."

Would she? Lovina smiled back in what she hoped was a natural way, and then she raised her voice so Johannes could hear her.

"*Yah*, I can go!" she said.

Johannes waved at Elizabeth and started across the grass toward his buggy again.

"Great!" he said, and he waited at the side of the buggy until she met him there. He caught her hand in his rough grip and helped her up with a strong lift. Her stomach fluttered as she slid into the seat and he hoisted himself up next to her. He shot her a smile and untied the reins.

He smelled good . . . a little musky, and a bit like wood shavings. He must have been working with wood this morning before he came out to see her. His arm brushed hers as he flicked the reins, and the horses started to pull the buggy in a circle to head back up the drive.

Elizabeth was pinning a dress up on the line, but her gaze lifted and caught Lovina's as they eased past her once more. Was Lovina worrying for nothing? If Elizabeth was lying to her, why send her off into town with Johannes? It didn't make sense.

"You smell like wood," Lovina said.

"*Yah* . . ." He chuckled. "I was fixing a stall in the barn, and I had to saw a few boards. I thought I'd cleaned up enough—"

"No, it's nice," she said. "I like that smell."

Perhaps that was something else she could identify

about herself. She liked the smell of sawed wood. And as the buggy bumped over a rock and then turned onto the road with the swinging rhythm of the horses' hooves, she looked over at this man who was supposed to be her fiancé.

He sat comfortably, his blue shirtsleeves rolled up his forearms, his legs spread so that his knee pressed against hers. His dark gaze flickered toward her. The last time they'd been alone together, he'd held her hand, but this time, he didn't make a move to touch her again.

"So . . . how are you?" Lovina asked.

"Not too bad." He shot her a smile. "It looks like things are going to get complicated with the cheese factory that buys our milk. They've decided to put all their records online. So . . . it just makes everything harder."

"What will you do?" she asked.

"My *daet* is going to talk with the neighboring dairy farmers today, and they'll all go talk to the bishop. We'll sort out something. No one ever claimed that living Amish was the easier path, right?"

She shook her head. "I don't know . . ."

His smile slipped. "Sorry, I forgot you don't remember. They don't say that, for the record. Our life is one of hard work, and I shouldn't complain when we come across a challenge."

His gaze moved back out to the road, and she watched him for a moment—the set of his shoulders, the way he held the reins. He was tense, like a spring.

"I'm one of your challenges, aren't I?" she asked.

"No!" He sighed. "I didn't mean it like that."

He flicked the reins as the horses began to slow, then

he leaned forward to look out a side mirror and put his hand out and beckoned for a car to pass him. When the vehicle was past, he glanced toward her again.

"I think my thirteen-year-old nephew has got a crush on a girl," he said.

"Probably normal?" she suggested.

"*Yah*, probably," he replied. "I told him if he talked to me about it, I wouldn't tell my sister, but I'm wondering if that was wrong."

Lovina shrugged. "I don't know."

"The thing is, I'm a little worried about Daniel," Johannes said. "He's a sensitive boy. He's . . . I don't know. Lovina, can I count on your discretion for this?" He turned and looked at her directly this time. "Or is that too much to ask? I used to talk this stuff over with you, and . . . I know it's different now, so I don't mean to put pressure on you, but . . ."

Johannes's gaze swung back to the road where there was an oncoming car. She watched him for a moment.

"Of course I can keep your confidence," she said.

Johannes's smiled slightly. "Good. Well, anyway, he got a little sewing kit from a friend of ours, and he's hiding it away. I don't know how to explain it. He's treating it like . . . a secret."

"As a gift for a girl?" Lovina asked.

"That's what I think," he replied. "He's just being . . . I don't know, evasive."

"And you think you should tell his *mamm*?" she asked.

"She sent him to us for a male influence," he replied. "I suppose I just feel the responsibility to help him out. And something feels . . . off."

Johannes glanced over at her and raised his eyebrows. She knew that feeling all too well these days. Something felt very "off" for her, too.

"You should probably listen to your instinct," she said.

"*Yah*?" He nodded a couple of times. "*Yah*, I probably should." He leaned toward her and nudged her with his arm. "It's nice to have you to talk to again."

She leaned toward him in return, and she settled against his arm, feeling the rattle of the buggy through his muscled triceps. One hand lay relaxed on his thigh, and without thinking, she reached out, slipping her fingers under his. His warm, rough fingers closed gently over hers.

Had that been terribly forward? She felt a sudden twinge of worry. She hadn't thought before she'd touched him.

"I'm trying really hard not to take any advantages with you," he said, his voice low. "I just want you to know that. I know your memory will come back, and when it does, I don't want you to think I . . . I don't know . . . overstepped when you were vulnerable."

"By holding my hand?" she asked.

"*Yah*, by holding your hand." His voice softened, though, and he squeezed her fingers.

"It's okay," she said. "I like it."

Here she thought she'd been the one to overstep. Holding this man's hand in the semi-privacy of the closed in buggy might not feel familiar, but it did feel honest. And she liked the feeling of his hand over hers, and the thick warmth of his muscled arm pressed against her side.

In all of this mess of unfamiliar new people and experiences, Johannes's strong hands and deep voice were a comfort. If she did truly have a history with these people, she could see why she would have chosen Johannes Miller. He felt safe.

Chapter Five

Johannes had told himself that he wouldn't hold her hand again, but it made a difference that she had taken his hand, didn't it? She might not have her memory back, but she was still a woman with her own free will. He ran his thumb over her soft skin . . .

They used to take long rides together holding hands when no one else could see them . . . And there had been the singings with the other young people when he'd be sitting on the boys' side of the fire, looking at her sitting with the other girls and thinking how wonderful it would be to finally claim her as his wife. He'd been looking forward to all the details of putting a home together with her. He wanted to build some of their own furniture, and he was putting money aside for things like dishes and linens—the sorts of things a new wife picked out for herself.

And he'd been thinking about what a relief it would be to come back into the house on a chilly evening to find Lovina waiting for him with food on the table. He'd be able to hold her then—and it would be good and proper for him to pull her into his arms and kiss her.

They'd be able to talk late into the night and then crawl under warm quilts together, two people in love with no guilt to stand between them.

Sitting with her in this buggy felt like starting over with her, in a way. She didn't remember anything about him, and he had a heart filled with these memories that meant absolutely nothing to her. But she was holding his hand, and he felt that surge of masculine victory he'd felt the first time he'd held her hand. So in a way, it was like starting their relationship over from scratch, except there was no guarantee that she would fall in love with him this time around. A woman's heart wasn't so easy to navigate, and he knew what an honor it was to have won it once— a big enough honor that he wasn't certain of doing it again.

The town of Bountiful, Pennsylvania, was popular with tourists. It was nestled in the center of verdant farmland, surrounded by mostly Amish farmers with a spattering of Englishers. The town itself was small and quaint. The downtown core was strongly Amish—Amish businesses flourishing as a result of the influx of tourists coming from all over the country. Amish and *English* cooperated and helped each other thrive. Ordinarily, they maintained an easy balance, and this new demand for emailed records was still frustrating Johannes.

On the west end of town, it looked no different than any other town in America—gas stations, strip malls, a few chain restaurants and hotels that catered to the visitors who traveled through, and *Englisher* subdivisions with houses and cars lining streets named after Pennsylvania Dutch founders of the town.

On both sides of the wide downtown streets, there

were parking spots that had hitching posts and were big enough for a buggy, allowing for easier Amish shopping and dining. The restaurant that Johannes chose wasn't an Amish-run establishment, though. It was an Italian eatery that he and Lovina used to enjoy with an almost rebellious relish. This was the kind of food they'd never find at home.

When Johannes had hitched the horses and given them some water and a feed bag on the ground each, he and Lovina went into the restaurant. Lovina took a seat by the window, and he went to the men's room to wash his hands after dealing with the horses. When he returned, the waitress was just leaving the table, and there were two menus waiting for them.

Lovina picked hers up, and as he pulled out his chair and sat down, he saw something flicker across her face—surprise, almost. Her face drained of color, and she opened her mouth as if to say something, but nothing came out.

"Are you okay?" he asked.

She didn't answer, but she turned the menu over, and pink flooded into her cheeks.

"Lovina?" he said.

"I remember this food," she said, looking up. "I remember spinach-and-ricotta-stuffed cannelloni, and lasagna, and . . . the pizza! I remember what it tastes like." She looked up, a smile brightening her face. "I remember what I like!"

"*Yah*!" He leaned forward. "You remember this place?"

She looked around her, down at the tablecloth, behind her toward the door, then shook her head.

"Not this place, exactly, but I remember places like

it . . . and I do remember this menu—I've seen this menu before," she said, tapping the laminated menu with one finger.

So it was coming back, and he felt a tingle run through him.

"We used to come here," he said. "We liked it. It was different from anything we could eat at home, and so I'd save my extra money and take you here once every few months."

"*Yah*?" She smiled at that. "What else?"

"You'd order the cannelloni. Every time. I'd try different dishes, and you'd try a bite of them, but you always ordered the cannelloni." He felt her shoe against his under the table, and he wished he could take her hand—but not in public. Not like this.

"Because I *love* the cannelloni," she said. "It's one thing I remembered, even back in the hospital. I know exactly what it looks like—served in these personal-sized casserole dishes, right? They're white?"

"*Yah*." He nodded. "Exactly!"

"And I like something . . . something like Italian soda?" she said. "I like that—don't I?"

"You do." He laughed softly. "And you'd take the leftovers home to eat later on. I think you shared them with your sister."

"Did I?" She shook her head. "I don't remember that. But it's starting to come back, Johannes. Finally! It's a relief to have some memories come back. I just can't connect them yet."

"Maybe I can help with that," he said. Did she remember any hint of *him*?

The restaurant door opened and a young Amish couple

came inside—Ben and Vannetta Albrecht. Vannetta spotted Lovina as she turned to look in the direction that Johannes was looking, and her face broke into a smile.

"Lovina?" She looked back at her husband and then hurried in their direction. "Lovina Yoder! You're back!"

Lovina smiled hesitantly. "Hello."

Vannetta rested a hand on top of her belly, and her words came out in a rush. "We've been praying and praying, and I told Ben that you'd come back. I told him I knew you well enough to know you'd definitely be back! And look at me! I'm due in two months!"

"Congratulations," Lovina said feebly. "That's . . . lovely."

"Where have you been?" Vannetta asked, lowering her voice. "No one knew where to look for you!"

"I don't know," Lovina said. "What's your name?"

Vannetta's face fell and her gaze flickered toward Johannes.

"What?" Vannetta asked weakly.

"She doesn't remember," Johannes broke in. "She's had an injury, and she has what we hope is short-term amnesia."

"Oh . . . Oh, Lovina . . . Really? Are you telling me you don't remember me? I'm Vannetta. I'm your *friend*. You stood for me at my wedding! I was going to stand for you at yours!"

"*Yah*?" Lovina asked hesitantly.

Ben arrived then, and the waitress came up with two more menus.

"Did you want to sit together?" the waitress asked brightly.

No, Johannes didn't want to sit together, but what was

he supposed to say? How was Johannes supposed to protect Lovina from knowing too much when there was a whole community who had known and loved her, and who would be chattering at her with complete abandon?

Ben met Johannes's gaze, then turned to his wife.

"I think Johannes and Lovina could use some time alone," Ben said, his voice low. "We'll sit over there, if you don't mind. Come on, Vannetta, we don't want to intrude. Do we?"

Ben looked pointedly at his wife, and her face colored slightly.

"Of course," Vannetta said. "Lovina, we'll talk later, okay?"

The other couple moved away as the waitress went to get them settled, and Johannes let out a slow breath of relief. He looked over at Lovina. She was watching the Albrechts with a strange look on her face.

"Do you remember them?" he asked.

Did she remember other friends before remembering him?

"No . . ." She looked back over at him. "I don't remember them. But the women who came to help with Elizabeth's quilt, and now this woman—Vannetta? They all talk like I've been gone for ages. How long was I in that hospital? And have I lived here my entire life? And what about nail polish . . . did I ever wear nail polish? Because I think I have the remnants of nail polish on my toes, Johannes."

He blinked at her. "What?"

"On my toes," she repeated. "I think I have the remnants of red nail polish on them."

"Maybe at the hospital?" he asked feebly.

"Do they do that at hospitals?" she asked.

"Maybe if you stay long enough?" he replied. "Maybe volunteers? You were there for a little while."

The waitress came back then, and they fell silent. The waitress pulled a pad of paper out of her pocket with a cheery smile. Lovina looked down at the menu.

"I'd like the cannelloni," she said.

"Great," the waitress replied. "And for you, sir?"

Johannes swallowed, his stomach feeling like it was filled with rocks. "Uh—the pepperoni and sausage pizza, please."

After taking the rest of their order, the waitress left, and Johannes leaned back in his chair. He wanted her to remember, but the one detail he kept conveniently forgetting was that her memories wouldn't necessarily match his.

Her memories included a year of *Englisher* living, and they also included a relationship that she'd been able to walk away from. He hadn't been able to cut off his feelings for her, even when she'd left him. He'd had a chance to marry a good woman, and he hadn't been able to take it, because she wasn't Lovina. Was there another boyfriend she'd recall when all this was over? Because she had had a life in the last year . . .

The food came quickly, and Lovina turned her attention to the Amish people she saw passing the window. A few waved, looking surprised, and a couple of them came into the restaurant to say hello. There were more explanations, more questions, and finally Johannes and Lovina finished their meals.

Johannes put a protective hand over her back as they headed past Ben and Vannetta's table on their way out of the restaurant. Ben's gaze sought out Johannes's, and for a split second, he felt like Ben understood. The other man gave him a slight nod, and Johannes nudged Lovina past them, toward the door and some semblance of privacy again.

Lovina might be back, and the community might be happy to see her, but time had marched on. Over a year had slipped away, and everyone's lives had moved forward without them. It was only Johannes and Lovina who were locked back in the past, beginning all over again.

Lovina got into the buggy and waited while Johannes put the feed bags into the back of the buggy and untied the horses from the hitching post. Their tails swished as Johannes worked, and she watched his strong hands— gentle, but competent. She shivered in spite of the warm day, her back still tingling where his hand had firmly guided her out the door of the restaurant. There was something about his touch—his confidence, his familiarity. It made her breath catch, and it made her imagine things she shouldn't . . . like what his kiss would be like. How his arms would feel wrapped around her . . . If he was indeed the fiancé he claimed to be, then those were some memories she'd like to get back, and the realization made her cheeks heat.

All of these feelings might be new for her, but they weren't for him, and she could feel that in the way his hand had moved against her back, knowing exactly how to guide her. If they'd been everything he'd claimed to each other, then *he* knew what *her* kisses felt like . . .

In the restaurant, he'd been calm, but there had

been a protectiveness about him. He wouldn't let anyone question her about what had happened, and he'd leaned forward, elbows on the table, staring directly at the people who'd stopped to talk.

He was standing guard, and the visitors seemed to recognize that. They were all strangers to her—talking quickly, asking questions, mentioning things she didn't remember—and it felt a little safer knowing that tall, muscular Johannes was cutting those overwhelming conversations short on her behalf. They had to get through him before they got to her.

Johannes led the horses out of the parking space, then looked up and down the road before hoisting himself up next to her, untying the reins, and giving them a flick. He leaned forward to check traffic out the side mirror again and then glanced in her direction with a small smile.

"So, how did you like eating out?" he asked.

"It was very nice," she said. "And those people all seemed to know me."

"That's how things work when you were born here," he said. "Eventually you'll remember that you know all of them, too."

How long would this take? It was difficult being told who she knew and who she didn't and having no way to verify any of it.

"How old am I?" she asked after a moment.

He cast her a sidelong smile. "Twenty-one."

"Oh. I only thought to ask now." She eyed him. He looked young—no gray in his hair, freshly shaven face, no lines around his eyes. "How old are you?"

"Twenty-four," he replied.

She nodded. "Hmm."

These were only numbers to her, but it was nice to know all the same.

"You didn't like those people coming in to talk to us," she said.

"It was fine." His voice low, deep, and his eyes were fixed on the road.

"That's not true," she countered. "I could tell. You hated it."

He sighed. "*Yah*, well . . . it's supposed to be fine. And it would have been if things were normal, but things aren't, are they? You have no memory, and I'm . . . . maybe I'm not wanting to share you quite yet. You don't remember *me*, Lovina."

"I'm sorry," she murmured.

"And you don't have to keep apologizing for that!" He shook his head, reining the horses in to stop at an intersection. When his turn came, he flicked the reins again and the horses started forward. "You were in an accident. That's not your fault. But what we used to be—it's really far from this."

"Because we were engaged," she said softly.

"Because we were *in love* with each other," he said, and he cast her a look so full of agony that her breath caught in her chest. "I knew you, and you knew me. We understood each other. We adored each other. We—" His voice broke.

For a few beats, neither of them said anything, and the clopping of the horses' hooves filled in the silence between them. She put her hand on his arm, and he clasped her fingers in a hard grip.

"So we start over," she said. There was no other choice.

He looked down at her with pain in his eyes, but he didn't answer. He was the one who needed comforting today, it seemed. He was the one with the broken heart, and she was the one who couldn't remember anything that they'd been to each other.

"I'm not trying to pressure you," he added. "I'm not trying to make you feel bad, or feel like you owe me anything. Because you don't. It's just difficult to step back."

Lovina sucked in a wavering breath. "We're out together, aren't we? That's something."

"You don't know what I mean," he said, his voice low. "I'm doing the right thing here. I'm . . . not assuming anything. You might not feel the same way the second time around. Just because you fell for me once—"

"We can get to know each other," she repeated.

He smiled faintly. "Maybe I'll be better at impressing you the second time around."

"You weren't very good the first time?" she asked.

"My hands were sweaty when I held your hand, and the first time I kissed you, I missed and kissed your ear," he said.

It was comical to think of having this big, handsome man be so flustered as to completely miss when trying to kiss a girl . . . trying to kiss *her*, more precisely. It was so different from the confident man she'd been dealing with so far.

Lovina laughed. "Really?"

"You forgave it, of course," he said. "Neither of us had any idea of what we were doing."

"And you do now," she breathed. She was the only one who didn't . . .

"I have a better idea now than I did then." His voice

was low again, and she felt a course of goose bumps move over her arms as he gave her hand a little squeeze.

"What else did we do?" she asked.

"Oh, I took you on drives and was too terrified to say much," he said. "I held your hand and memorized what your fingernails looked like, and how your hand looked in mine . . ."

Lovina looked down at his hand gently covering hers. His was sun-browned and broad, strong.

"You must have talked eventually," she murmured.

"*Yah*, of course," he said, and he gave her fingers another squeeze. "But that was thanks to you. You knew how to get me to open up. You asked me about my *daet*, and my family, and about what I liked about farming . . ."

"Should I ask that now?" she whispered.

"All right." He smiled, his gaze flickering down at her. "What would you like to know?"

"About your *daet* and your family," she said. "To start."

"Well, like I said before, my *daet* is a dairy farmer. And my *mamm* died when I was a teenager, and I'm the second youngest in the family. My younger sister got married last fall to a boy she met in another community. She went out there to stay with one of my *daet*'s cousins, and she met him."

"Is he nice?" she asked.

"*Yah*. My sister talks very well of him in letters, and we see them from time to time. He's quite shy—not a big talker—but he's smitten with my sister, which is what counts."

She smiled at that.

"My oldest sister, Linda, was already married when my *mamm* passed, and she came to stay with us for a few

weeks during the time of the funeral and all that,"
Johannes went on. "She's strong—really strong. She's the
kind of woman who can hold up a whole family. Her
husband passed away a few years later, and I went out
to help her through the funeral, and I got to know my
nephew better."

"Daniel," she said.

"*Yah*, Daniel." He smiled. "He's a nice kid. I can see
my sister in him, but also his *daet*. He's got his father's
mannerisms."

"Do you think Linda will get married again?" Lovina
asked.

"Apparently, there is a man who's interested," he
replied. "I'm not sure how good a man he is, though. He
seems to be hard on Daniel, and I don't like that. She
needs a good man, not just any man who will provide for
her. I know that women have the pressure to find another
husband once they have *kinner* to feed, but . . . I don't
know."

"You worry about her," Lovina said.

"*Yah*. I do."

"I daresay you are a very noble man, Johannes," she
said quietly.

He didn't answer.

"I wish I could tell you about my family in return. That
seems like the right thing to do," she said.

"You still could," he said.

"You know them better than I do," she replied with a
short laugh.

"That's okay," he said. "I still want to hear it."

Was he really playing along with this? She looked up
at him and then readjusted her position.

"Okay . . . well, I have one sister, who seems quite nice . . ." she began.

And for the rest of the drive home, she did her best to describe Elizabeth, Isaiah, and Bethany the best she could. She asked about her father, who she hadn't seen much of since being picked up at the hospital, and Johannes told her that she'd had a bit of a strained relationship with him, but he wouldn't say more. She pointed out the odd way Elizabeth and Isaiah had of looking at each other when she asked questions, and how they all warmed up to her like sunshine when she entered a room. She talked about Baby Mo, who was adored by everyone, even when he was cranky, and about the sweet life of taking care of that home and entertaining the baby that she'd settled into rather comfortably.

She talked about the quilt she inexplicably knew how to sew—how it was progressing, and how it was planning for Elizabeth's marriage to a man who had been to prison. But Elizabeth was the one who could see deeper, somehow—that was all anyone said. And no one in the family really questioned that upcoming wedding. Not in front of Lovina, at least. Even with her lost memory, that felt strange.

All the same, Elizabeth seemed to be completely headlong in love with him . . . Lovina had seen them together. And Sol Lantz was just as in love with Elizabeth. Their eyes sought each other out in a room, even when they were on opposite sides of it. And Elizabeth blushed when Sol murmured things that only she could hear. What they felt for each other was palpable in the room. And in a matter of weeks, Sol and Elizabeth would be married. They'd have a home of their own—Sol had already rented a little house, and he was working hard to fill it with furniture.

Johannes turned the horses into the drive, and he pulled them to a stop several yards from the house. There were no windows in direct sight of them, and when she looked over at him, she found his dark gaze locked on her.

"It's nice to get to know you," she said quietly.

He laughed softly. "I have to admit, it's rather nice to get to know you like this, too, with just you—you and your observations."

They were still seated quite close together, and his arm was pressed against hers. The leather buggy seat squeaked as he turned toward her and slid his arm along the back of the seat. They were inches apart, and his knee touched hers, but nothing else. His gaze dropped down to her lips, and she felt her heart skip a beat.

"Is this how you used to drop me off?" she whispered.

"*Yah,*" he said. "Just like this."

His gaze moved up to her eyes, then he reached out and brushed her bottom lip with the pad of his thumb. He dropped his hand.

"And we'd talk about things?" she asked hesitantly.

A smile touched his lips at that. "A little bit. We didn't always talk . . ."

And somehow she knew exactly what he was thinking. He wanted to kiss her. She could remember something faintly—the touch of lips against hers, breath against her cheek, the smell of musk and man . . . Would he kiss her now?

She leaned forward ever so slightly, but Johannes didn't close the gap between them. For a moment that hung between them like an eternity, his gaze lingered on

her lips, but he didn't make a move. Lovina pulled back,
embarrassment flooding through her. If he used to kiss
her . . . why not now? Her cheeks flamed with heat, and
just as Johannes was about to say something, the side
door to the house opened and Isaiah came outside. He
was holding Mo in one arm, and when he saw the buggy
he waved.

"You're back!" Isaiah called. "I came home early to
fix a leak in the stable roof! Do you have the time to help,
Johannes?"

Johannes looked over at Lovina, and he sucked in a
breath as if he was about to speak again, but then he
stopped.

"It's fine," she said, blinking back tears that threatened
to rise. "Go help him."

"I could come by the house afterward for pie," he said,
and he caught her eye with a pleading look.

"*Yah*, that would be nice," she replied, but her voice
was tight.

Johannes hopped down from the buggy, and Lovina
did the same. She flicked her skirt straight again after
reaching the ground, an automatic gesture, and she
caught her brother's easy smile in her direction.

"I won't keep him too long," Isaiah said. "Do you want
to take Mo? Bethany and Elizabeth are changing linens
upstairs, so he was getting in the way."

"*Yah*, of course." She held her arms out for the chubby
baby.

"I'll help you unhitch," Isaiah said to Johannes.

As Lovina made her way back toward the little house,
she looked back over her shoulder toward Johannes. He

glanced up at her once, and his gaze caught hers for one intense moment. Then he turned away.

What had happened there in the buggy? If she was his fiancée, why hadn't he kissed her when he had the chance? He'd told her before about the passion in their relationship. Why hold back now?

And then a possibility that explained it all came rushing in like cold water. Everyone kept talking about the relationship they used to have . . . but maybe his feelings had changed, and he hadn't kissed her because he hadn't wanted to. Simple as that.

Chapter Six

It took a couple of hours to patch the weak spot in the stable roof, and the entire time he worked on it, his mind kept slipping back to Lovina. He'd almost kissed her— he'd only barely stopped himself from falling right back into old habits with her. But how would he be able to explain himself after that?

She's *wasn't* his fiancée. Not anymore. And he needed to put his own life together. Did he really expect that Lovina's memory would come back and she'd just choose the life she'd left? It might be what her family was hoping she'd do, but it wasn't a reasonable expectation. So what was he doing to himself? This was just punishment.

Isaiah asked him a few questions about how his sister was doing, and Johannes answered as honestly as he could. But what could he really say? She'd remembered some food, and he'd been falling in love with her again. But he wasn't about to admit to his feelings.

When they finished nailing down some new shingles on the roof of the stable, Johannes went toward the ladder to go down, and he paused when he spotted Lovina standing on the porch. She was watching them work, a peculiar look on her face. Johannes raised one hand in a wave, and her fingers fluttered in response, then she descended the steps and headed toward the stable.

Johannes came down the ladder, and when Isaiah emerged outside, his gaze flickered between the two of them.

"Maybe I'll just head in and see how Bethany is doing," Isaiah said. He was giving them some privacy.

Isaiah strode toward the house, and Johannes cleared his throat. He wasn't thinking straight right now, and he knew it. And he needed to behave well so that when he told his father how things had gone, he wouldn't feel guilty or have to hide anything.

"I should probably head home," Johannes said. "This took longer than I thought, and my *daet* needs help with the milking."

What he really needed was some time alone to sort out his own feelings—get them back under control—and milking was a good enough activity to allow him to do that.

Lovina looked at him uncertainly. "Okay."

Johannes fetched his horses from the corral.

"I could help," Lovina said.

He didn't really want the help—he wanted space. Or rather, he needed space, because being this close to her wasn't helping him to keep perspective here. She looked at him, her blue eyes filled with misgiving.

"Do you remember how to do this?" he asked her.

"*Yah*, I think I do." She reached for the straps to secure the horse in place. Johannes watched her fingers moving deftly.

They worked together in silence until the horses were

both hitched, and then Johannes led the horses around and up the drive a little ways. He could make excuses, say he was getting the horses into shade, for example, but it wasn't that. It was to give him and Lovina just a little more privacy. The buggy would shield them from view.

Lovina licked her lips and dropped her gaze.

"Is something wrong?" Johannes asked.

"I could ask you the same thing." She tucked a stray tendril of hair back under her *kapp*.

"Everything is fine," he said, and he moved closer, looking down at her face—the faint freckles over her nose, the pale lashes that looked so much longer when he was this close to her. Why did looking down into those blue eyes always unhinge him like this?

"You—" She took a step back. "Earlier, when we arrived, you had the chance to kiss me, Johannes. And you didn't."

He smiled uncertainly. "Your brother came out, and—"

"It wasn't my brother who stopped you. You had the chance, and you didn't." She raised her gaze to meet his, and he saw something close to anger flashing there. "You aren't acting like a fiancé. Apparently, we've been planning a wedding, and I don't have a wedding quilt, and you don't even kiss me!"

So he'd offended her by not kissing her . . . If only she knew the self-control it had taken to keep himself in check.

"I'm trying to be respectful of what you've been through," he said, choosing his words carefully. "You don't remember me, or us, or . . ."

"I might not remember the past, but I know what I see

in front of me," she said, and her voice shook. "And you don't love me—"

Those words slipped past whatever fences he'd been putting up around his heart, and he stared at her in disbelief.

"What?" He caught her hand and pulled her closer. "You honestly think I don't love you?"

That had been the problem all along—he did! He loved her when he shouldn't—when it was wiser to fix his sights on other, more viable women. He was the idiot who couldn't stop loving her!

"If you loved me, you wouldn't be holding yourself back," she said. "I think you're being nice. I think you feel bad about my accident, and—"

"You have no idea what I'm feeling!" he shot back. "You think I don't love you, Lovina? I've been thinking about nothing but you since you left! I've been worrying about you, praying for your safety, and wondering why you didn't come back!"

His voice shook and he pressed his lips together, trying to regain control. He was saying too much.

"Then why haven't you kissed me yet?" she whispered.

Because it was the one thing still holding his heart together . . .

"It seemed wrong to kiss you like I wanted to when"—he swallowed—"when for you we've hardly met."

"I *know* we haven't just met," she said. "It just seems like you might be holding back for a reason, and—"

"What reason?" he asked gruffly, and he slid one hand behind her neck, pinning her to the spot.

"Maybe your feelings changed . . ." Her breath was shallow, her chest rising and falling with every intake, and he could see the tremble of her pulse at the base of her neck. She thought he didn't love her . . . She actually thought that he'd rather not pull her back into his arms where she used to belong?

"Are you saying you want me to kiss you?" he asked, his voice coming out in a growl. Because he hardly had a thread of restraint left inside of him.

"*Yah* . . ." she breathed. "I do."

It was the only encouragement he needed, and he pulled her against him more roughly than he'd intended, and traced her lips with the pad of his thumb. He wanted this more than she could imagine, he was sure, and when she sucked in a little breath, he lowered his mouth over hers, claiming her. For a moment she seemed stunned, frozen, and then her eyes fluttered shut and she leaned into him. He kissed her with all the pent-up passion he'd been holding back all this time, sliding one hand down her back to her waist, where he held her firmly against his body. He wanted more than this, more than even a fiancé could ask for, because nothing was going to be close enough in order to touch the loneliness at his core. He deepened the kiss until he was afraid he'd cross a line too many and have something serious to apologize for. She pressed closer against him, and he broke off the kiss with ragged breath.

He'd take this too far if he didn't stop now.

Lovina leaned her cheek against his shirt, and he could feel the patter of her heartbeat against his body. Her breath was coming fast, and when she pulled back and looked up at him, her cheeks were flushed.

"Like that?" he murmured.

She didn't answer, and he didn't really expect her to. She'd asked to be kissed, and if he were a different man, or if they had a different past, he might have been able to give her a chaste little peck on her lips, but there was no way he could hold himself to that.

Lovina took a step away from him, and he felt a wave of regret.

"I hope I didn't scare you," he said.

"No, it's okay . . ." She took another step back, and behind her the side door opened and Bethany appeared at the open screen, the baby on her hip.

"Did you want to come in for pie, Johannes?" Bethany called.

She wasn't really asking him in for pie; she was reminding him of the boundaries, and he'd plowed right over them just now.

"No, I'll head home!" he called back. "But thank you."

He shot Lovina a weak smile. Would she forgive him for that kiss when her memory came back?

"You'd best get inside," he said. "Your family is waiting, and I have to help my *daet* with the milking, so . . ." He licked his lips, and she stared at him mutely for a moment. "That was why I was holding back . . . for the record," he added.

Had he upset her? Guilt wriggled up inside of him, but then she said, "Will you come back to see me again?"

She was asking, and he was powerless to refuse her.

"I can come tomorrow," he said. He'd be back in time for milking. "Maybe a picnic by the creek. We used to like that."

"That would be nice," she said, and a smile tickled her lips.

He shouldn't be doing this. He was galloping past all of the boundaries he'd set up . . .

"I'll see you then," he said.

Without another word, Lovina turned back toward the house. He watched her go with a lump in his throat. He shouldn't have kissed her like that—it had been wrong. But if he had to do it all over again, he couldn't say that he'd choose anything different.

She asked to be kissed . . . Gott help him if she asked for it again.

Lovina hadn't expected a kiss like that, and as she walked back to the house, her lips were still moist from his. That was her first kiss . . . the first she could remember, at least, and it had made her heart nearly beat out of her chest, and her knees felt wobbly even now . . . Perhaps asking for that kiss had been naive on her part. She'd thought that Johannes had been making nice, hiding some lapse in their relationship, perhaps, but a kiss like that one?

The way he'd pulled her in, the urgency of his hands sliding up her back, his lips covering hers . . . His body had been hot against her, and she had felt the trembling limits of his self-control as he'd broken off that kiss.

She wasn't sure what she'd expected, but not that . . .

The buggy rattled on down the drive, and she turned and watched it go. There had been more between them than she'd guessed, and she sucked in a shaky breath.

"Has Johannes gone, then?" Bethany asked as Lovina came back in through the side door.

"*Yah*, he . . . had to help with milking, I think," Lovina said.

That was what he had said, wasn't it? It all felt a little blurry now.

"Did you have a nice lunch?" Elizabeth asked, coming down the stairs. She was carrying a bucket and a mop, and she put them down next to the kitchen sink.

"*Yah*, it was very nice," Lovina said, and she forced a smile that she hoped looked natural. "They had my favorite dish there."

"*Yah*?" Elizabeth dried her hands on her apron, her eyes brightening. "You remembered it?"

"I knew what the foods were," Lovina said. "I recognized the menu . . . and I know that probably sounds silly—"

"It doesn't sound silly!" Elizabeth burst out. "It sounds wonderful! It's coming back!"

For the next few minutes Elizabeth and Bethany chattered away, seemingly overjoyed at some memories returning. They talked about Amish foods and about restaurants they enjoyed in town, not seeming to require much input from Lovina, and she was left to her own thoughts, which kept circling around that heart-pounding kiss. He'd been holding himself back because *that* was how he felt . . . and he hadn't wanted to scare her.

She wasn't scared of him, exactly, but she was a little unnerved by her own very physical response to him. Was that her memory coming back that drew her to him, or was it something else . . . something more carnal, and more dangerous? How wicked did it make her that she was hoping to see the edge of his self-control again?

The sound of hooves and buggy wheels pulled Lovina out of her reverie, and she went to the window to look out. Was it Johannes coming back? Elizabeth met her at the window, and for a moment, they both watched as an older man jumped down from the buggy seat. It wasn't Johannes . . . but he did look a little familiar. He'd been there at the hospital to bring her back to this house, but she hadn't seen him since. She watched as he moved around the single horse that pulled his buggy, his movements confident and sure. Isaiah met him and they started unhitching together.

"Daet's here," Ellizabeth said, and it was like her voice echoed in the back of Lovina's mind. She'd heard that before—many times . . . *Daet's here*.

"Our father?" Lovina asked.

"*Yah*. Do you remember him at all?" Elizabeth asked.

The man? No. But her sister saying the words—that felt familiar. It was hard to explain, though, so she said, "No, not really."

The baby's cry started upstairs, and Bethany headed up the stairs, leaving Lovina and Elizabeth alone.

"Don't we have a mother?" Lovina asked.

"She passed away when you were a toddler," Elizabeth said. "Daet raised us alone after that. He never did remarry. Mamm had been the only one for him, he said, and he couldn't imagine being with anyone else."

Elizabeth's voice was quiet, and Lovina watched as that older man slid a hand down the horse's flank and he released the last strap and pulled the leather away. That man was her father. Isaiah led the horse toward the corral, and the older man looked toward the house.

His hat sat on top of gray hair, and his eyes looked sad. She knew her father's name was Abe Yoder—they'd told her that much—and she searched the lined face, looking for some lurking memory . . .

Abe Yoder saw them in the window, and the lined face crinkled up into a smile as he headed toward the house. Lovina pulled away from the window. Why was remembering a family so difficult? Why could she recall a restaurant menu, the timber of her sister's voice, but not her own father? That didn't seem right.

Elizabeth went to open the door, and she and Abe murmured in the mudroom for a moment before they both came back into the kitchen.

"Lovina!" Abe said, holding out his arms to her. "Come give your father a hug."

Lovina hesitated, looking at the man's face. His eyes were warm, and he blinked back some emotion. She moved toward him, and he enfolded her gently in his arms, giving her a squeeze and then releasing her. He smiled down into her face.

"You look like you're keeping well," he said.

"*Yah*. I'm fine," she said.

"Good." He patted her shoulder. "Good. I'm glad. I hear you've been seeing more of that Miller boy."

"Johannes?" she asked, and she felt some humor touch her lips.

He wasn't quite a "boy," now, was he? He was every inch of him a work-hardened man, and he'd shown her a side of himself that she wasn't going to forget.

"*Yah*. I always did like him. Is he behaving well?" Abe asked.

"Remarkably," Elizabeth cut in with a small smile.

Well, it would seem that no one had spotted that kiss, and it was just as well. She felt the prickle of goose bumps on her arms.

"I'll start cooking," Elizabeth said, and when Lovina made a move to go help her, she added, "Lovina, you visit with Daet. I'll be fine."

Lovina watched her sister head to the stove, and she looked back at Abe. He nodded toward the kitchen table, and they both took a seat, Lovina sitting opposite her father. For a moment, he just looked at her with that smile.

"Do you know me?" he asked gently. "You can be honest. You won't hurt my feelings."

"No," she replied. "Sorry."

He nodded and dropped his gaze. "It will come back. The doctors are certain that it will."

"*Yah*, that's what everyone keeps saying," she replied.

"You had a happy childhood," he said. "Your *mamm* died when you were little, but I devoted myself to you *kinner*, and you three were very, very loved."

"I'm glad . . ." She wasn't sure how to answer that. It was a childhood she couldn't recall. Johannes had mentioned some tension in their relationship, though.

"You and I used to take walks down the road to our neighbor's fruit stand when you were about this high," her father said, measuring a height next to him with one hand. "And we'd buy enough fruit to carry in a basket back home again. You used to be the one to choose the fruit you wanted so that you and your sister could make pies."

"Johannes said something about me making pies, too," Lovina admitted.

"You used to like blackberries the best," her father said. "Johannes liked your apple pies, but you, my dear girl, liked blackberry."

Lovina smiled. "Did I?"

"You're a young woman who knows her mind," he said, and then his face colored slightly. "You knew your feelings, maybe I should say. You knew what you liked, and you knew what you didn't. You had strong opinions, too."

"Is that a good thing?" she asked with a rueful smile.

"Depends on who you ask," her father said with a chuckle. "If you ask your *daet*, I say it is a very good thing. Put on the right path, that's called strength of character."

There were footsteps on the stairs outside, and the side door opened and then banged shut again. Her brother would be done with the horses.

"I used to be a preacher," her father went on. "And you and your sister and brother would sit at the front when I preached—your brother on the men's side, and you'd sit with your sister on the women's. And you'd fix me with this direct stare of yours while I expounded upon the Word—it was hard not to smile at you!"

"You aren't a preacher anymore?" she asked.

"No." He shook his head, but he didn't elaborate.

A loving father who would spend time with her and take her for walks . . . a preaching *daet* who would try not to look too jovial while he preached, but who had a

hard time because his daughter was watching him . . .
And blackberry pie! These stories were lovely—they
were a life she longed to remember!

"So why can't I remember it?" she asked, her voice
shaking.

Isaiah came into the room then, and Bethany came
down the stairs with the baby in her arms. They all turned
toward her at once, and she felt that strange intensity
from them all over again. This kept happening!

"You're all acting so strangely!" she burst out. "All of
you! You keep doing that!"

"Doing what?" Elizabeth asked, drying her hands on
a towel.

"Staring at me like this," she said. "And you tell me
these lovely stories that I can't recall! You tell me things
I said, and things I did . . . You tell me things I liked. But
I can't remember any of it! It's like you aren't my family
at all, and you're all just pretending!"

The words came out in a rush, but this was her actual
fear. What if this life they described wasn't actually hers?

"We aren't pretending," Isaiah said. "I can promise
you that. You're very much our little sister. We wouldn't
be going to all this trouble if you weren't."

"Then why can't I remember you?" Lovina demanded.
"Why can't I remember a preacher father and a fun-loving
brother and sister? How come the only *clear* memory I
have is *English*?"

The room stilled, and Lovina could hear the tick of the
clock behind her on the wall.

"What?" Elizabeth was the first the break the silence.
She came back to the table and pulled up a chair next to
Lovina. "You remember something?"

"I don't remember *this*," she said, glancing around the room. "Any of it!"

"What do you remember?" Isaiah asked, his voice low.

"It isn't even a full memory," she said. "I remember sitting on a bed. I'm wearing blue jeans. I have a laptop computer on my lap, and I'm watching a movie. There's a digital clock on a bedside table next to me. I have a cell phone in my hand and someone texts me a message asking if I want popcorn. It feels . . . natural."

Everyone was silent, their eyes fixed on her. No one spoke.

"That's all," she added. "But I know it's a real memory and not something I dreamed or something like that, because my toenails used to be painted red. I can see some polish around the edges of my toes."

"We know what is right and wrong," her father said slowly. "And sometimes we rebel. That doesn't mean you aren't Amish, my dear."

"What does that even mean?" she demanded. "It all sounds very nice, but it doesn't answer my questions, does it?"

"You believe that we're your family, at least, don't you?" Elizabeth asked, putting a hand on her arm.

"Your voice is familiar," Lovina admitted, swallowing.

"Mine?" Elizabeth whispered.

"*Yah*, I could remember your voice saying 'Daet's here,' and I remember hearing you say that before. Many times, I think," Lovina replied.

And there was Johannes, the man she didn't remember, but whose kiss was too heartbroken and urgent to be anything but sincere. The way he'd pulled her against him . . . She wrapped her arms around her middle.

"So it is coming back," Abe said, and he sounded so calm and reassuring that Lovina looked up at him hopefully. "Lovina, my little sunbeam, it's going to be okay. You're home where you belong. If you need time to remember, that's okay. We have plenty of it."

Still not an answer.

"Why do I remember *English* things?" she pressed, looking around the room. "If I'm Amish, why do I remember *that* so clearly?"

"Because you had a Rumspringa," her father said at last. "You spent a little bit of time away from us with some Englishers. We didn't like it, but I suppose you needed to experience a different way of life for a bit. And I suppose . . . it left an impact."

Isaiah exchanged a look with Elizabeth, but Abe didn't take his eyes off of Lovina. He smiled at her encouragingly.

"Do you remember getting into trouble for nail polish when you came home from a friend's house?" he asked with a twinkle in his eye. "I made you rub it off with paint thinner, and we had a long talk about modesty and a woman's true beauty lying in her heart, and not in makeup or paint, or other fancy things the Englishers do to their bodies to try and look appealing . . . We talked about a woman's character, and her love for her family, and her family's love for her."

Was that all it was? Was she remembering some brief rebellion? Had she painted her nails again and then rubbed it off?

"I don't remember that part," she said.

"I wasn't the perfect *daet*," Abe said quietly. "I tried—as we all do—but I wasn't perfect. But I'm still here, my girl. And I know you. You're kind and smart. You've got a very quick wit about you, and you've always been one to question authority."

"I don't think—" Isaiah began.

"No, no," Abe went on. "It's not bad to question the rules. When we question them, we realize why we follow them, and they become a personal choice instead of an order."

Lovina looked at the older man's face—the lines around his eyes, the warmth in his gaze, the way his lips turned up into a half smile when he spoke. His beard was grizzled and gray, but she could almost see a version of him in her mind's eye with a beard that was dark brown like mahogany wood, and eyes without the lines surrounding them . . .

"As we go to sleep, we thank Thee for this day," she murmured, the memory coming back with the lilt of a childhood rhyme. "We ask Thee to help us choose the right, in work as well as play . . ."

" . . . Make us humble and kind, grateful and good," her father continued, tears shining in his eyes. "Give us only enough so that we choose what we should. And when we awake, give us strength for the rest—"

"And keep us together, happy and blessed," she concluded.

"Amen," her father said, and he wiped a tear from his cheek. He reached across the table and clasped her hand in his. "That was the prayer we said every night when I tucked you into your beds when you *kinner* were small."

"We'd say it together, the three of us," Isaiah said. "And then I'd go into my bed across the room, and you and Elizabeth would curl up in your bed together. You had squeaky springs."

"And we'd whisper after the lamp was blown out," Elizabeth said. "We could hear Daet downstairs, and we'd whisper about all the little secrets that *kinner* hold. Do you remember that?"

She didn't remember being tucked in, or the whispering with her siblings after the light went out, but the words were sharp in her memory now. And she remembered rolling over, hearing the squeak of springs beneath her.

"I think I remember . . . some of it," she said.

Elizabeth slipped an arm around her shoulders, and Isaiah did the same for his wife, who now stood at his side.

"Well, *we* remember," Elizabeth said. "We had a good childhood."

"It'll come back," Isaiah said. "The doctor said it would."

"Of course," Abe said with a teary nod. "Just a matter of time."

Chapter Seven

Johannes opened a drawer in the kitchen and rummaged around. He was looking for scissors. He had a fraying lace on one of his boots that was bothering him, and he wanted to trim it. But he couldn't see the scissors, so he opened another drawer, and another.

Johannes felt about as frayed as that lace. All day, he'd been thinking about Lovina and that kiss . . . He was kicking himself for it. Kissing her like that—it was wrong. She didn't remember him, their relationship, or how *she'd* felt! And asking for a kiss wasn't the same thing as asking to be kissed with all the pent-up passion inside of a man.

The kiss had been honest on his part, but he'd also meant to hold himself back more than he had—to stop short of the kind of kiss that would sear through his own blood and show her exactly what had been boiling beneath the surface all this time.

Because she couldn't handle it. She couldn't even remember him, or the life she'd lived in the idyllic town of Bountiful. She was vulnerable, fragile . . . and he was supposed to be protecting her!

He slammed shut another drawer.

"What are you doing?" Bernard asked, coming into the kitchen with a slab of beef wrapped in paper.

"Looking for scissors," he said. "Is that dinner?"

"*Yah*, Arnold traded it to me for more help with his fence this morning," Bernard replied. Arnold was an *Englisher* neighbor, a nice enough fellow who insisted on paying for the help he received—and sometimes that payment came in the form of meat.

Bernard slapped the wrapped meat onto the counter and opened a cupboard to pull out a roasting pan. Then he tore open the package and dumped the thick, red cut of meat into its depths.

"Excuse me, son," Bernard said, reaching past him to open a cupboard and pull down some spices. Then he set to seasoning the meat in his haphazard way—a little of this, a little of that. He sniffed at a bottle, and then shook some on top.

His father's arrival was a welcome interruption to his own self-recriminations. He'd been going over it in his head all morning, and from no angle did he look any better.

"Were you using the scissors?" Johannes asked.

Bernard opened another drawer and pulled out an old pair of scissors—they were dull and needed sharpening.

"Thanks," Johannes said, accepting them. They'd have to do. But he'd bought a new pair of sharp shears not too long ago, and it was irritating not to be able to find them.

"So Paul, Amos, and I talked to the bishop today,"

Bernard said. "And he says he and the elders will pray over it, but they're leaning toward allowing cell phones for business purposes on the farms."

"You'd keep them in the barn, I suppose?" Johannes said.

"*Yah*, of course," Bernard said. "We could charge the cell phone with the generator. It would cost to buy it, and there would be a monthly fee. I can't say I like that very much."

"How much would it cost?" Johannes asked.

Bernard shook his head. "I have no idea. But other communities have been using cell phones for safety for some time. And I know we have the one phone for community use, but having a phone on the farm might be useful. Did you read about the Amish man who broke his leg out in the field and used a cell phone to call for help?"

"*Yah*, I think I did," Johannes said.

"And then Elizabeth Yoder used our community cell phone when she was being harassed by those local trouble-makers," Bernard said. "There are safety issues to keep in mind. We need to rely on each other—that's why the Ordnung keeps us from adopting the *Englisher* conveniences. But there is the argument that we also shouldn't be left like sitting ducks for the criminal element to take advantage of. And I think we in Bountiful have experienced a little more of that than most."

Johannes squinted at his father. "You want a cell phone, don't you?"

"All I'm saying is, it's worth discussing," Bernard said.

"But I'll accept what the bishop and the elders agree upon."

Johannes smiled ruefully. Yes, it looked like Bernard had warmed up to the idea.

"Where is Daniel?" Johannes asked.

"The last I saw him, he was heading out to the barn to feed the calves," Bernard said.

Johannes looked out the window. The sun was getting low in the sky.

"This will be good," Bernard said, surveying the meat in the tin roaster.

"*Yah,*" Johannes agreed, looking into the pan.

Bernard headed for the stove and sank down to his haunches. He pulled open the oven door and reached for the kindling.

"Would you mind checking on Daniel?" Bernard asked. "It's been a few hours. If nothing else, bring him in so we can spend some time with him."

"*Yah,* I'll go find him," Johannes replied. He cut the piece of lace from his boot, and it took a couple of tries to get through it. Then he put the scissors back into the drawer.

Johannes headed out the side door, his boots thunking down the steps, and then he headed in the direction of barn. The barn was a five-minute walk from the house, and he passed the chicken coop, the stables, and the corral as he listened to the far-off lowing of the cattle.

Johannes was frustrated, and it wasn't because of missing scissors or a frayed lace. He was upset with himself for that kiss, and he was starting to resent his role in Lovina's recovery. He knew what the Yoders were hoping—that she'd remember loving him, and not remember her year away. But that wasn't reasonable . . . and Johannes's own hopes right now weren't terribly reasonable, either, because he found himself hoping for another chance to pull her into his arms and have some release for the mounting pressure inside of him.

He pulled open the barn door and looked inside. The calves were in their stalls, all seeming content enough, which suggested full bellies. He let the barn door swing shut behind him, and he ambled down the stalls, stopping at one large stall where three bucket-fed calves were lying in the hay, milk still on their chins. He stopped and looked around. Where was his nephew?

Johannes heard a shuffling sound overhead in the hayloft, and he headed for the ladder that led up. He climbed the rungs and made it to the top. The hayloft had a few bales still stacked, but it was mostly empty, waiting for a new harvest and fresh bales to feed the cattle through another winter. The large back doors were flung open, and he could see his nephew seated in the light of the lowering sun, hunched over something, his attention absorbed.

"Daniel?" he said.

The boy startled and turned, shoving whatever he was working on behind a bale of hay. His face flushed red. As Johannes stepped up onto the floor of the loft, he spotted the new scissors laying on the bale of hay his nephew had just been sitting on.

"What are you doing?" Johannes asked.

"Nothing." Daniel pushed some unruly hair away from his forehead.

"How long have you been up here?" Johannes asked.

"Awhile," Daniel said. "The work is done. Dawdie said I could do what I wanted when I was finished."

"So what are you doing?" Johannes pressed. He walked over to where his nephew had been sitting, and Daniel moved to physically block him. Johannes's first thought was of dirty magazines. The Englishers sold them, and sometimes Amish boys got their hands on them, but how Daniel would have found any was beyond Johannes.

"Now you're making me worried," Johannes said. "Daniel, I'm serious. What are you doing out here?"

Daniel licked his lips, which were suddenly pale, and he swallowed. "Sewing."

"What?" Johannes laughed in surprise. "I'm not joking, Dan. What are you doing? I was your age once, too. Hiding a sin only makes it worse, you know. The guilt gets you."

Johannes reached behind his nephew into the crevasse behind him, and his hand closed down on something sharp.

"Ouch!" He pulled his hand out, and there was a dot of blood on his finger.

Daniel reached into his hiding spot and pulled out a wad of fabric. He smoothed it out carefully, but he wouldn't look up. Sewing. He hadn't been lying about that.

"Can I see that?" Johannes asked.

Daniel didn't say anything, so Johannes picked it up and looked at it. It was patchwork—the kind women did for quilts. There were tiny pieces of fabric sewn together, but the pattern wasn't evident.

"You're really *sewing*?" Johannes murmured.

"*Yah.*"

"Why?" Johannes asked feebly.

"I don't know." Daniel looked away.

"You have the good scissors, too," Johannes said, picking them up. "Daniel, I don't get it. Why are you doing this? Did you damage something that you're trying to replace, or—"

"I like it," Daniel said.

"Sewing." Johannes sighed. "Daniel, this is women's work. I know you spent a lot of time with your *mamm* and sisters, and you've probably seen them work on enough quilts, but . . ." He reached out and put a hand on Daniel's shoulder. "Look, you're here with us for a while, and we're going to do things the manly way, okay?"

Daniel held out his hand for the fabric, and Johannes was tempted to keep it and throw it away, but he handed it back. Daniel smoothed it and carefully folded it before pushing it into his shirt.

"Did your *mamm* teach you how to sew?" Johannes asked.

Daniel shook his head. "No."

Then Johannes remembered that sewing kit that Sovilla had sent back for Daniel and her words of warning that he was a sensitive boy . . .

"Not Sovilla—" Johannes said.

"No, not her," Daniel said testily. "I taught myself. I just . . . I could see how it worked, and it's not like I'm making a woman's quilt. I'm not doing a Wedding Ring pattern or a Star Quilt or a Basket Block . . . I'm just . . ." Daniel shook his head. "Never mind."

"You're just what?" Johannes asked.

"I can see a better way to do it," Daniel said, and for the first time he lifted his gaze to meet Johannes's, and he saw a gleam that hadn't been there before. "It's about the colors and the textures. I don't care for patterns. I can make pictures!"

"Pictures," Johannes said uncertainly.

"*Yah*. Look—" Daniel pulled out the fabric again, and he smoothed it out. "You see? I'm doing the blue of the sky right now, but you don't just do one block of blue— that's fake. Real sky has different bits of color in it. So I have the light blue, and the slightly darker, and then there's the icy blue that's almost white, and then some pink in there, too. I mean, look outside—"

Johannes looked out the open loft doors, then back at his nephew.

"So, maybe you can't see it yet," Daniel said, the enthusiasm waning. "But when I'm done, you will."

Quilting. His thirteen-year-old nephew was quilting like the women did . . . . And maybe he wasn't following the set patterns, but he was still sitting over his bits of cloth with a needle and thread.

"That's called a scrap quilt," Johannes said quietly.

"*Yah*," Daniel agreed. "But it's not just scraps, it's a *picture*."

It was still a *quilt*, and Johannes looked at his nephew for a couple of beats, and all he could think was how much easier it would have been to confiscate a dirty magazine. How were they going to explain this to his sister? Or did she know already, and that was part of her reason for shipping him off to spend time with the men?

Johannes rubbed a hand over his face. "Okay . . . Let's get back to the house," he said, for lack of anything better to say.

Daniel looked down at the fabric and folded it once more.

"Maybe just don't do that anymore," Johannes said.

"What?" Daniel said.

"Just stop doing it," Johannes said. "It's women's work. You know that. You're not a little boy anymore—you're almost a man. It's time to act like one."

Daniel looked up at him in silence, then pressed his lips together. Was that acceptance, or silent defiance? Johannes wasn't even sure. Maybe he'd been too harsh, but it had to be said.

"Dawdie is starting dinner," Johannes added, softening his tone. "And maybe I can show you how to do some carpentry or something. That's fun."

And it was more masculine, more appropriate.

He headed for the hole in the floor and the ladder leading down. He tucked the scissors into the waist of his pants and started down. Daniel needed time with men more than Johannes had previously appreciated.

The next morning, after breakfast was made, chores were complete, and a load of washing had been hung out on the clothesline, Lovina went outside to work on the flower garden in the front of the house. There were a few pots of flowers hanging from hooks on the porch, but the main flower garden in the front was quite spectacular.

Inside the house, Moses was crying loudly—the big, angry, hiccuppy kind of crying that wasn't going to be soothed very easily. She could hear Bethany's voice through an open window—the tone, not the words. She sounded tired, and a bit frustrated.

Isaiah had already left for work early, and Lovina stood outside by the flower beds, her mind still going over her most recently recovered memories.

The prayer that had come back to her mind the day before when their father had visited had been an unexpected nugget, and this morning, a few more memories from her childhood had surfaced. She remembered lying in a bed with her sister next to her. They were both little girls, and she remembered her feet being cold. They cuddled up close to each other to get warm. It must have been winter. She had another memory of standing on a porch on a summer evening watching two dragonflies and hearing her father's voice calling her in for worship. They were sweet memories—and she smiled now thinking of them.

Lovina had gone a couple of weeks now with no memories at all, so having something come back was a relief. Not only was it reassurance that this was her family and she belonged here, but it was nice to know that this quiet, happy life truly was hers.

Because life here was lovely—the rhythm of the days, the work interspersed with laughter and chatting. It was an event when her brother got home at the end of his work day at the book bindery, and Bethany would go wash her face and comb her hair once more before he arrived. Lovina doubted that Isaiah even knew his wife did that.

And then there was Johannes. She'd had a hard time accepting that they really had been engaged. It had just felt unbelievable somehow. He was so good-looking, so confident. His gaze could pin her to the spot, and his kiss . . . Oh, that kiss! She still wasn't sure what she thought of it, but even remembering his fingers on the back of her neck, his lips on hers, she felt a shiver.

If this community was hers for sure and certain, and this family, then it would seem that Johannes was part of that. That tall, handsome, protective man was truly hers . . .

She knelt down in the dirt and started pulling weeds and dropping them into a bucket. She absently listened to the cry of the baby back in the house—he was calming down a little bit now. She worked her way through one section of the flower garden, the bucket of weeds steadily filling. She didn't notice the buggy that had pulled into the drive until it was halfway to the house, and she looked up in surprise at the clop of hooves.

It wasn't Johannes, who she was expecting to come later and take her for that promised picnic. This was a woman with two little girls on the front seat next to her. She was a serious-looking woman, and she held the reins like she was used to the task. The buggy was pulled by a single horse, and she reined in next to the garden.

"Good morning," Lovina said, looking up at her.

"Hello." The woman smiled hesitantly. "You must be Lovina."

"*Yah.*" Lovina pushed herself to her feet and brushed her hands off.

"I'm Sovilla," she said.

Sovilla seemed to be waiting for Lovina to react, so Lovina smiled.

"Nice to meet you," Lovina said.

The side door of the house opened and Elizabeth appeared on the step.

"Hi, Sovilla!" she called. "Girls, come on inside! I've got pie!"

Sovilla turned and helped the girls down, then they scampered toward the house, their little *kapp* strings trailing out behind them.

"Those are my daughters," Sovilla said. "Your sister has offered to watch them. I have a job interview in town."

"Oh?" Lovina brushed her hands again. "That's nice. What kind of job?"

Elizabeth stayed on the step watching them, and Sovilla waved again.

"I'll be just a minute!" Sovilla called, and Elizabeth disappeared back into the house.

"It's for a tourist location," Sovilla went on. "They need tour guides. They've got a house—a regular, Amish one—and Englishers get to walk through it and be all amazed at everyday things."

Sovilla shot her a smile, and Lovina couldn't help but chuckle.

"Well, I hope you get it," Lovina said.

"Thank you." Sovilla paused. "I hope there are no hard feelings between us."

Hard feelings? Why? Lovina frowned, looking the woman over.

"I don't remember you," Lovina said.

"We've never met, actually," Sovilla said. "But I'm the one Johannes was going to marry, and . . . I just want you to know that he was in love with you, and I knew it. That's why we called off the wedding plans. There was no point in marrying a man still in love with someone else. He adores you."

Lovina blinked. Johannes—the Johannes who had kissed her with such passion that she still felt a little breathless at the memory—had been going to marry another woman? None of this made sense!

"What?" she said feebly.

"They didn't tell you that . . ." Sovilla breathed, a look of horror coming to her face.

"No." Lovina glanced over her shoulder toward the house. "No one told me that!"

Least of all Johannes. He hadn't breathed a word . . .

"Oh!" Sovilla's face turned red. "I really stepped wrong, didn't I? I'm really sorry. I'm only making things worse—when you want to talk to me, I'm very willing. That's all I'm trying to say."

Sovilla retreated toward the house.

"Sovilla, wait!" Lovina called.

The other woman turned, her expression strained. Her face was blotched with red, and she shrugged helplessly.

"I'm sorry!" Sovilla repeated.

But it wasn't an apology that Lovina needed most right now. She closed the distance between them, glancing nervously toward the house, and lowered her voice.

"There is a lot they haven't told me," she said quietly. "And I've noticed the holes in the stories. It doesn't all make sense. People treat me like I've been gone for ages, and you're telling me you were going to marry my fiancé? My family makes it seem like I was gone for a week or two! Obviously, I don't know what's happening, and I have a right to know!"

Sovilla was silent for a moment, and she seemed to be considering her options.

"If you could just fill me in, I'd be really grateful," Lovina said, and she glanced quickly toward the house again. Bethany was in the window watching them now. There wasn't much time if she was going to get a hint of what was going on.

The side door opened again and Elizabeth appeared.

"Thank you for watching the girls for me!" Sovilla called brightly. "I really appreciate it!"

"It's not a problem," Elizabeth replied. "They're such sweet girls. It'll be fun to have some more *kinner* in the house. I was going to make cookies with them."

"They'll love that!" Sovilla replied brightly. "I shouldn't be too long. I'll come back right after the interview."

"Take your time," Elizabeth said. "Lovina, did you want to come help with the girls?"

Her sister wanted her inside—she could feel it.

"I'm not done with the garden yet," Lovina replied.

"Oh—" She could see her sister casting about for some excuse to call her in, so Lovina turned her back on the house and marched back toward the buggy. She heard Sovilla and Elizabeth exchange a last few pleasantries, and then Sovilla's footsteps on the gravel came up behind her.

"I deserve to know!" Lovina said quickly, whirling around.

"I have to rely on your sister and sister-in-law to help me," Sovilla said hurriedly. "And I can't go about alienating people who are going make it possible for me to start over. My husband is dead, and I have two daughters to raise. It's not simple for me."

"I won't tell them what you've told me," Lovina pressed. "I'll remember eventually, won't I? This might just help the process."

Sovilla was silent for a moment, then she sucked in a shaky breath. "What do you want to know?"

"Where was I?" Lovina asked.

"You left the community a year ago. You jumped the fence and went *English*. We have no idea where you were, because the next time anyone saw you was in that hospital, and they picked you up and brought you home."

"I was gone a *year*?" Lovina whispered. Was that where those nagging *English* memories were coming from?

"*Yah,*" Sovilla said softly. "And in that time, my Rueben died in a farming accident, and the communities tried to arrange a marriage between Johannes and me. We were both grieving. I was grieving my dead husband, and he was grieving you."

"But you didn't marry him, obviously," Lovina said weakly.

"We both thought we were willing to go through with it," Sovilla said. "He's a good man, but he loved you still. And I could tell. Then they found you at that hospital, and I couldn't compete with a woman who had Johannes's heart. I called it off. And he was grateful that I did, might I add."

Johannes had been getting ready to marry another woman . . . a woman with *kinner*. He had been intending to move on to a new family. No one had breathed a word of this, least of all Johannes. They all said that Lovina and Johannes were engaged . . . Her head was spinning.

"So Johannes and I weren't engaged anymore," Lovina clarified.

"No, you weren't," Sovilla said quietly. "But he loves you. He was so heartbroken when you left him, and time didn't heal those wounds. He just kept hoping he'd see you again. That man loves you, Lovina. Desperately."

Lovina sucked in a shaky breath. "Thank you for letting me know."

"You're welcome." Sovilla reached out and touched her arm. "I would never overstep. I've been married before. I've loved a man so deeply that his death rocked my entire world. I have no interest in moving in on another woman's man, okay? I promise you that."

"Thank you," Lovina said weakly. "I appreciate it."

"I'd stay longer, but I have to get to that interview," Sovilla said, and she looked at her watch. "I'm sorry."

"It's okay," Lovina said.

Sovilla looked over Lovina's shoulder, and Lovina looked back, too, to see the two little girls standing on the side porch.

"Becca, Iris, you girls be good, now," Sovilla called. "I'll be back soon!"

Then Sovilla hoisted herself back up into the buggy and gave Lovina another apologetic look.

"I really am sorry," she said.

Lovina nodded, and Sovilla made a clucking noise and flicked the reins, sending the buggy lurching into motion.

Elizabeth came down the steps, and Bethany called the little girls back into the house. Lovina could feel the tension crackling in the air.

"What did she say to you?" Elizabeth asked.

How much should Lovina say? She couldn't hide that they'd spoken, but she didn't want to break Sovilla's confidence, either. She'd taken a risk in saying as much as she had. Her sister was watching her with a cautious expression on her face, and Lovina heaved a sigh.

"She said Johannes loves me," Lovina said at last.

"*Yah*?" Elizabeth didn't seem convinced.

"Really loves me," Lovina said. "He doesn't want anyone else but me . . ."

Elizabeth smiled at that. "That's the truth. He doesn't. He's been in love with you since . . . oh, I don't even know how long. He started walking with you and giving you special attention when you were fourteen and he was seventeen. It was only friendship then, but he never did go give any other girl attention. It was always you after that."

"*Yah*?" Lovina turned toward her sister.

"I don't think that kind of love is a regular occurrence," Elizabeth said. "Johannes is the kind of man who would wait for you for as long as it took. And not because it's a choice, but because that's how much he loves you. . ."

This much sounded true. If he'd been unable to move on, and was back at her side after she'd left him for a year . . .

"Is your Sol like that?" Lovina asked.

"*Yah*." Elizabeth nodded. "He's exactly like that."

"I feel like you're not telling me everything, trying to protect me," Lovina said.

Elizabeth was silent for a moment, then she said, "It isn't all pretty and perfect, but I love Sol so much. Not everything in life is easy or comes along in the ideal way. But it's worth it . . . It really is! So *yah*, I've been trying to protect you from some of the hard things . . ."

"I wish you wouldn't," Lovina said. "I wish you'd just tell me the truth."

Elizabeth licked her lips and looked away. Would she tell Lovina the truth—that she'd been gone a year? Would she tell her what had happened?

"Do you know that Sol was willing to take a beating to protect me, and he didn't even give it a second thought?" Elizabeth asked.

No, Elizabeth wasn't going to, and maybe Lovina didn't want to hear it from Elizabeth. She wanted Johannes to tell her what had happened, because he was the one who should have said something from the start. He was the one who'd nearly married someone else!

"Somebody beat up Sol?" Lovina asked.

"Oh, Sol is a good man, and the time he spent in prison wasn't entirely his fault. Do you want to hear that story?" Elizabeth asked. "The real, unvarnished one?"

"*Yah*, I want to hear it," Lovina said.

Maybe it was time to hear a few honest, true, difficult stories from her family. They'd been trying to spare her from the truth, but she was tired of caution. She needed to hear how things really were. They could start with Elizabeth's story, and today when Johannes came, she'd ask him to tell her theirs.

She deserved the truth.

Chapter Eight

Johannes sat in the Yoder kitchen, watching as Bethany and Lovina put together a picnic lunch. He'd brought some cheese and roast beef sandwiches, and that had been declared "a very nice start" by Bethany, and they'd set about putting more items into a basket.

Apparently, Sovilla had dropped her daughters off to be watched while she went to a job interview, and the littlest girl, Iris, was playing with a doll, trying to feed it a spoonful of jam. No one seemed to notice just yet the mess she was making, and Johannes watched her in silence. She would have been his daughter, if he'd done the will of the community and married her *mamm* . . .

"Where are you going?" Becca asked, pausing at his chair and fixing him with a direct look that seemed just a little too grown-up for her four years.

He cleared his throat. "Uh—on a picnic."

"Are you taking me and Iris?" she asked.

A couple of weeks ago, her *mamm* had been telling her that Johannes might be her new *daet*. Did a child this young understand how quickly and thoroughly things could change? He felt a pang of regret.

"Not this time," he said. "I'm very sorry, Becca."

And he meant for more than the picnic. If he brought the girls on a picnic, it would only be more confusing for them. "It's very nice to see you today."

"My *mamm* is getting a job," Becca said. "Like daets do. She's going to go to work, and I don't know who will take care of me."

Her lip quivered, and she looked up at Johannes hopefully.

"Oh, Becca . . ." His heart stuttered, and he looked down at the small, mournful face. She'd lost her father in the last year, and he couldn't be the replacement. Now her mother would have to find a job because there was no husband to provide for them. And that was his fault— partly, at least.

"Hey . . ." he said, leaning forward. "Your *mamm* loves you very much, and we're not going to leave her on her own. We're a community. We help each other."

"I miss Mamm," Becca whispered, and tears welled in her eyes. What did this little girl care about a community of strangers when her *mamm* was out looking for a job that would take her away from her and her sister? He hadn't married Sovilla, and she and her daughters would suffer for it.

"She'll come back soon," he said with more confidence than he felt, then he looked over her head toward her little sister. "Did you notice Iris got into the jam?"

Becca turned then and sighed. "Iris, you can't do that! Dollies don't eat jam!"

And she turned away to her toddler sister, leaving Johannes to sit in his own sense of responsibility for all of this.

Lovina came to the table with a picnic basket, and Johannes stood up and picked it up for her. It was moderately heavy.

"Girls, we're going to make cookies!" Bethany said brightly to Becca and Iris. "Oh, dear, has someone gotten into the jam? Hold on—I'll get a cloth—"

And the bustle of a busy kitchen continued as Johannes carried the basket out the side door, Lovina close behind him. The screen door bounced shut behind them, and he headed down the stairs. He could still hear Bethany's cheery, maternal tone as she chattered to the girls.

"Is something wrong?" Lovina asked.

Johannes had been looking back at the house, feeling a flood of guilt. He obviously wasn't hiding it very well.

"No." He forced a smile. "It's fine."

Lovina didn't say anything, but she eyed him uncomfortably.

"We can walk to the creek from here," he added. "Apparently, it's just over at those trees. It's not too far. We used to do it all the time at a different creek. But Elizabeth says there's a nice little grassy spot by the water."

"*Yah*, okay," she said.

Johannes switched the picnic basket to his other hand to leave his hand closest to Lovina free to hold hers, but she stayed a proper twelve inches away from him, and he tried not to feel hurt by it. They were starting over, after all.

"Sovilla came by to drop off the girls," Lovina said. "And we talked a little while."

"Oh?" His heartbeat sped up and he glanced down at

her. She wasn't looking at him; her blue gaze was locked straight ahead.

"She filled me on a few things," Lovina said. "Things you didn't tell me."

She looked over at him then, and her gaze was filled with sharp recriminations.

"Like what?" he asked.

"Like the fact that you almost married her," Lovina said.

"That wasn't exactly—" He cleared his throat, his mind spinning. How much had Sovilla said? "It wasn't like that! Bishop Lapp had spoken to the bishop from the Edson community, and they needed a husband for Sovilla. It wasn't like I fell in love with her, it was—" He looked over at Lovina miserably. "You'd been gone for so long . . ."

The one detail they'd been keeping from her. She'd been gone, and he'd been trying to go on alone. He hadn't been betraying anything—Lovina had already left him.

"How long?" she asked.

"A year."

There was no surprise on her face. She met his gaze, then nodded. "*Yah*, that's what Sovilla said, too."

"She told you?" he asked, and he stopped walking and turned toward her. They were past the house, the stable, and the chicken coop, and open field lay before them. No one would overhear them here.

"She said I left the community," Lovina said. "I ran away."

"You did," he said, swallowing.

"So why didn't you tell me that?" she demanded, and he saw the old fire flare up inside of her.

"Do you remember it now?" he asked.

"No!" She shook her head. "I don't remember any of it! But you could have told me that! I have this memory of sitting on a bed watching a movie on a laptop, and I thought I was going crazy! My *daet* said I had a little rebellious streak . . . But my nails were painted rather recently, and . . ." Her chest rose and fell with her quickened breath. "You all *lied*!"

"We didn't lie!" he shot back.

"No? It sure sounds like one to me!" she retorted.

"We had to let you remember something good first!" he said. "You had a whole life here, Lovina! You were *born* Amish, raised Amish . . . You only left because of your *daet*!"

"My *daet*?" Her eyebrows rose. "You mean that sweet man who used to pray with me when I was a little girl? I remembered that when I was with him. He nearly cried when he realized I was starting to remember something. He's the reason I left?"

So she was remembering some pleasant memories of her Amish upbringing. He pulled off his hat and rubbed a hand through his hair. What was he supposed to do now? She was furious that they hadn't told her everything, but there was a whole lot more to tell . . . Was it time to fill her in? Or would he only make things worse?

Johannes looked back toward the house. Could he live with himself if he continued the deception?

"Keep walking," he said, his voice low. "I'll tell you everything."

"What problem did I have with my father?" she asked.

"He joined an *Englisher* fraud ring and helped rob our community of people's hard-earned savings," he said. The words felt heavy, like a weapon, and saying it out loud like this to her made them sound almost fictional.

Lovina was silent, and he looked over at her. Her face had turned white, and her shoe caught on something and she stumbled. He shot out a hand and caught hers, and she didn't pull away.

"You were enraged," he went on. "At the time, Elizabeth didn't even believe it, and Isaiah was a complete wreck. He'd wanted to be a preacher like your *daet* was, and with your father's crime, he'd lost his *daet*, his role model, his hope at ever preaching . . ."

"My *father* did this?" She stared up at him, aghast. That was the same look on her face from the first time she'd found out . . . The crushing betrayal . . .

"*Yah*, he did." He couldn't make that part easier. "He was caught and arrested. Your family's farm was taken away to pay back the people who'd been swindled—that's why you're out here with your brother—and your *daet* was put into prison."

"But he's here," she countered. "I saw him yesterday."

"He got out early on good behavior," Johannes replied. "He's still on parole. He has to visit a parole officer every week and account for his time."

She was silent, and they walked steadily in the direction of the trees that lined the creek that passed through the back end of this property.

"So I left because of that?" she said woodenly.

"You'd asked me to go visit your *daet* in the prison," he said. "But I was really angry with him, too. My *daet* had put some money into that scam fund, and we still haven't seen a penny of it back. You wanted to see him, talk to him face to face, and I was so furious with him for what he'd done that I couldn't go along with you. Maybe if I had—"

He bit back the words. It didn't matter now. What did matter was why she had left without him, because he'd never been completely sure about that. He'd been reeling with his own emotions, too, and she'd just . . . left.

"Why did I leave, though?" she pressed.

"I'm not entirely sure," he replied. "You left a short letter."

"What did I say?" she asked.

"You said you couldn't live with the shame of what your *daet* had done and you were leaving for good. As if I hadn't been affected by all of it, too! I was supposed to move on."

"So we are definitely not engaged," she breathed.

They reached the trees, and Johannes put the picnic basket down in the grass. The creek was nearly overgrown with grass along the banks, but the water trickled past, babbling over stones and making a tinkling sound as it went. The breeze was cooler here by the water, and the shade made the air almost chilly.

"No, we aren't engaged," he said, his voice low. "We were, though, before all of this. We'd been planning a life together. We were going to get married and live with your family for the first year, the way we were supposed to, and . . ." He swallowed. "But my *daet* was perfectly happy to have us at the farm with him after your *daet*'s arrest. We could have kept moving forward with our plans. My heart hadn't changed."

"But mine did . . ." she whispered.

Was that a memory, or a conclusion? He watched her pale face, looking for a hint, but her thoughts were locked away.

"I'm sorry I didn't tell you sooner," he said. "I was hoping—" He swallowed. "I was hoping you might remember what we had before you remembered why you left me."

"Was there anything else to make me leave? Anything else you aren't telling me?" She looked up at him, searching his face. Those large, liquid eyes that had always made him feel like he could drown in the depth of them were moving over his face. She wanted answers, too.

"I've told you everything now," he whispered. "I was hoping you'd tell me."

Lovina sighed, eyeing him for a moment as if deciding if she believed him, and then turned toward the creek. She walked to the edge and looked down, the wind rippling her dress around her slim legs, outlining her form. She was beautiful, and even looking at her a few paces off, he felt himself wanting to close to the distance, pull her into his arms, and somehow forget all the complicated misery between them.

"Maybe your *daet* is the key to everything," he called after her. "It was his crime that started all the craziness around here, and it was his crime that drove you away. I'm not saying everything will go back to the way it was, but maybe remembering him will unlock the rest of it for you . . ."

Because hiding her father's crime didn't seem to be working anyway.

Lovina's eyes were fixed on the water flowing past, tugging at the long grass that drooped into the water and trailed along with the current.

Her father—the few memories of him that had surfaced had been connected to some deep emotion. Lovina loved her *daet*, and remembering that she loved him, and seeing how much he loved her, too, had been an incredible comfort. She had a *family*, and as strange as everything felt here, she did belong.

Last night, she'd lain in bed, feeling so deeply grateful for those few memories that she'd prayed for the first time in a long time, pouring out her limited memories and her unlimited worries to her Maker. And she'd cried into her pillow for the first time since she'd arrived in Bountilful, too, because she felt like she could finally start letting go, and maybe start trusting this family who were so insistent that she belonged here.

Because she'd seen it in her father's eyes.

And that *daet* was a criminal?

And then there was Sovilla . . . the one the community and everyone had wanted Johannes to marry. She'd seen him in the kitchen with Becca—how the little girl had looked to him in that hopeless, heartbroken way. That little girl had gotten attached . . . Johannes's connection to Sovilla wasn't one without emotion. Whatever he'd felt for her, he'd gotten attached to them, too.

Lovina turned back toward him and found Johannes spreading out a thin, worn quilt on the grass.

"A whole year!" she said, and Johannes stopped what he was doing and straightened. "A year!"

"*Yah*." He nodded.

"A lot can happen in a year, Johannes . . ."

"I know it."

A man could marry someone else . . . a community could close the gap she'd left behind. What had *she* done with that year?

"Did I write to you?" she asked. "Or call?"

He shook his head. "No."

"Did I contact anyone?" she asked. "My family?"

"Not that they told me," he said. "I always asked if you had, and they always said no."

"So you believe them," she said.

"*Yah*, I believe them."

Lovina's heart hammered hard in her throat. She had walked away . . . she'd turned her back on everything—everyone. Had it been stupid, or was it warranted? She wished she could remember that much. But it would seem that she'd disappeared for a year, and Johannes had been expected to help her recover her memory now that she was back. So that was why he'd seemed so distant and strange for a man who wanted to marry her. He wasn't her fiancé!

"Do you wish you'd married her?" Lovina asked.

Johannes frowned. "What?"

"Do you wish you'd done it?" she asked. "You were left alone here, and I didn't write, or call, or . . . You were *alone*. And those little girls—I saw the way Becca reached out to you. They know you. They seem to really like you, too."

"They're sweet *kinner*," he said. "This mess isn't their fault."

"Sovilla was supposed to be your comfort, wasn't she?"

The words almost stuck in her throat. Lovina had broken his heart, and this other woman—this seemingly very worthy woman—was supposed to make up for that. Johannes was silent, his dark gaze pinned on her as if he was about to say something, but held himself back.

"And you were supposed to be *hers*!" Lovina pressed on. "You were supposed to raise those girls and provide for them, but you couldn't because I came back. I ruined it."

She could see it in her mind's eye now . . . Sovilla—sweet, kind, and decent—needed a job or a husband, and a husband was much preferable. Johannes, who had been abandoned, would have needed to move on. It all made perfect sense.

"You didn't ruin anything," he retorted, his voice a low growl. "Your *daet* finding you in that hospital was a miracle!"

"Did you even want to play along with this whole plan to get me to remember?" she asked, shaking her head.

"Of course I did!" he snapped, and for the first time she saw anger burning deep in those soulful eyes of his. "I *prayed* for you to come back! I prayed for that miracle! And if you think I could just turn my back on you—"

"But apparently, I turned my back on you!" she shot back. "Don't tell me that year did nothing to you!"

"You want to know what that year did?" He took three brisk strides and closed the distance between them. "It broke my heart." His voice cracked. "It gutted me. It left me worried about you every waking hour—worried about those Englishers who take advantage and hurt people."

"And you never once thought that maybe the girl who left you wasn't worth waiting for?" she demanded. "Maybe I'd stopped loving you back!"

"Is that what you're telling me?" he asked woodenly. "That you had stopped loving me?"

"I don't remember!" she shouted. "I have no idea! I don't know why I left! I don't remember any of this! I don't even know who I was!"

Johannes's Adam's apple bobbed as he swallowed. Did she want him to say she was worth all of that heartbreak? That he was fine with all of this? That he could be patient and wait while they started all over again? Maybe . . . It might make her feel better if he did.

"I didn't *choose* to wait for you . . ." His lips trembled as the words came out. "Do you think I decided that I'd just put my heart on a shelf and put my life aside for a woman who might never return? No! I *wanted* to move on! And when your family found you, I knew that you'd eventually remember whatever very good reason you had for walking out on me. So I'm telling you straight—I *wanted* to love someone else. I wanted to stop loving you, Lovina! But I couldn't! This was no choice! This was a living hell!"

She stared up at him, her breath caught in her throat. His blazing eyes were locked on hers, and there was a twitch in his jaw, betraying the effort it took to hold back his emotion.

"Was there another man in your life?" he asked, his voice tight.

"I don't know . . ." she breathed.

He licked his lips, his eyes raking over her face before he dipped his head down and caught her lips with his. This kiss was different from the last one—it was filled with pain, and it burned with longing. His lips moved over hers, locking her to the spot and tearing open whatever reluctance she had left. But he didn't touch her—didn't pull her against him, or slide his arms around her. His kiss was only that—his lips searing against hers. Then he pulled back, and she was left with her breath coming in gasps and her knees weak.

"Why did you do that?" she whispered.

"I don't know," he said, echoing her last words to him. "I shouldn't. I know that—whatever heartbreak I endured, you couldn't have gone through the half of it. It was your choice to leave, and you never tried to contact me . . ."

"Maybe I don't want to remember after all," she said, tears rising up inside of her. "I've had a chance to remember growing up here—a little bit of it, at least. I remember my family—being a little girl with a *daet* who adored me. And I can see what a good man I had in you. Maybe I don't want to remember anything more than that! Maybe I can stop remembering here and just start over—"

"It's what your family wants," he said, his voice thick. "But I don't want to start over."

His words felt heavy and hard.

"It might be easier," she said hopefully. "We could go for walks, and talk, and—"

"No, it isn't easier," he said, cutting her off. "Not for me! If you don't remember what we were, then what is this to you? I'm just some man who loves you more than makes sense, and you're just a woman who doesn't love me nearly enough."

Lovina wiped an errant tear off her cheek.

"Then what if you helped me remember us?" she whispered, turning back toward him. "What if you showed me what we were to each other?"

"I'm not sure I dare," he murmured.

"Why not?" she said.

"Because I promised your family that there were lines I wouldn't cross," he said, his eyes blazing.

"Then don't cross them. There must be something that you can show me that doesn't jeopardize our reputations."

"All right," he said. "I used to play with your fingers."

He reached out and took her hand in his. His broad, work-roughened hand moved down her fingers, and he touched the very tips of them. She felt a shiver run down her spine, and she held her breath.

"And I used to tell you that you reminded me of that first spring melt—that feeling of wild relief." He smiled faintly.

"And what would I do?" she whispered.

"You used to run your hand up my arm," he said.

"That's all?" she asked, and she let her fingers trail up his muscular arm, pausing on his hard bicep. Her breath caught. He was a very handsome man, she had to admit . . .

"Sometimes," he said softly. "You'd put your cheek against my shoulder and you'd say . . ." He swallowed.

"I'd say?" She leaned her cheek against the top of his arm and she breathed in the scent of him—musky, manly.

"You'd say I smelled nice," he said with a self-conscious laugh.

She pulled back, warmth hitting her cheeks. She'd just been thinking that . . .

"Johannes," she said softly.

"*Yah*?"

"Would you kiss me again?" she whispered.

"Are you sure you want that?" he asked. "That's one of those lines, you know. I'm not your fiancé anymore. You should know that."

"I'm sure." She lifted her gaze to meet his and sucked in a wavering breath. She wanted to see what his kiss was like when it wasn't angry or heartbroken. What had his kiss been like back when everything was happy?

He stepped closer and he put one hand on her cheek and then bent down, his warm lips covering hers. His kiss was slow and gentle. Not one part of his body touched hers except for his hand on her face, and she felt his thumb tug on her bottom lip as he parted her lips and deepened the kiss. And there was something that felt so close to a memory—it tickled the back of her mind, surging closer to the surface. It was in the scent of him, the gentleness of his touch . . .

Then he pulled back, those dark glistening eyes meeting hers.

"That was nice," she breathed.

He chuckled. "You always said that. Do you remember?"

"Almost," she said.

"That's a no, then," he said.

"I feel like I *could* remember . . . it's close," she said.

"That's a step forward, then," he said.

She reached out and touched his arm again, running her fingers over his shirt and pausing on the solid muscle. This was familiar—the feeling of the cotton under her fingers, the way her heart sped up, the way his arm felt . . . It was like it had happened before, but it wasn't a memory of a distinct time . . . More like déjà vu. Where had she heard about déjà vu?

He caught her hand and pulled it away from his arm.

"I don't think you know what that does to me," he said with a small smile. "And we're trying to stay within appropriate boundaries."

"Oh . . ." She felt the heat in her face again, and she pulled her hand away, putting it behind her back. "Sorry."

It wasn't only about her memories anymore, was it? Johannes's feelings were involved, too.

"It's okay." His dark gaze was locked on her, then he sighed. "We need to eat that food."

"Oh . . . right."

The picnic basket sat beside the quilt that lay over the long grass, waiting for them. It was a distraction, at least, and that might be for the best right now.

When she finally remembered the whole of their story, the reasons she had felt she had to leave and never come back, were these sweet memories going to be ruined, too, like her memories with her father?

That was what she was afraid of right now, that all the lovely possibilities she could see at the moment would be shattered when she remembered why she'd left all of this behind. If her own father was a criminal, who was Lovina Yoder? And did she dare to find out?

Chapter Nine

Johannes drove the buggy home that afternoon, and he took his time unhitching the horses and brushing them down. He needed to think this through.

Lovina wanted to remember, and he wanted to help her, but this felt wrong. She could still quicken his pulse and absorb all of his thoughts, but she *had* left him. And a lot had happened in the last year.

When his grandfather died, Solomon had been off making dangerous connections with bad Englishers. And Johannes had felt the loss of Dawdie Menno very deeply. It was Abe Yoder who preached at the funeral, talking about man returning to dust from whence he came, and the hope of eternal glory. It was Abe Yoder who'd put his arm around Johannes's shoulder and said, "Your grandfather loved you very much. He was proud of you."

And those words had slipped down into Johannes's heart, because while he'd known his grandfather had loved him, that he'd been proud of him was what he'd needed to hear—that Johannes, with his ordinary abilities, was enough to make old deacon Menno Miller proud. Abe Yoder knew how to give hope.

How was it possible for a man like Abe Yoder to be such a meaningful part of Johannes's life, and yet also be the reason that everything tore apart?

What would Dawdie Menno say if he were still here? What advice would he give Johannes about how to deal with all of this?

He'd likely point him back to the community and the faith. He'd say something about how Gott gave them community for difficult times like these, and how he should rely upon the support network supplied by Gott Himself.

His grandfather the deacon . . . his wisdom had always been simple and to the point, and it never varied too much. Do the right thing. Stand tall, even when it's hard. Trust the faith. Why was it that every time his grandfather gave some of this advice, it felt new?

"Johannes?" Bernard poked his head into the stable.

Johannes roused himself from his thoughts and pushed his hat back on his head. He hung the last bridle on the wall.

"Hi, Daet," he said.

"You're back," Bernard said. "Good. I haven't seen Daniel in a while. He was supposed to be back by now to dig up potatoes, but I have to go start the milking."

The tradition of men passing down the wisdom of how to be a good man—it was ages old. Dawdie Menno had been the solid example Johannes had needed, and maybe Johannes was going to be what Daniel needed.

"He's probably at the calf barn," Johannes said. "I'll go get him, then we'll help you milk."

"Thank you, Son." Bernard tapped the door frame and then disappeared again.

Johannes walked briskly toward the calf barn, and when he pulled open the heavy door, he saw the calves had been fed again—the buckets were standing empty, and the calves looked calm and full.

At least Daniel was taking this responsibility seriously.

"Daniel?" he called loudly.

"*Yah*?" Daniel's head appeared at the opening to the hayloft.

"What are you doing up there?" Johannes asked.

"Nothing—I'm coming—" Daniel disappeared back into the loft, and Johannes eyed the empty space speculatively. Was he sewing again? Had he disobeyed Johannes's direct order?

"I want an answer, Daniel," Johannes called. "What were you doing?"

The boy reappeared at the opening and started down the ladder. When he got to the bottom, his cheeks were flushed, and he wouldn't meet Johannes's gaze.

"Were you sewing again?" Johannes asked.

"I'm sorry I was late," Daniel said. "I should have watched the time better. But Dawdie said I could go explore or play, or whatever, so I wasn't doing anything wrong."

"You were working on that quilt, though," Johannes clarified.

"*Yah*."

Johannes rubbed a hand over his eyes. He was so tired of all of this. Daniel needed some straight advice—the kind Dawdie Menno might have given.

"I don't have the energy for this," Johannes said. "If I didn't have as much going on right now, I'd take my time, talk to you over a few days, maybe . . . but I'm not going to do that."

Daniel took a step back, eyeing him warily.

"You're too old to spank, Daniel," he said dryly. "And I'm not your father, so I wouldn't try. Instead, I'm going to just tell you this straight. I'm not going to cushion your feelings."

"Okay . . ." Daniel said.

"That's woman's work," he said bluntly. "There are some chores a man needs to know how to do. You should be able to sew a seam shut if it splits. You should be able to fry a steak, cook a stew and scramble an egg. You should be able to wash and hang your own clothes—and trust me, if you haven't learned those skills yet with your *mamm*, you'll be learning them here with us. That's just plain survival. But quilting?"

Daniel licked his lips, but didn't answer.

"You might be good at something, but it doesn't make it yours to do!" Johannes went on. "I might be capable of making a good roast beef, but once I'm married, I'm never making one again, unless my wife is ill or injured. Because that's not my domain! And Daniel, there isn't any explanation for why a single man would need to make a quilt!"

"I told you before—it's more of a picture."

"Then paint it on the side of a barn!" Johannes said, shaking his head. "Whittle it with wood! Carve it into the side of a chest! Why must you *sew* it?"

"Because I can see how it will work with the colors and the textures—" Daniel seemed to see Johannes's expression, because he paused for a moment. "And because I'm better at it than my sisters."

"You've been quilting at home?" he asked. "Does your family know?"

"I hid it," Daniel said. "But I can see my sisters' work, and I'm better at it than they are. Plain and simple."

So he had a man's sense of competition . . . He eyed his nephew in silence for a moment.

"Okay, go get it. I want to see," Johannes said.

Daniel headed up the ladder again, and when he came back down, he had his folded fabric in one hand. He carefully unfolded it and held it out. It wasn't complete, or even close, but he'd finished a corner—sky in various hues and textures that almost looked like clouds if he squinted, and beneath that were some trees in crimson and mustard yellow. The seams were tight, the stitches almost invisible. This would be easier if the boy weren't so obviously talented . . .

"All right," Johannes said quietly. "I'll admit that I'm impressed."

"*Yah?*" Daniel took his work back and refolded it.

"Sit." Johannes nodded toward a couple of stools along the wall, and Daniel went over and perched on the edge of one. Johannes sat down next to him and sighed.

"Here's the thing, Dan," he said. "Your *mamm* sent you out here to learn how to be a man. You've got her and your sisters, not a lot of male influence at home. So I've got to try and explain some stuff to you, and I hope you'll be patient."

"I'm not like a girl," Daniel said irritably.

"I know," Johannes said. "You aren't at all. You're tall and strong, and you contribute some real, hard work. But as you get older—starting now, actually—you've got to think about how you're going to fit into your community."

"I have friends," he said.

"I know, but I meant—" Johannes sighed. "Next year is your last year of schooling, and you'll need a job. But as an Amish man, you have to find something that fits in with the community, right? And you've got to look at the kind of life you want, and what it will take to get it."

"I don't show anyone my sewing," Daniel said. "If that's what you mean."

"It's pretty close to what I mean," Johannes admitted. "There's men's work and women's work, but more than that, there's a community of men you need to get along with. And men who do well are the ones who find a need in the community and fill it. For example, a farmer is always needed. But we also need woodworkers, fence makers, horse trainers, farriers, shop owners, preachers—" He stopped at that last one. "You can't make a future out of sewing. Not as an Amish man. Even if you're better at it than the women. It's just not going to be accepted."

Daniel nodded. "I know that."

"Okay, that's a start," Johannes said.

"It's just that I really like it," Daniel said quietly. "I think about it a lot. I plan it out in my head before I go to sleep."

Johannes met his nephew's earnest gaze. He really did love to sew, didn't he? He sighed.

"Okay, well, enjoy it or not, the other question you have to ask yourself is if you want to go the rest of your life hiding it," Johannes said. "And if you make something, and sell it, how do you explain where it came from? Do you pretend your wife made it? That's a lie that will require more lies to cover it. And as you tell the lies that allow you to sell your work, it affects your soul. Lies change you on a fundamental level. They turn you into a liar."

"I won't sell it, then," he said.

"Will you tell your wife about it?" he asked. "And how will she feel? Now she's got a secret to hide, too. And secrets are a lot like lies in how they affect a person."

Daniel was silent.

"The safest way to live a life is to be honest," Johannes said. "Trust me, I know from experience. And if you can see that this thing isn't going to help you get the life you want, it's probably safer to just let it go."

An image of Lovina rose up in his mind—Lovina as she was now, confused and hopeful, but poised to remember every single reason she'd left them to begin with. Was Lovina Yoder going to help him achieve the life *he* wanted in his community? He was giving advice that he didn't seem strong enough to follow himself, because he *should* let Lovina go . . .

"What kind of life do you want?" Johannes pressed.

"I want a good job, and a nice buggy, and I want to court a pretty girl," Daniel said.

"All very good things," Johannes said, nudging his nephew with his elbow. "A girl would find a boy who sews better than her . . . hard to understand."

"*Yah* . . ." Daniel heaved a sigh.

Making his point didn't feel as good as he'd thought it would. But a boy had to learn the rules of manhood sooner or later. If he didn't, he'd never fit in. Still, that glimmer in Daniel's eyes when he'd explained how he created his quilted pictures had gone out, and Johannes felt a twinge of regret.

"Hey, it isn't so bad," Johannes said. "You've got skill

with color and texture and dexterity that can be put to good use in other ways. What about leatherwork, for example? You could create saddles that the Englishers would pay a fortune for."

"*Yah*, maybe." Daniel stood up and looked down the floor. "I promised Dawdie I'd help with the milking, though. I should do that."

"*Yah*, that's probably best," Johannes agreed, and he paused for a moment, feeling like this hadn't quite gone as well as he'd hoped. The boy might see his point, but Johannes still didn't feel quite right. "Are we okay, Daniel?"

"*Yah*." Daniel looked over and met his gaze, but he looked deflated, and a little sad. That wasn't quite what Johannes had hoped to do . . . Dawdie Menno would have done this better.

Would Linda be relieved or annoyed at how he'd handled this? Because while he might have solved the sewing problem, Daniel looked dimmer now. Johannes had messed this up somehow.

Daniel headed for the door and Johannes heaved a sigh. Sometimes that leap into manhood meant accepting disappointment.

Daniel would be better for it . . . wouldn't he?

That evening, after dinner had been eaten and the dishes done, Lovina stood by the kitchen window, her gaze following the meandering path of a cat as it sauntered across the yard. It paused by the chicken coop, but the rooster's angry glare sent it on again.

Bethany sat at the kitchen table with Mo in her arms

and a baby blanket over one shoulder as she fed her son. Isaiah sat next to her with a pen and paper in hand, and he bent over a letter that he was writing.

"Should I say how much Mo weighs now?" Isaiah asked his wife.

"*Yah*, that would be a good detail to add," she agreed. "And that he likes to clap his hands."

"Hmm." Isaiah kept writing, his lips pressed together in concentration.

Elizabeth brought a tub of chocolate ice cream to the table with a stack of bowls, and Lovina couldn't help but look over in interest.

"I think we could use a treat," Elizabeth said. "Don't you, Lovina?"

"*Yah,*" Lovina said, but she glanced back over at her brother. "Isaiah, who are you writing to?"

"Micah," he said.

"You're honest about Micah being Mo's biological father," Lovina said. "Why aren't you honest with me?"

Her brother stopped writing and looked up. "What do you mean?"

"You've been hiding things," Lovina replied. "Like how long I was gone. And what our father did to land him in prison."

Isaiah put down his pen. "You remember?"

"No!" She swallowed hard. "Everyone keeps asking that! I shouldn't have to remember something in order to be told the truth!"

"Did Johannes tell you?" Elizabeth asked.

"Does it matter who told me?" Lovina asked. "I was

gone for a year! And you all made it seem like I'd vanished for a few days."

"We had a good reason for that," Isaiah said. "You don't remember what it was like when Daet was arrested, but it was horrible. We all lost pretty much everything. We lost our home, our good reputations, our own father. And *you* were crushed."

"So you lied to me," she said woodenly.

"The last time you found out about Daet's crime, you went *English*!" Elizabeth shot back. "You're our baby sister, and we were trying to protect you!"

"So that's why I left, then?" Lovina asked. "Because I couldn't deal with Daet's crime?"

"It's what you said in the letter," Isaiah said. "Wait—"

He pushed back his chair and headed down the hallway. He came back a moment later with a grubby piece of paper in one hand. He passed it over to her, and she looked down at her own handwriting—she recognized it.

Dear Isaiah and Elizabeth,

I'm leaving. I can't do this anymore. I can't live a life where I'm the daughter of the man who did this horrible thing. I'm sick of it! What is any of this worth if our own father could steal all that money?

I know you don't believe he did it, Lizzie, but I do. He stole it, and he told us that stealing was wrong. He lied, and he told us that lying was wrong.

> *Who are we? Why do we bother living away
> from the Englishers when we're no better?*
> *Please give the other letter to Johannes for me.
> I can't face him. I know he wants out of our
> engagement. I can see it in his eyes—he's panicked.
> I'm giving him the way out.*

> *Lovina*

Lovina's heart pounded to a stop. Johannes had wanted out of the engagement? Had her instincts about his feelings for her been right?

"Where did I go?" Lovina asked, looking up from the letter.

Her brother shook his head. "We don't know. I promise you that. When he got out of prison, Daet asked the police to help him find you. We were all really angry with him for his crime, and we blamed him for your leaving—for obvious reasons. And he wanted to find you. It wasn't like we hadn't looked. We searched, and so did Johannes. But Daet wanted to start all over again. As it happened, you had that accident and the hospital was looking for your next of kin at the same time Daet started asking questions. So we found you—and we came to get you. But we don't know where you came from, or what you were doing in Erindale."

Erindale . . . No, it didn't sound familiar to her, but at least some of the details in her history were starting to come together. Where had she gone? Where had she lived where she'd been able to paint her nails and watch movies on a laptop? She'd had a life the last year.

"What was I dressed in when they found me?" she asked.

"Jeans," Bethany said softly, interjecting for the first time. "And a T-shirt. You had running shoes and socks, and your toenails were painted red. They said when you woke up, the red nail polish was upsetting you, so they found some polish remover and took it off for you."

"I was upset?" she asked, her voice trembling.

"We Amish don't paint our nails," Bethany said. "Maybe that was why."

Lovina nodded slowly. "I might remember that."

There was an image in her mind of painted toenails. Nothing more than that, but the image was a vivid one. There were white sheets, too, and her legs had been bare. Was that in the hospital? Maybe.

"You had no ID on you," Isaiah added. "You had some cash in your pocket, and that was all. You were riding a bike, so you had some scratches and bruises. It was a hit-and-run—nobody saw who did it. But some passersby saw you on the road and called an ambulance."

"How long was I at the hospital before you came for me?" she asked.

"A week," Isaiah said. "But we hadn't seen you in a year."

Do you know what year this is?

Who's the president right now?

Where do you live?

She could remember the questions the doctors and nurses had asked her over and over again. They'd make notes on charts and look at her with expressions of sympathy. There was that one nurse who had given her extra puddings with her breakfast tray. And she'd brought the magazines, and chatted with her for a few minutes when she could.

"I think you could use a treat," the nurse would say with a wink.

They'd felt sorry for her.

Lovina looked toward the tub of ice cream. "Could I have some?"

"Uh—" Elizabeth cleared her throat. "*Yah*, of course . . . Lovina, do you forgive us?"

Lovina looked at the faces around the table—her brother and his wife, her older sister—they all looked stricken, deeply apologetic.

"It was hard to keep up the deception," Isaiah said. "We didn't want to, and we were planning on telling you everything eventually, but we didn't know how to do it."

"Lies are like that," Lovina said softly.

"We are sorry," Elizabeth said, her voice shaking. "You know everything now. You left Johannes, so he isn't your present fiancé, although you did love him very much before you left."

"Did you tell him what I wrote to you?" she asked.

"*Yah,*" Isaiah said. "He read it. He knew what you said."

Lovina nodded. "And there's nothing else? I'm not going to find out you've got some other secret hidden away?"

"There's nothing!" Elizabeth said earnestly. "I promise you. This is everything we know—it wasn't much to begin with."

But it was more than Lovina had heard before.

Elizabeth started to serve bowls of softened chocolate

ice cream, and for a few minutes, everyone turned their attention to the frozen treat.

So this was her family . . . the people who'd come for her, who'd brought her home, and who'd tried to hide the worst part of their history from her. These were the people who were determined to see her get better. These were the people who wanted to see her reunited with Johannes, and somehow, she couldn't blame them for that. Johannes was a good man, and they obviously had meant a great deal to each other before she'd left.

But who had been in her life the last year away from home? Anyone at all?

There was the rumble of an engine outside, and Lovina went to the window and watched as a police cruiser came to a stop. Two officers got out of the car and came toward the house.

"What is it?" Isaiah asked, and he headed toward the side door. There was a knock just as he got to the door, and he pulled it open.

"Hello," Isaiah said in English. "Can I help you?"

"Hello, we're looking for someone who was reported missing—Lovina Yoder. According to Erindale Hospital, a Jane Doe who was in an accident was identified as Lovina Yoder and came back to this address. We're doing a wellness check, just making sure she's okay."

Lovina's heart skipped a beat. Police . . . the very thought of them made her heart squeeze, and she wasn't sure why.

"Is there a Lovina Yoder here?" the first officer asked.

"I am." Lovina's voice felt rough in her throat.

"We're doing what's called a wellness check," the officer said repeated. "It's good to see you, Miss. You were reported missing from your job, and your employers just wanted to make sure you were okay."

"A job?" she asked, and a flicker of hope ignited inside of her.

"You didn't have a job?" the officer asked, eyebrows rising. He pulled out a notebook. "Do you mind answering a few questions for us?"

"If you spoke to the hospital, you know about her amnesia," Isaiah said. "She doesn't remember too much yet. But some of it is coming back."

"I don't remember the last year," Lovina said. "I didn't know I had a job. But I'd like to hear about it."

"Apparently, you were a support worker for a young disabled woman in a wheelchair," the officer replied. "You lived with the family, and you disappeared a couple of weeks ago. At first, they thought you might have quit, but after some time, they just didn't feel comfortable with that explanation and asked us to look into it."

Lovina searched her mind, looking for some image, some memory of this job they were describing. Was that where she'd been painting her nails? *Had* she quit?

"I was on a bike when I had the accident," Lovina said.

"They mentioned that. They said you used to borrow one of theirs."

"Oh . . . I must owe them a new bike," she said faintly.

"I don't think that's the worry," the officer said with a kind smile. "They were more concerned about your safety. They wanted to make sure you were all right. They said if we found you that we should tell you that there are no hard feelings, and they are sorry if they offended you."

"I don't remember what happened," she admitted with

a shake of her head. "But do you have an address, or something, so I can contact them?"

"Yeah, sure," the officer said. He pulled out a piece of paper. "It's all written down there. On our end, we'll let them know that we found you with your family, and that you're in one piece. If you'd like to contact them further, it's up to you."

"Thank you," she said, and she opened the page to see an address typed there, along with a phone number.

She'd had a life in a place called Erindale, and a job. And the people she'd worked for had been looking for her. The officers were seen out, and Lovina sat in stunned silence, her gaze moving over that address.

"Maybe you did quit," Elizabeth said, and Lovina pulled out of her reverie.

"They wouldn't have been looking for me if I quit," she replied.

"Maybe you left for good reason," Elizabeth said. "Maybe you were coming home."

Without any form of ID, without bags, without her Amish clothing? Did that seem likely? Lovina wasn't even sure. Maybe it made perfect sense if she'd been running away from something.

"It was just a job," Isaiah said quietly. "It's not like they were your family."

And maybe her siblings were right, but Lovina knew that she'd need more than assumptions. She needed a few answers of her own, and she wasn't going to get them here in Bountiful.

Chapter Ten

Two days later, Johannes and Bernard decided that it would be good for Daniel to go along with Johannes to help Solomon build the eck decorations. The eck was the corner of the room where the wedding party would sit for the reception, and it was the groom's responsibility to decorate it using his skills with woodworking. This was all part of the male experience, and it would be good for Daniel to participate in a rite of passage like this one.

Johannes hadn't mentioned the quilting to his *daet* yet. He was still hoping his last, frank discussion with the boy would take care of the issue and there would be no need to involve anyone else.

Solomon had been working on the decorations for a matter of weeks, and he needed some help with the finishing polishes and then needed to transport everything to the Yoder acreage, where the simple wedding would take place.

But it wasn't the eck that had Johannes's thoughts as the buggy rattled down the road toward the Lantz place; it was Lovina. The last time they'd talked, he'd told her everything he knew, and still there was this connection between them that just wouldn't sever. Was he a fool to be holding on to that? Or maybe he should just be wiser and feel the pain, and let it heal, and then let her go. Because she would have time to think everything over, too, and she might come to the same conclusions she had before.

She wouldn't even be back in Bountiful if it weren't for that accident, so it wasn't like she'd changed her mind before she lost her memory, was it?

"Have you ever seen an eck made?" Johannes asked, pulling his mind back to his nephew at his side.

"No," Daniel said. "When my sister got married, her husband made his eck with his brothers."

And didn't think to include Daniel—although, that had been a few years ago. Daniel would have been nine or ten at the time, and maybe a little too young to include. Johannes looked over at the boy.

"It's a chance for a man to show his woodworking skill," Johannes said. "Everyone sees what he can do."

"Is Solomon any good?" Daniel asked.

"Not bad," Johannes replied. "He's out of practice working with wood, though. He left the community for a few years, and he's suffered for it. Maybe let that be a lesson to you that you can always come home again, but it doesn't replace the time you were gone. And the skills a man needs are honed over time. You can't just skip that. There's no shortcut."

"*Yah* . . ." Daniel looked out the side of the buggy.

Was Johannes lecturing too much? Maybe. It was a hard balance to find—making a man out of a boy, but not driving him away in the process. As for time away, Lovina had been gone for a long time, too, and maybe he needed to face that things weren't going to be the same again, no matter how much he wanted the clock to go back.

The Lantz home was coming up. They had a produce stand that was set up this time of year, and wooden baskets of fruits and vegetables were on display for passing vehicles. A car was stopped at the side of the road, and Aunt Anke, Solomon's mother, stood serving her customer.

Johannes reined in the horses and turned down the drive. He waved to Anke, who waved back with a broad smile.

"Hello, Johannes!" she called.

The Englishers looked over at him in curiosity, openly staring as they turned into the drive.

"Who knew we were this interesting, huh?" Johannes said, shooting Daniel a smile.

"Why do they do that?" Daniel asked.

"I guess they like horses?" Johannes joked. "We're different. People stare. What can you do?"

"So how come it's a good thing for us Amish to be different, and a bad thing for one Amish man to be different from the others?" Daniel said, looking out the side of the buggy, away from Johannes.

"Because when you're Amish, you have your community, but if you're one Amish man who's different, you stand utterly alone," Johannes said. "That kind of loneliness is harder than you can imagine."

And Gott had given them community for a reason. How many times had his grandfather told him that? People might be frustrating, but they were necessary to growth and maturity. Sometimes even to survival.

"I thought being different built character," Daniel said. "That's what Mamm says."

Johannes glanced over at his nephew as they approached the stables. He reined in the horses and pressed his lips together. Stand for what was right—even if it meant standing alone. That was what the Amish taught, and Johannes agreed. Mostly.

There could be hard consequences for doing the right thing, but why court those consequences unnecessarily?

"Tell you what," Johannes said. "My cousin Solomon is different—especially now that he's been to prison. You keep your mouth shut and help us with the eck. But pay attention. You're going to see what it's like to be different."

Why couldn't *kinner* ever see what the adults were trying to spare them from?

Solomon came out from around the stable, and he waved at Johannes with a grin. Solomon was a muscular man—much more so than he'd ever been as a teenager. He'd done a lot of working out in prison, and the defined muscles still hadn't softened since his return. His sleeves were tight around his biceps.

"Hi!" Sol called. "You made it!"

"This is my nephew, Daniel," Johannes said as they jumped down from the buggy. "Linda's son."

"Oh, *yah*?" Solomon gave Daniel a nod. "Your *mamm* used to tell *my mamm* when she saw me skipping school."

Daniel smiled hesitantly. "That sounds like my *mamm*."

When Johannes looked over at his nephew, he saw him eyeing Sol's muscular physique. Amish men didn't lift weights or work out, so the muscles they built were honed on the farm. Amish men were strong, but Sol had taken that a step further that would make the old people shake their heads and cluck their tongues. Sol still stood out, no matter how much he wanted to blend back in again.

Solomon led the way into the stable. There was an empty work area in the back where Solomon had the windows propped open for a breeze, and the decorations for the eck were leaning against one wall.

"I don't know if it's much good, but—" Solomon took off his hat and slapped it against his thigh. "But it's this window frame, see? And we'll hang it up with these hooks from the ceiling, and behind the frame, Elizabeth wants to hang up the wedding quilt."

"It sounds really nice," Johannes said.

"And then there's these shelves we'll put on either side, and each of us will put some items on the shelves from our families that they're giving to us to start our home," Solomon went on. "I'm going to put some chisels that used to belong to your grandfather before he passed away, and this hammer he gave me when I was twelve or thirteen. And Elizabeth is going to put some other little items—that's up to her. But we'll have to mount them to the wall without doing too much damage. I made the shelves both sixteen inches wide so they can be mounted right to the studs, see?"

"I thought you'd go simpler," Johannes said.

"*Yah*, well . . . maybe I should have." Solomon rubbed his chin.

"No, it's good," Johannes said quickly. "It's a small wedding. That can be nice—a little more private."

"*Yah*, only about thirty or forty people," Solomon said.

"Oh, and my *mamm* needs you to try on your shirt. We'll be wearing green, you and me."

"Why so few people?" Daniel asked.

Both men looked toward him, and Solomon put his hat back on his head.

"Because they're the only ones who care about the wedding, I expect," Solomon said. "I made a lot of people angry."

"Going to prison, right?" Daniel said, his tone a little too knowing for comfort.

Johannes put a solid hand on Daniel's shoulder. So much for keeping him quiet and explaining things later. The boy winced.

"Nah, it's fine," Solomon said, shooting Johannes a grin. "Yes, Daniel, I went to prison. I got out not too long ago, and now I'm marrying Elizabeth. That's a lot for people to get used to all at once, and it's going to take some time to get people to trust me again. It also means that most of the people who do come to this wedding are only going to be there for the gossip. They don't actually wish me well."

Daniel's eyes were wide, and he dug one boot into the concrete floor. "What did you do to get put in prison?"

"Hung out with the wrong friends, mostly," Solomon replied. "I put having friends above doing right. It's better to be alone and right with your conscience than to have friends and get tugged into bad things. I learned that the hard way."

Johannes sighed. Not exactly the lesson he was aiming at for Daniel, but Solomon wasn't wrong, either.

"But what did you *do*?" Daniel pressed.

"I drove a car that was helping my friends get away

from a robbery they'd just committed," he replied. "Here's a piece of advice for you—if you have friends who say, 'Don't ask for details, it's for the best that you don't know too much,' don't do whatever it is they want you to do. The court doesn't believe you when you say you didn't know."

"Okay . . ." Daniel murmured.

"The Amish way of life is the better way," Solomon said earnestly. "Living *English* might seem fun, and free, and . . . I don't know, it may be really tempting to jump the fence and see how the rest of the world lives, but there are traps there you aren't ready for. And people who claim to be your new family will throw you under the horses' hooves just so you have to share the blame."

Daniel didn't say anything. Was this too much information for the boy, or was it just good sense to tell him a few truths plainly? He only had one more year of school and then he'd be working, just like every other Amish boy that age. There were temptations out there, just waiting for him. Johannes and Solomon turned toward the shelves, and for a couple of minutes, they discussed their plans for finishing them up.

"Maybe I can help with waxing the shelves," Daniel said after a moment.

"*Yah*. Thanks," Solomon said. "Here—" He passed him a tub of wood wax and a rag. "Your uncle and I will go unhitch."

Daniel started prying the lid off the wax can, and Johannes followed his cousin out of the stable as they headed to the buggy.

"I didn't know you had my grandfather's tools," Johannes said.

"*Yah*, he gave me a few," Solomon said. "When my *daet* passed away, your grandfather took me under wing a bit, showed me how to fix some things, how to do some basic woodworking."

"*Yah*, I remember that," Johannes replied.

"Your grandfather was special," Sol said. "I don't know what it was, but he saw the world in a way that made everything fit into place, you know?"

"*Yah*," Johannes agreed. "He was."

"I wish I could see the world like he did all the time," Solomon said. "Instead of just when we listened to him talk. Do you think that comes with age?"

"I hope so." Johannes cast his cousin a wry smile. "Maybe it comes with experiencing enough, too. I don't know."

They started unhitching the horses, and for a little while, they worked in silence.

"So am I the morality lesson for the kid today?" Solomon asked as he loosed the first horse.

"A bit," Johannes said. "I'm sorry. But it's not the lesson you think."

"No?" Sol asked.

Johannes loosed the second horse, and he and Sol led them by the bridles toward the corral.

"Dawdie Menno isn't here to give Daniel some talk that he'd take to heart and never forget. So, for better or for worse, it's falling to me," Johannes said. "I want Daniel to learn that being part of a community is worth protecting, and that you *have* to belong. There really isn't another option. You can't be *too* different, you know?"

"*Yah,*" Solomon agreed.

"And you're working hard to fit back in after everything," Johannes went on. "I wanted him to see that fitting in was worth it to you personally. Because I had a feeling he'd look up to you."

"Look up to me?" Sol said. "Why?"

"Look at you," Johannes said with a grin. "You're like a bull."

"Ah." Sol chuckled. "Right. I'm trying to keep the muscle up so that no one thinks of coming around to harass my family again. That's the only reason."

There was probably a small amount of vanity in there, too . . . and the possibility that Elizabeth secretly liked it.

"Well, it's still impressive," Johannes admitted.

"So, the kid . . . he's different?"

Solomon cast him an unreadable look over the horses' backs. Then he pulled open the gate and they ushered the horses through.

"Different" could cover a whole lot of space, but Daniel's secret hobby wasn't one for Johannes to tell. He was trying to stop this before it got out of hand. There were a couple of beats of silence between them, and Solomon held his gaze, waiting for an answer.

"It's not a big deal," Johannes deflected. It could be worse, at least.

"Hmm." Solomon turned back to the buckles and said, "Can I say something about that?"

"Sure," Johannes said.

"Sometimes it's better to let someone be different and

find their path here in the Amish life than it is to hammer him into a space he doesn't quite fit and chase him away."

Johannes eyed his cousin. "I'm not hammering him. Or chasing him off."

"I know, it's just . . . sometimes being different isn't the end of the world. That's all I'm saying. I was different. I'd have been better off staying put instead of trying to find my place out there."

"Is that why you left?" Johannes asked. Was that why Lovina had left? Had Johannes been expecting too much from her? Had he been putting on pressure without even realizing it?

"Partly," Solomon replied. "In order to come home, I had to learn to be myself and . . . find my place, even if it was on the edges, you know?"

"But you don't want to stay on the edges," Johannes pointed out. "You want a proper Amish life. That includes community."

"Yeah, but now I might not have much choice about being on the edges," Sol replied. "Sometimes you get pushed there. My past isn't going to disappear."

But Daniel still could decide to conform a little better, because a man who quilted . . . that was more than just living on the edges. That wasn't going to be acceptable in any possible way.

"The thing is," Solomon said, lowering his voice as he locked the gate once more, "the whole *Englisher* world isn't made up of criminals and prisons. That's the problem. There are good people out there, too—people with solutions and wider minds than we tend to have here in Bountiful. They are kind people who like to help— who believe in Gott in their own ways. I got to know a

Catholic priest who was just as good of a Christian as Bishop Lapp." He paused, then shrugged. "Don't make your nephew search too hard to find his place here with his own people—because he might find it over the fence. The one thing about Englishers—they like to help more than you think."

Johannes swallowed hard. That hadn't been his intent with his nephew, but the warning was well taken. There had been an *Englisher* life that had held Lovina for the last year, too. And his deepest fear was that her *Englisher* experience was sweeter than her Amish one, that there was some other man who'd made her happier than he'd managed.

And maybe he'd have to accept it.

"I'll watch that," Johannes said, clearing his throat. He glanced back toward the stable. He could see Daniel bent over the shelf through the open window.

But why, of all the things that could make a boy different, does it have to be quilting?

Lovina stood by an open window, trying to catch a breeze. The stove was lit, and even with all the windows and doors propped open, the kitchen was hot.

"But why do you want to go back to Erindale?" Elizabeth said, brushing a stray tendril of hair off her face. She stood at the counter rolling out cinnamon roll dough with a wooden pin. "Lovina, I don't see the point!"

"Because it was my life for a year," Lovina said. "And I need to know what happened."

"It was a mistake!" her sister said, and she put the rolling pin down with a thunk. "You jumped the fence.

You left our home, our way of life, and our faith behind you. You abandoned Johannes! It's dangerous out there, Lovina. Do you have to repeat a mistake just to be sure of it?"

Was it a mistake? Lovina had been hit by a car or truck or something. But that could happen here—there were vehicles on all the roads. And her job had been working with a disabled woman. She'd been helping . . . at least it sounded that way.

"I had a job," Lovina said.

"You could have gotten married and cared for your own family," Elizabeth said. "What more important job is there?"

"Some people need more care," Lovina said. "And maybe there was something meaningful that I was doing out there—"

"And if there was?" Elizabeth came around the counter and crossed her arms under her breasts. "If you had some meaningful job out there that made you feel like you were doing something important, would you go back to it?"

Lovina sighed. "I want to remember. I need to know why I left before I can choose to stay. Don't you see that?"

"Or maybe this is a gift, Lovina!" Elizabeth said earnestly. "Maybe Gott allowed you to forget and start over like a whole new creation, and you're throwing that gift back in His face."

"To forget my family?" Lovina's voice shook. "To forget my father, memories of my dead mother, the man I left behind who never seemed to stop loving me? That was a *gift*? Maybe Gott wasn't involved in this, Elizabeth. That's a possibility!"

"Gott is involved in *everything*," her sister shot back. "And He doesn't make mistakes!"

"Then Gott was cruel to do this to me!" Lovina felt tears prick her eyes. "I'm home, but I don't know who I am! I know I left. I know I was unsatisfied here, or I never would have gone. I know my father is an ex-convict—"

"So is Sol, Lovina," Elizabeth said, warning in her tone. "People can change."

"Maybe you're the one who needs to believe in people completely changing and leaving their mistakes behind!" Lovina retorted. "Maybe you want to believe that whatever happened to Sol out there isn't a part of him, because that makes *you* feel more comfortable!"

"Oh, I know how much a part of him those years are," Elizabeth said, her voice low and angry. "He has nightmares. He feels like people are coming up behind him when they aren't. He's still lifting heavy things to keep his muscles because it makes him feel safer! He's still struggling with how he's going to fit in here—but he's *chosen* us. He doesn't *want* to go back!"

Lovina dropped her gaze. She'd gone too far—she shouldn't have said that. She knew how much Solomon and Elizabeth loved each other. But at least Solomon had his memories intact—he knew *why* he was staying.

"Okay," Lovina said.

"So maybe learn to ask what's happening before you decide to throw around your accusations, Lovina!"

Her sister was angry, and Lovina deserved that.

"I'm sorry, Elizabeth," she said. "I'm just . . . I'm frustrated. I need answers."

Elizabeth sighed and shook her head. "Can't you find them here?"

"I haven't yet," Lovina replied. "And I can't just live my life with half my memories. You don't know what it's like—everything is confusing. You can't put down roots when they've been cut off!"

Elizabeth met Lovina's gaze, and for a moment neither of them spoke. Then Elizabeth turned back to the counter and reached for the butter.

"That is a good point," Elizabeth said quietly. "I'll admit to that. And I can understand how confusing all of this would be for you. I'm just scared to lose you again."

Lovina wished she could say that it wouldn't happen, that she'd come back and everything would be just like it was now . . . She wished she could say that her days would be made up of cooking and sewing, quilting and helping out with little Mo, and she would continue seeing Johannes and looking forward to those heart-pounding kisses. But she couldn't promise anything—she didn't *remember*.

Outside, a buggy turned into the drive, and Lovina shaded her eyes to see who it was. She'd just been thinking of him . . .

"Johannes is here. And Solomon is with him," Lovina said. "And a boy."

"Are they?" Lovina saw her sister's cheeks pink, and she smoothed a hand down the front of her apron. "Sol must be bringing the decorations for the eck. He said he was coming sometime today. I'll hurry up and get these cinnamon buns into the oven. They'll take a few minutes to unhitch."

Elizabeth had a beautiful life here in Bountiful. She had a man she loved, a life that made sense to her, and things to look forward to. It would be lovely . . . but it was possible that Lovina was different than her sister. Elizabeth's hands sped up, and she deftly sprinkled cinnamon over the layer of butter, then reached for the tub of brown sugar.

"Let me finish that," Lovina said.

"Do you mind?" Elizabeth asked hopefully.

"It's for your wedding," Lovina said. "I remember how to do this. Where is the pan?"

"Here. It's already greased." Elizabeth turned to the sink to wash up, and then pulled off her kitchen apron. "Thank you, Lovina. I appreciate it."

Lovina watched as her sister headed for the side door, a spring in her step as she felt her hair and *kapp* with her fingertips before disappearing outside. This was Elizabeth's life . . . it was Bethany's life, too. Upstairs, Lovina could hear her sister-in-law's bucket of soapy water scraping against the floorboards as she mopped the upstairs bedrooms. Those were women who had found their place, who had made a home.

If only it could be that easy for Lovina.

Lovina washed her hands and then picked up the brown sugar. She spread a generous amount over the dough and then began to roll it, starting at the ends and rolling it over her palms to get it started.

Her fingers knew the job rather well, it seemed. She must have done this task a thousand times, even if she didn't remember it, exactly.

Was it enough to have the muscle memory of a life? Would she ever get it all back again—like other people had?

When Lovina slid the pan of cinnamon rolls into the

oven, the side door opened, and she looked up to see Johannes.

"Hello," he said.

"Is that your nephew with you?" she asked.

"*Yah*, that's Daniel. He's looking at your new chicks in the coop," he replied.

So they had a few minutes alone, it would seem. Johannes glanced around the kitchen, and she heard the sound of the bucket moving upstairs again. She felt her pulse quicken, and she brushed the flour from her hands. Johannes's dark gaze locked onto her, and she felt her cheeks heat. They were alone for now . . .

"They're very excited about their wedding, aren't they?" she said. She didn't need to say who. Johannes smiled, and he moved around the table, coming closer to where she stood at the counter.

"We used to be like that," he said, his voice low.

"Were we?" she asked uncertainly. And she'd left? She couldn't imagine Elizabeth leaving Sol . . .

"Before your *daet*'s arrest," he qualified. "It was different afterward. It was hard for both of us in different ways, I suppose. We didn't understand each other well enough."

Lovina nodded. "The police came to find me yesterday."

"What?" He looked startled, and she smiled ruefully at his response.

"It was a wellness check," she said. "I had a job in Erindale, they said. And my employers were worried about me. They left an address."

"What kind of job?" he asked.

"Working with a woman in a wheelchair," she said.

"That's all I know, and I don't actually remember it, but I want to see them. I had a life over there—I'd like to know more about it."

Johannes was silent, but some color drained from his face.

"And before you try and convince me not to, I've had this discussion with both my brother and my sister— repeatedly," she said. "I need my memories back, Johannes. I need to know what my life was."

He chewed the inside of his cheek. "Okay . . . What do you want to do?"

"I wanted to ask you—" She felt a pang of caution. This might be too much to ask . . . "Johannes, would you come with me?"

Johannes licked his lips and looked to the side toward the kitchen clock, but his gaze was turned inward.

"To Erindale?" he asked at last.

She nodded. "I need answers! I need to see what kept me away for a whole year. And I don't want to go alone."

Johannes moved closer, stopping inches from her side so that she had to tip her face up to look at him. He reached out and touched the top of her apron, his fingers moving slowly over the fabric, tracing a line across her collarbone. She felt a shiver move down her arms.

"Is this familiar at all?" he asked, his voice low.

"What?" she asked feebly. Him being so close? Him touching her with one fingertip making her whole body yearn for more? The way her heart was skipping a beat at the thought of a kiss . . .

"I mean you asking me to go with you . . . does it feel familiar?" he asked quietly, and he dropped his hand.

Oh, that. She shook her head.

"Because you asked me to go with you before," he went on. "You wanted to see your *daet* in prison—you needed answers. And I said no."

Lovina felt the air rush out of her lungs. So it was too much to ask. She was trying to put her own worries and uncertainties onto his strong shoulders, and he had every right to turn her down. But how would she find the place? She wasn't sure she could do it alone, and her siblings certainly weren't going to take her out there.

"I'll figure something out," she said, and she reached for a cloth to wipe the counter—something to focus on in her embarrassment.

"Hey—" He caught her hand. "I said no a year ago when you wanted me to go to see your *daet* in prison, and I regretted that choice. I should have gone with you, because you were going whether I went with you or not. I'll go with you to Erindale."

"You will?" She looked up with a flood of hope.

"*Yah* . . ." He touched her cheek, and then dipped his head down and brushed his lips against hers. "As long as your family is okay with it, I'll go with you."

"Thank you," she breathed.

"But you have to promise you'll come back," he said. "If I take you out there and you don't return, they'll blame me. And I don't think my reputation could take much more of a beating."

How much of that was a joke? She wasn't sure, and she smiled faintly. "I'll come back with you. I just need to see it. I need to know what I was doing out there. I need to remember something."

He nodded. "Okay."

There were footsteps on the stairs, and Johannes took a step away from her, making the air between them suddenly feel like a chasm. The door opened and the boy came inside. He looked around uncertainly. He was tall, a little gangly, and starting to fill out like an adolescent, but there was still something of the child in him.

"Could I get some water?" Daniel asked.

"*Yah*, of course," Lovina said, but she sounded just a little too bright and cheery in her own ears. She moved away from Johannes toward the kitchen sink. She turned on the water and reached for a clean glass.

"Sol and the other lady are kissing," she heard Daniel say when her back was turned. She felt some heat hit her own cheeks. Given a little more time alone, she and Johannes might have been doing the same thing.

Lovina handed Daniel the tall glass of water, and she gave him a reassuring smile.

"They do that," she said with a chuckle. "I suppose it's a good thing they're getting married."

Daniel's face turned red, and he laughed. "*Yah*. I guess." Daniel emptied the glass and handed it back. "Thanks."

"I should get back out there," Johannes said. "I'm pretty sure I'm obligated to noisily interrupt them or something."

Lovina exchanged a mildly embarrassed look with Daniel.

"Whatever you think is best," Lovina said.

This could have been Lovina's wedding . . . the

excitement, the anticipation, the happiness could all have been hers. But something had held Lovina in Erindale, away from this man who made her stomach tumble and her cheeks blaze.

What would make her do that?

Chapter Eleven

Johannes and Daniel helped Solomon unload the eck decorations, and a blushing Elizabeth headed back to the house. The wedding would take place under a tent, which meant reconsidering how they'd set up the eck without a proper corner.

"We'll have to make a frame," Johannes said. "There's no way around it."

"It shouldn't be too hard," Solomon replied, "if we can get the lumber and make two walls. Tobias Lapp still does drywalling, doesn't he?"

"*Yah,*" Johannes said. "That's a good idea. If we asked for his help, I'm sure he would. We couldn't waste any time, though. And we'll have to have the frame done first."

"It would look good—a false corner—the shelves hung on both sides," Solomon said. "I wonder if we could hang a rod for the quilt to drape over, like the quilt displays in the fabric shop . . ."

The details were slowly coming together, and for a few minutes they discussed the logistics of making sure it would stay upright and support the weight of the shelves as well as a quilt. As they talked, Daniel went to watch a new colt play in the grass outside.

"It's strange to see Linda's son," Solomon said, nodding toward Daniel, who was standing within view with his foot on a fence. "He looks like her."

"*Yah*, I know," Johannes agreed. Daniel had Linda's sandy blond hair and her soulful eyes. He had her grin, too, when he was just about to laugh at something. It made Johannes miss his oldest sister. "The older Daniel gets, the more he looks like our side of the family."

Johannes crossed his arms over his chest, his mind moving back to the house where the women were working. Solomon was getting married, and Johannes couldn't help the twinge of envy he felt. In a matter of weeks, Solomon would have his wife in his arms and would start growing that married beard. Solomon, who'd jumped the fence and been incarcerated. It hardly seemed fair.

"You don't approve of me marrying Lizzie, do you?" Sol asked, his voice low.

"What?" Joannes turned toward his cousin. "I didn't say that."

"You don't have to. I can see it, and you're not different from anyone else," Solomon replied. "You think she'd be better off with someone else."

"I think—" Johannes was silent for a moment, wondering what he could safely say. "I think if you marry her, you'd better stay on the straight and narrow. You're choosing the Amish life—*for life*."

"I'm choosing *her* for life," Solomon said. "And that's the easy part."

Johannes nodded. Sol was in love—it was plenty obvious. And Elizabeth felt the same way. And Solomon had found his way to belong . . . Johannes didn't begrudge people a life together.

"I'm happy for you," Johannes said, and he paused. "And seeing as you're just about one of Lovina's family, I might as well tell you that Lovina wants me to take her to where she used to work in Erindale."

Sol's eyebrows went up. "Does she remember it?"

"I think she's trying to," he replied.

"What did you tell her?" Sol asked.

"I said I'd do it," Johannes replied.

Sol nodded and was silent for a moment. "I mentioned it before, but it isn't all bad out there. There are some people who live really beautiful, Christian lives."

"And you think . . ." Johannes swallowed. "You think Lovina had one of those beautiful lives?"

"It's possible," Solomon replied. "I know what you are all afraid of—that she'll want to go back. She didn't contact anyone, and it wasn't because she couldn't. She *chose* not to. We all know that, right?"

This was supposed to be helpful? This was all common knowledge, and it stung every time he thought of it. He didn't need it repeated to him over and over again as if he'd never considered the fact that Lovina had been able to walk away that successfully.

"*Yah*, I know," Johannes muttered.

"It's why Isaiah and Elizabeth hope she only remembers the Amish," Sol said. "But it won't work. When she remembers, she'll have to make her peace with her time away."

Or with her Amish roots . . . and regardless, she'd have a choice to make all over again.

"She's going to be different than she was before," Sol went on. "I'm saying that as someone who's been away. You won't be able to go back to what you two used to be. It's not possible. Time away changes people, and your brother and sister haven't gotten to the point where they feel okay with that yet."

"But who was she out there, past the fence?" Johannes murmured, more to himself than to his cousin.

"That's what you have to find out," Solomon replied. "Look, Johannes, you loved her. But the woman you loved is in the past. She's different now. And even though this family is counting on you to work miracles, you've got choices to make for your own future, too." Solomon's gaze was steady, earnest. Then the other man shrugged and rubbed a hand over his chin. "And that's all I'm going to say about that."

When Johannes and Daniel arrived back at the farm, Johannes's mind was still chewing over what Solomon had said. He was right—there were choices to make on both sides. Technically, Johannes could choose a life with Lovina, if she'd have him, that wouldn't follow the Amish ways. That was in the realm of possibility, but it wasn't the life he wanted. It wasn't the life they'd wanted together when they'd fallen in love.

Had that changed for her?

And if it had, would it give him the closure he'd need to move on and marry a woman who wanted an Amish life with him? Maybe it would make an inevitable good-bye easier.

But his heart clenched at the thought. She'd only just gotten back. Give her time . . . Miracles happened, didn't they?

That evening, when Johannes told his father the plan, Bernard was silent for a few beats, chewing the inside of his cheek.

"What do you think?" Johannes pressed.

"I don't think you have a choice," his father admitted. "She's going, and she's asking you to go with her. I think if you're there, you'll at least be a physical reminder of the Amish life for her. There's a better chance of her coming home for good that way."

A better chance was not necessarily a good chance, though.

Bernard went upstairs and came back with a roll of bills. He peeled them off, one by one, counting as he did so.

"How much will it take to pay for taxis, food, maybe a few nights at a motel?" his father asked.

They discussed the cost, including a little bit of emergency money, and his father handed over the cash.

Daniel's gaze was locked on that roll of bills.

"That's a lot of money, Dawdie," Daniel said.

"It only spends once, though," Bernard said, giving the boy a meaningful look. "Remember that. You have to be ready for emergencies, and that is what this money is for. Has your *mamm* talked to you about taking care of money yet?"

Daniel shook his head. "Not really."

Bernard regarded the boy for a moment, then he took one more bill off the roll and handed it over to him.

"Make that last for your entire stay here," Bernard

said. "Think before you spend, and if you can keep some in your pocket to go home with, even better."

It was a fifty-dollar bill—a large amount of money for any boy to have to himself. It wasn't like he needed anything. And Heaven knew that Bernard had never passed over that kind of cash to Johannes growing up.

"Thank you, Dawdie!" A grin split Daniel's face.

Johannes smiled at his nephew's excitement.

"What are you going to do with it?" Johannes asked.

For a second, there was a flicker of misgiving in the boy's eyes, and then he said, "I'll buy something small. Just a little thing, and then I'll save the rest. Like Dawdie says, it only spends once, right? I might need something later. Or my *mamm* might."

Was Daniel thinking about his quilt? Maybe. But how he'd manage to buy sewing supplies without Bernard noticing, Johannes had no idea. They were probably safe on that front, at least for now.

"I'll go back to talk to Isaiah later on tonight," Johannes said. "I can't take Lovina anywhere without the blessing of her family."

Bernard nodded soberly. "Maybe she'll see that the *Englisher* life she's imagining wasn't as glittery as she thinks. Something just out of reach has a way of seeming so much more appealing than it really is."

"Am I doing that with Lovina?" he asked. "Am I remembering things better than they were because she's just out of reach?"

His father reached over and patted his shoulder.

"Would I be better off marrying someone I feel less passionately about?" he pressed. "Someone stable, kind, able to commit to me and an Amish life?"

Bernard was silent for a moment. "There is something to be said for stability, son. The passion, the heartbreak, the ups and downs—they get a little old over time. There will come an age where the happiest moment you can think of consists of lying in bed next to your wife, talking about spring planting . . . and knowing that tomorrow and the day after and the day after will be just the same. No drama. No heartbreak. Just . . . life."

"With the right woman," Johannes clarified.

Bernard shrugged. "*Yah . . . Yah*, I agree, with the right woman. But spring comes every year, and we plant. We weed. We water. We harvest . . . It's good to know that your wife is happy with those regular rhythms and she'll be by your side for it all. A contented life depends upon someone who finds pleasure in the work. There is a practical side to choosing a wife."

It was only then that Johannes noticed his nephew's gaze locked on them. They were saying too much.

"You remember that, too, Daniel," Bernard said, putting a hand on his grandson's shoulder. "A woman needs to be able to count on you, but you need to be able to count on her, too. Stability matters. Remember that."

Daniel was thirteen. He likely wouldn't remember it, but it had been driven home for Johannes. The life he longed for with Lovina might not be possible any longer.

"I don't need your permission, Isaiah," Lovina said, shooting her brother an annoyed look. "I'm of age."

Johannes sat at the kitchen table, his hands folded on the tabletop, his gaze fixed on a space about a foot in front of his face. The baby was sleeping in a cradle by the stairs, and Bethany and Elizabeth stood in the kitchen watching in uncomfortable silence.

She might be of age, but it seemed that even Johannes was waiting for her family to give their permission for this trip. Because living here meant doing things the Amish way, and it meant getting permission, and not tipping the wagon. And she hated that right now! This was her life!

"And how do you expect to get to Erindale?" Isaiah retorted. "If you want to go, you'll need money and a driver."

"So now I'm held hostage?" Lovina crossed her arms over her chest. "Because from what I've heard, that didn't work the last time!"

She was angry, and the words were out before she could even think better of them. She wasn't really threatening to walk out, because he was right. She had no way to get to Erindale, and no money of her own. She also had no memory to guide her, just a hope that some familiar sights might spark something.

"I'll pay for it," Johannes said, and his gaze flicked toward Lovina. "Before anyone starts throwing out threats they don't mean."

She felt the chastisement, and her cheeks heated. No, she hadn't meant it, but she was angry. Everyone in this room had a stake in controlling her choices, hemming her in. Every single person in this room wanted her to stay home, including Johannes. He'd agreed to take her, but not because it was his first choice.

"It's not about the money," Isaiah retorted.

"Johannes said he'd take me," Lovina said. "And I'll promise to come back home with him, if that makes everyone feel better. I'm not trying to take off again, I'm trying to remember my own life!"

Her brother rubbed his hands over his face. "There is a huge order we're working on at the book bindery, and if you could wait a couple of weeks, I'll take you myself—"

But she didn't want her brother along for this trip. It wasn't that she didn't love him, or trust him, but he was more inclined to order her around, speak for her, try to protect her as if she were a little girl still. Johannes was still a risk, but less of one than her brother.

"I'd rather go sooner," Lovina said, and she glanced toward Johannes. "With Johannes."

"Why the rush?" Isaiah asked.

"Would you want to put off digging up your own memories, Isaiah?" she asked. "Would you be willing to just wait around for a couple of weeks?"

Her brother met her gaze, and for a moment all she saw was stubbornness, but then he sighed.

"No," he admitted. "I wouldn't."

"I'll bring her home again," Johannes said, and he flicked a serious look over in Lovina's direction. "That's a promise."

She wasn't quite sure what he meant by that. How far was the tall, broad Johannes willing to go to bring her home? But it was fine. She'd come home, and whatever she learned about herself, and about her life, could be processed here with her family. She could agree to that.

"You'll come back?" Isaiah asked her.

"*Yah,* Isaiah. I'll come home," she replied. "Of course."

Her brother looked over toward Bethany and Elizabeth in the kitchen for the first time.

"What do you two think?" he asked.

"Lovina, you'll miss Service Sunday," Elizabeth said. "That could spark memories, too. You'd see old friends, and worship. It's important."

But somehow, the thought of attending a Service Sunday left a knot of unexplained dread in her stomach. She didn't need sermons and community—she needed answers out there with the English.

"I need to see what I left in Erindale," Lovina said quietly. "I'm coming back, though. I promise."

The room was silent for a moment, and Isaiah locked eyes with his wife. Something unspoken seemed to pass between them, and then Bethany smiled faintly.

"It's up to you, Isaiah," she said. "But like she says, she's grown."

"Are you okay with this, Lizzie?" Isaiah asked.

Tears stood out in Elizabeth's eyes. "At least we have an address this time."

Elizabeth's chin trembled, and she blinked a couple of times.

"I said I'd come back, Elizabeth!" Lovina said.

"I know. But there was a time you swore you'd never leave, too."

A promise she couldn't remember making.

"Okay," Isaiah said, his voice low. "Then you have our blessing. But, Lovina?"

"*Yah*?" she said softly.

"Not everything is as sunny as it appears at first look, okay?" he said.

Including this life here in Bountiful. She'd been learning that over that last couple of weeks, too. A wedding planned for her sister, who was marrying an ex-con. A father who loved her dearly who'd defrauded the community. But she knew what he was trying to say, and until she had her full memory back, she wasn't going to make a choice one way or the other.

"I just need to remember," Lovina said. "And maybe when I do, I can explain myself to all of you. I have a feeling I owe you all that much."

Elizabeth looked away, and Bethany dropped her gaze, too. Only Isaiah kept his head up, and she saw the uncertainty in his eyes. Johannes was silent, and he didn't look worried. But then, he'd be with her, and maybe he knew just how far he'd go to bring her home again.

For the first time since Lovina had woken up in that hospital bed, she felt like she had some control.

Her memories were out there. It was time to go get them.

Mid-morning the next day, a taxi arrived at the house. Johannes was already inside, and he got out to help her put her backpack into the trunk. Lovina hadn't packed much—going with fewer clothes and toiletries seemed to make her siblings feel better, and so she packed a nightgown, two dresses, two kapps, and the underthings required. If the experience was going to spark memories, then a couple of days should be enough. And then she would return as promised.

Lovina's brother was already at work, and Bethany and Elizabeth stood on the side deck, Moses in his mother's arms.

"Be careful!" Elizabeth called as Lovina got into the back seat next to Johannes.

"I will!" she called back.

But she knew that caution wasn't what her sister really wanted from her. She wanted her defenses up, like a good Amish woman, refusing to be enticed by the *Englisher* world. She might not remember her time with the Englishers, but she knew it was a little too late for that.

"All right," the driver said. "So we're off to Erindale now, are we?"

"*Yah*, thank you," Johannes said.

The driver put the car into gear, and they rolled forward. It was a different feeling from the jolt and jiggle of a buggy, but it was familiar, too. Lovina reached for the seat belt without even thinking, and as it clicked into place, she felt more than familiarity—she remembered doing this before. Many times. She knew to buckle up. She knew the feeling of sitting back and looking out the window. She knew that cracking the window open just a little with that button could give her a finger of fresh air to help with the motion sickness.

But it was more than knowing how to ride in a car. Another memory floated to the surface of her mind. She saw herself in the back seat of a vehicle, and sitting next to her had been a young woman with thin legs and one hand that didn't stretch out all the way. The young woman's hair was done in a style that was too young for her years—a half ponytail on top of her head with a purple elastic—although the young woman's mother had done her best.

"I remember her . . ." Lovina breathed.

"What? Who?" Johannes reached for her hand, and his strong grip closed over hers.

"The young woman I worked with," Lovina said. "Her name is Carrie, and I remember her."

Johannes stared at her, and Lovina felt her breath speed up. She remembered driving somewhere with Carrie and her parents, but it was in a minivan, not a car. They were higher on the road, and there was more space in the vehicle. The had separate seats instead of a bench seat.

The smell was similar, though, the scent of air freshener and stuffiness. She remembered feeling excited to be going out somewhere, seeing the other cars slip past outside the window, and listening to the low voices of Carrie's parents as they talked from the front.

"What is she like?" Johannes asked.

"She has cerebral palsy," Lovina said. "I can't explain it well. I never did understand it all the way. But she's in a wheelchair, and her body doesn't do what she wants it to. But she's smart, and sweet, and often misunderstood. Her parents are trying to give her a full life, and they need someone to take Carrie out and do things with her—independent from them. Carrie needs to be a full person, not just someone's child."

It was flooding back into her head—this part of it, at least. And she could feel the irony of her own present situation. She was pushing against her family's wishes to keep her home, to keep her identity locked down with her own family. But she needed more than that, too— even without an intact memory. She needed to be more than someone's child, or someone's sister.

"And her parents?" Johannes asked.

Lovina searched her memory for the people she remembered murmuring from the front of the vehicle.

"I can't quite remember them . . ." She leaned her head back, sifting through these new memories. "And I don't remember how I got there . . . or who they are, or . . ."

It was frustrating getting back so much in a rush and yet realizing that it was still just a fragment of memory floating in a sea that she couldn't recall.

"Are they good people?" he asked, his voice low.

"I don't know . . ." But she'd stayed, hadn't she?

"Hey, it's a really good start!" Johannes said.

She looked over at him, and he gave her a reassuring smile.

"It is," he insisted.

The taxi turned onto a main road and they picked up speed. It was coming back, and she felt a surge of relief at the realization. She was starting to remember more, and she felt an unbidden wave of happiness to be speeding down the highway toward Erindale.

It felt like freedom.

For the first hour of driving, it was farmland—mostly *English*, but Johannes did spot a few typically Amish homes with laundry flapping on a line. There must be a small Amish community out here, but he hadn't heard of it. Maybe it was New Order.

An hour by highway was much farther than Johannes had ever driven his buggy, and he noted the changes in the crops—corn and wheat gave way to oats and barley. There was one field he recognized as soybeans, and another he was relatively sure was tobacco, but he couldn't be certain. They were big fields, though—the *English* kind that required tractors and sprayers—and the farmhouses couldn't be seen in the distance, they were so far off.

Johannes watched as the farmland melted away outside the taxi window and a spattering of housing developments began to appear. There were construction businesses—large vehicle rentals, prefabricated homes, a window company right next to a lumberyard. There were billboards for new apartment complexes, all promising luxurious living at phenomenal prices just outside the city limits of Erindale, and Johannes could feel his blood pressure rising. It was so busy, so close together, so . . . *English*.

He looked over at Lovina. She'd been sitting perfectly still this whole time, her knees pressed together and a sparkle in her eyes that he couldn't deny. This was exciting for her. She didn't feel the same anxiety he did, obviously.

"Do you recognize any of this?" he asked her.

"Not this," she replied, but it didn't seem to dampen her good spirits.

When they got into the city, the driver followed his GPS, the little mechanical voice telling him when to turn. It was a strange feeling—no time for a man to think things through, or discuss an upcoming turn with someone else. Just this bodiless, oddly cheerful voice saying, "Stay in the left-hand lane, and at the next intersection, turn left."

They eventually made their way into a subdivision with large houses packed closely together in a way that made a man feel like his breath was restricted. There were beautiful lawns, though, and tall trees stretching over the street, a few patches of the leaves turning yellow.

"It's there," Lovina said, pointing ahead to a large three-story house with yellow siding and white trim. There was a wheelchair ramp that led up to the front door, and a beautifully arranged flower garden lined the front of the house. The lawn was greener than was natural—probably because of chemicals and sprays, he imagined.

It was an *Englisher* foible—the need to perfect everything, even nature. They couldn't let a lawn fade with the season, as if there were only beauty in green grass and white snow, not in the journey between.

There were no vehicles on the driveway, and Johannes realized then that he had no plan for what to do if this family wasn't home today.

The driver pulled up next to the house and quoted Johannes the price. It was a little more than he'd anticipated, and he paid the bill. The driver popped the trunk, and he and Lovina got out and took their bags.

"You want me to wait—see if your friends are home?" the driver asked Johannes.

There was shadow in the front window, and the door opened just then, a middle-aged man appearing in a pair of khaki pants and slippers.

"No, I think we're fine," Johannes said. "Thanks, though."

"Have a good day," the driver replied, and he got back into the driver's seat, then started to back out of the drive.

"Lovina?" the older man said. "My goodness, we were worried about you! The police said there was an accident, and you were fine now, but—"

Johannes looked over at Lovina, who was looking at the man hard. She was trying to remember—he could almost see the effort.

The man's gaze moved over to Johannes, and he gave him a smile.

"I'm Gordon Maitland," he said.

"Johannes Miller," Johannes replied.

They shook hands, and Gordon glanced over his shoulder at a woman who had appeared in the doorway.

"This is my wife, Aline," he said. "And you are—?"

"A friend of Lovina's," he replied.

"Right. We had no idea what happened to her," Gordon said. "We thought maybe she'd quit. I mean, we've had other workers find other jobs, and they've left pretty abruptly. We didn't think Lovina was the sort to leave without a goodbye, but being Amish and all . . ."

"You thought she'd come home?" Johannes asked.

"Yes, pretty much," he replied.

Aline came up then, and she smiled hesitantly at Lovina.

"We had no idea you'd been hurt, Lovina," Aline said quietly. "We thought you'd quit! And I know that's terrible. But we did start looking for you, and the police said that your family had brought you home, and"—Aline shrugged helplessly—"I had no idea you were hurt! Are you okay now?"

"Her memory isn't back yet," Johannes said quickly. "She was hoping that a visit here might help her recover more of it."

"Oh . . ." Aline nodded. "Do you remember us, dear?"

"A little," Lovina said slowly. "I remember a pink apron. With ruffles. And lace."

"Yes!" Aline laughed. "Yes! That's my apron. You loved it—I let you wear it whenever you cooked."

A very *English* apron—it sounded rather gaudy to

Johannes. Amish women didn't wear lace and ruffles. There was something deeply beautiful about a simple white apron. But it wasn't just the description of it that sat wrong for Johannes; it was the fact that her memories were coming back for her now, faster and faster.

And none of them were Amish.

Johannes watched as Aline slipped an arm around Lovina's shoulders. "You both must be hungry—that's a long drive. Carrie is in the backyard right now. Come on in."

Johannes didn't move at first—his mind was spinning—but Gordon shot him a friendly smile and angled his head toward the house.

"Come on in," Gordon said. "We were about to make lunch—burgers and fries, if you like that. I could throw another couple of patties on the grill."

It did sound good, actually, and Johannes's stomach growled.

"Thank you," Johannes said.

He followed the older man into the house, and Johannes glanced around at the decor. The sitting room had a piano, and the couch had a floral pattern on it. A bookshelf held a few books, but mostly little ornaments. It was overwhelming—a little stifling.

"Different than you're used to?" Gordon asked perceptively.

Johannes felt his face heat. "*Yah*, just different."

"Lovina had the same look on her face when she came in the first time," Gordon said. "I suspect it's an Amish reaction. Lovina said that Amish homes are more streamlined—less froufrou."

"*Yah*," Johannes admitted.

"Well, a woman makes a home, and my wife made this one," Gordon said with a grin. "I imagine it's the same for you all."

It was, actually, and that was why the choice in a wife was such a careful one. A woman made an Amish home—her heart was the center of it. Her cooking, her love, her fastidiousness created the environment for a family to thrive. And two years ago, he'd chosen Lovina to be that woman.

Gordon led the way into the kitchen. Aline started an electric kettle, and Lovina looked around. He watched her face, seeing the uncertainty battle with the flickers of something else—was she remembering this place?

"Would you like to see your bedroom?" Gordon asked.

"Yes," Lovina said, and Johannes noted that she sounded more *English* now, her accent changing. "I really would."

"Why don't you both come up?" Gordon said.

They followed the man upstairs. There were family photographs on the staircase wall, and Johannes followed the both of them to the second floor, and then on up to the third. There was a sitting room up there with a couch, a small table, and a window overlooking the backyard. Johannes looked down to see a woman sitting in a wheelchair out there. She looked like she was dozing.

"That's Carrie," Gordon said. "She falls asleep out there in the fresh air. With all the medication she's on these days, she needs the extra rest."

Johannes nodded. "Oh, okay."

Lovina went into the bedroom, and Gordon nodded toward the window.

"I'm going to start up the barbecue," he said. "You two come on down when you're ready. I know Carrie will be happy to see Lovina, even if it is just for a proper goodbye. It was tough on her when Lovina didn't come back. She was really heartbroken."

Johannes didn't know what to say to that, but Gordon didn't seem to expect an answer. He headed back down the stairs, and Johannes went over to the bedroom doorway.

Lovina stood in a smallish bedroom. There was a bed on one side of the room, and next to it was a little side table with a digital clock. A standing wardrobe dominated the far side of the room, along with a mirror. The gabled window looked out over the front yard, over the trees and the street. Lovina went over to the bed and sat on the edge.

"I remember this room," she said, looking up. "That memory I have of sitting on the bed with a laptop computer—it was here. And that little bird's nest made of grass—it was from here, too. I made it for Carrie in the back yard."

Johannes pulled open a wardrobe door, and inside he saw some *Englisher* clothes—blue jeans, shirts . . . and hung to one side there was a single Amish dress—a little worn, the apron still crisp and white. It was the dress she'd worn when she ran away, and the realization brought a lump to his throat.

"This is yours," he said, fingering the cotton.

Lovina came to his side, and she looked into the wardrobe. Her gaze moved slowly over the small, neat piles of clothing. He let his hand fall from the fabric of her dress, and she smoothed a hand over it gently. Her blue gaze rose to meet his.

"You remember this, don't you?" he murmured.

"*Yah*." She nodded slowly. "I do."

She'd been in this house all of half an hour, and she had memories of this house, of her life here.

"Do you remember these people?" he asked.

"A little bit," she said. "I remember that apron—"

"But the people," he pressed.

"I'm starting to," she said, and her voice caught. "I'm sorry, Johannes! I know it's terrible that I'm remembering them first. I know it!"

But she couldn't help it, could she? And he'd be a jerk to blame her. However her memories came back, that would be a good thing. She needed to know who she was and remember her own history.

But why couldn't she remember *him* this easily? Why were her memories of him locked under layers of memories with these Englishers? They seemed like pleasant people, but they weren't *her* people, were they?

"It's fine," he said, swallowing a lump in his throat. "It's good that it's coming back."

"Is it?" she asked.

"*Yah*, it's fine." Because that was the only acceptable thing to say.

Her blue gaze met his, and his heartbeat pattered faster in the depths of his chest, and with every beat it declared that she was his, not theirs! He longed to catch her lips with his and reassure himself of the connection they shared. He'd been fighting it up until now, and all he wanted was to pull her close and feel how she leaned into him, how she caught her breath when he deepened a kiss . . . His arms ached for it, but that was selfish. This wasn't about reassuring himself.

Johannes slipped a hand behind her neck and pressed his lips against her forehead.

"We should go down," she said.

"*Yah*." He released her.

He looked around the room one last time before following her out to the steep staircase.

For an entire year he'd wondered where she was, if she was safe, if she was alone. And not once had he imagined a life like this. She'd had a whole upper floor in this large, somewhat wealthy home, it seemed. She'd been valued, treated kindly, and missed when she vanished.

All while he'd been lying in bed awake at night, praying for her safety, for her return . . . and as the months had worn on, as he'd started to ask Gott to help him let go and move on, his heart had been tangled up in her. And all that time, she'd been *here*.

She'd been comfortable. She'd been *just fine*.

And it would seem that his heartbreak had been very one-sided.

Chapter Twelve

Lovina felt a difference in Johannes—the tension and discomfort seemed to swirl around him, pushing everyone else away. He kept looking around at things—the pictures on the walls, the patterns on the wallpaper, the ruffles on the curtains. She noticed those details, too, but his disapproval almost emanated off of him.

"Be polite," she whispered.

"What?" Johannes looked over at her.

"You're scowling," she said. "And it's rude."

"Sorry." He smoothed his expression.

"This is their home," she reminded him in Pennsylvania Dutch. "And we might live differently, but we can't just openly disapprove of *English* ways. Not in an *English* home."

"I know," he said. "I'm sorry. I'll keep a lid on that."

"This isn't bad for them," she said. "They don't live Plain, but they *are* good people."

"You remember that?" His voice was low, his jaw tensed.

"*Yah* . . ." She shrugged helplessly. She could remember family worships downstairs in a sitting room with floral prints and an abundance of tiny decorations. She could remember honest, heartfelt prayer in a kitchen with a woman who wore glittering earrings and whose wedding rings had a diamond as big as a spring pea. They were *so English*. "Johannes . . ."

"It's fine," he said. "It's good that it's coming back. You were right about coming here, I guess." He licked his lips. "For your memory, at least."

But she could still see the sadness there, simmering under the surface, and she felt caught between two worlds already—the Amish family who had come for her, and the *English* people who hadn't. All the same, they were a part of her history here, and while she could remember feeling safe here, she'd also been deeply lonely.

When they got to the kitchen, Aline smiled at them.

"Gordon is firing up the barbecue," she said. "Johannes, our men take great pride in their barbecue skills. I'm sure Gordon would like a hand."

Johannes looked over at Lovina, and she shrugged weakly. Amish men didn't take pride in their cooking, but she knew that Johannes knew how to cook . . . how did she know that? But she did. Johannes didn't have a *mamm* at home, and he and his father did all the housework and cooking between them.

"*Yah*, I can go see," Johannes said.

He paused at the patio door, fiddled with the handle of the screen, and then pulled it open. Lovina could see Carrie in her chair. She was awake now, and she looked somberly toward her.

"I should go say hi to Carrie," Lovina said.

"She'd appreciate it," Aline agreed.

From the young woman's hurt expression, it looked like Lovina had an apology to give, too. She followed

Johannes out the screen door and then pulled it shut behind her. She crossed the grass toward the young woman in her wheelchair, and she pulled up a lawn chair next to Carrie and sat down.

"I was in an accident," Lovina said. "That's why you didn't hear from me."

"That's what they told me," Carrie replied. "Are you okay?"

"I still don't remember everything," Lovina said. "I've got a few bruises, but I'm okay."

"I thought you quit," Carrie said. "It isn't like it hasn't happened before. I had a worker who walked out in the middle of the day. She had other plans and had figured out a new job she liked better."

Lovina swallowed. That sounded terrible—a young woman being treated that poorly by a person hired to help her.

"I didn't do that," Lovina said softly. "But I understand why you thought I had, considering I just disappeared on you. I was in a hospital for a week. They said I was riding a bike and I got hit by a car . . . or truck. They still don't know who hit me. I hit my head pretty hard, and I lost my memory. My family found me and brought me home to Bountiful. I don't remember my family properly, even . . . It's really weird. It's like . . . everyone is a stranger I'm getting to know all over again. I don't even remember the man I was supposed to marry."

"Johannes," Carrie said.

"*Yah*. That's him," Lovina said, and then she frowned. "Did I talk about him?"

"You talked about him quite often. You broke up with him," Carrie replied, and she awkwardly pushed herself up in her chair. She rolled her head over to look at her with a clear, serious gaze.

"What did I say about that?" Lovina asked. "I don't remember."

"You missed him," Carrie said.

"Oh . . ." Yes, she could remember a surge of deep sadness associated with this place—loneliness that nearly rocked her.

"And you thought he'd be happier without you," Carrie said. "You also thought that he'd never love you enough to leave the Amish community with you."

Lovina licked her lips. "All probably quite true."

"You didn't want to be Amish anymore," Carrie said. "You asked me to teach you how to be . . . regular."

"Regular." Lovina inwardly winced at that word. The proper term was "*English*," but the English didn't always know that. So she'd decided to leave. For good. She'd suspected as much ever since she'd learned she'd been gone for a year, but having it confirmed still felt like a jolt.

"Was I learning?" Lovina asked softly.

"You were." Carrie shot her a smile. "And you liked it."

Lovina smiled faintly.

"You loved watching movies," Carrie went on. "And you bought some regular clothes, but you always said you felt a little bit guilty in them because it showed your legs."

"*Yah*?" She'd had that memory of herself wearing jeans. Apparently, her guilt hadn't held her back.

"And you wore perfume, too," Carrie said. "My mom gave you some of hers, and you said that Amish women don't do that, so having some perfume of your own was so luxurious. But you liked bubble baths most of all. And bath oils, and scented creams, and all that girlie stuff."

An image rose in her mind of a bathtub with a ring around the edge.

"Did it make the tub filthy?" Lovina asked.

"Of course!" Carrie laughed. "And then you'd scrub it out, and you'd always come up with some Amish proverb about work."

"*Yah*? What kinds of proverbs?" Lovina asked.

"Oh, how working together is as good as play, or how a job well done proves the character of the woman," Carrie said, and she shook her head. "But you could make a tub shine, Lovina!"

Lovina couldn't help but laugh at that. "It's coming back."

"Do you remember *me*?" Carrie asked, her smile slipping.

"I remembered you on the taxi ride over," Lovina said, and she reached over and took Carrie's hand. "That might not sound like much, but trust me, it's huge."

Tears misted Carrie's eyes. "I'm glad. Because I was praying you'd come back."

Just like her family had been praying, and Johannes, too . . . But whose prayers would Gott answer? Because they were all praying at cross-purposes. Maybe He'd answer Lovina's . . . if she could ever figure out what to ask for.

"What happened the day I left?" Lovina asked. "Did we argue? Was I upset?"

"Not at all," Carrie said. "It was your day off. You wanted to go for a bike ride. You always borrowed my mom's bike when you did that. So you left on your bike ride, and you just . . . didn't return. It was so weird."

"But you thought I'd run away," Lovina said.

"It happens sometimes," Carrie said. "I don't just mean workers leaving me, but Amish people go back. And it isn't like you'd have a phone there or anything. We knew you were lonely. It wasn't a shocking thought that you might return. We hear stories about that kind of thing when Amish young people leave, and then go back again."

"I didn't have a wallet on me or anything," she said. "I hadn't packed."

"You didn't bring that stuff with you when you rode," Carrie said. "You said that Amish people didn't bring ID and purses and cell phones every time they left the house. You used to say it was silly."

"Maybe not so silly after all," Lovina said, and she exchanged a rueful smile with the young woman.

"But that's true—the fact that you hadn't packed was weird for us. We waited to hear from you, my parents drove around looking for you, and then an ex-Amish woman from church told us that her guess was that you'd gone back home."

"Oh . . ."

"But that didn't sit right with us. So my parents eventually called the police, and that's how we found you."

Lovina looked over at Johannes, who stood on the deck next to Gordon. Johannes's arms were crossed over his chest as he watched Gordon flip hamburger patties. His gaze flickered up toward her and met Lovina's with a look of such intense longing. But then he looked away again, and Lovina's breath was stuck in her chest.

Those kisses they'd shared, the feeling of his strong fingers closing over hers, the sensation just before he kissed her, when she could feel the whisper of his breath touching her lips . . . She might not remember the relationship she'd had with Johannes in the past, but something was certainly growing in the present.

"Carrie, can I ask you something?" Lovina said, turning back toward the young woman.

"Of course," Carrie said.

"Did I have a boyfriend here?" she asked.

"Why, do you remember one?" Carrie asked with a teasing smile.

"I need to know," Lovina said. "Did I . . . I don't know . . . Was there a man—"

"No," Carrie said. "You were always here with us, or out with us. If there was a boyfriend, I would have noticed. Trust me."

Lovina let out a slow breath. "Good . . ."

"Why is that good?" Carrie asked.

"Because I don't want to have to explain myself to another man," she said.

She didn't want to explain that she hadn't remembered him . . . and she hadn't been true. And she didn't want to have to tell Johannes that there had been someone else, either. The thought of the hurt in his eyes—

"That's him, isn't it?" Carrie asked. "The one you broke up with when you came to Erindale."

"*Yah*. That's him." Lovina forced a smile. "And he's enough complication, I can assure you."

Aline brought a platter of buns and some condiments out onto the patio table, and Lovina rose to her feet. She should help—that was hardwired into her very soul.

"Time to eat!" Gordon announced with a smile.

Carrie smiled broadly. "I love burgers."

The scent of barbecued meat wafted through the summer breeze, and Lovina pushed Carrie's wheelchair over the soft grass toward the ramp that led up to the deck. It was a gentle incline, and when she got to Johannes's side, she looked up at him with a smile.

"Let's say grace," Gordon said.

As Gordon said a brief blessing, Lovina felt Johannes's arm pressing gently against hers, and when they lifted their heads, Aline smiled and beckoned for them to start. The next few minutes were spent loading up their plates and settling in to eat.

"Have you seen enough?" Johannes asked when everyone's attention was focused on their food.

"What do you mean?" she asked.

"Are you ready to go home tonight?" he asked hopefully. "We could be home for Service Sunday."

The old wave of panic at the thought of a Service Sunday sank into her middle. Why did she always have this reaction lately? What was it about an Amish worship gathering that left her feeling an urge to run?

Lovina looked over at the Maitland family—Aline wiping a dab of catsup off of Carrie's cheek, and Gordon chewing a big bite of burger, a contented look on his face. The last hour had brought back more memories for her than two weeks back in Bountiful.

Was it just the timing? Or was there something more bundled up with this *English* home that she needed to discover?

"I want to stay . . ." she breathed. And she didn't want to go anywhere near a Service Sunday in Bountiful . . .

Johannes stiffened. She knew how it sounded.

"For another day," she hurriedly added. "I'm remembering more, Johannes."

Could he understand how much she needed this? And was he that miserable here with a friendly family who wanted to feed him?

"With a little more time, I'm sure more will come back," she added. "Do you know what it's like to be trying to catch your memories again? It's like trying to trap a bit of eggshell in a bowl of egg whites. It keeps slipping away! And here . . ."

She looked around herself at the deck, the house, the bushes, and a hammock tied between two trees . . . What was it about this place that was bringing back the memories so much faster? It made no sense, but it was *working*!

"Okay," he murmured.

"*Yah*?"

"*Yah*. Okay. I have money for a hotel, and we can get two rooms," he said.

He was already planning ahead, and it was reassuring. She was safe with him here with her.

"Everything okay?" Aline asked, and Lovina realized they'd been speaking in Pennsylvania Dutch by themselves.

"We were just talking about our plans," Lovina said. "I know tomorrow is Sunday and that will mean church, but I was hoping to come see you again tomorrow afternoon before we go back."

"Lovina, you have a bedroom here," Aline said with a smile. "Stay with us! You're welcome to go to church, or just have a relaxing day here. We'd love to have you, regardless. You're like family now. And we can make up a bed in the living room for Johannes. It really is no inconvenience."

Lovina looked over at Johannes, and she could see the hesitation in his eyes, but he nodded.

"Thank you," he said. "That would be nice. Just one night. I promised her family I'd bring her home, and I mean to make good on that promise."

He turned to look Aline and Gordon each in the eye, and Gordon nodded.

"I understand," Gordon said. "One more night. You have obligations."

"I do," Johannes replied.

Obligations to return her to her family. Everyone else thought they knew what was best for her. Something seemed to pass between the two men, and when Lovina looked up, she found Carrie watching her father and Johannes with an openly curious look on her face. She widened her eyes at Lovina, and they both smiled.

Men . . . Maybe Lovina didn't understand them terribly well, but she knew that Johannes was only trying do the right thing by everyone in his own world.

Johannes wanted to bring her home, but there were answers here . . . she could feel it.

For the rest of the day, Johannes kept his thoughts to himself. Gordon and Aline seemed genuinely happy to see Lovina again, and they asked her what she could remember about her accident and talked about the chances of catching the perpetrator of the hit-and-run. They seemed to want someone to pay for what had happened to Lovina.

They all took a walk together to a local park and fed some squirrels. Carrie would hold some nuts in her lap, and the squirrels would climb her legs and come sit there on the arms of her chair, shoving as many nuts into their cheeks as they could manage.

Some people the Maitlands knew stopped to say hello and asked questions about Amish life . . . It was a pleasant day. Or it should have been. Maybe Johannes could have felt more comfortable with it if his cousin's words didn't keep ringing through his mind—there were good people amongst the Englishers who wanted to help. It would be easier if these people were obviously heathen or something. But they weren't. They were kind, considerate, sincere, and hospitable. If they were submerged in the Amish culture, they'd fit in just fine.

It wasn't supposed to be like this past the fence. It was supposed to be more like Solomon's experience, with his criminal associations. It was supposed to lead to immediate, negative consequences.

That evening, the family had worship together in the sitting room downstairs. They were reading from a devotional book aimed at young women that Carrie seemed to really enjoy. Then Carrie's father carried her upstairs so she could get ready for bed, and Johannes and Lovina were left alone downstairs. They sat on that floral couch— the pattern so busy that it felt almost sinful—and Johannes looked over at her.

"They're nice, aren't they?" Lovina asked.

"*Yah*, very."

"I'm remembering more," she said. "I was so lonely

when I arrived. I remember standing outside in the backyard and holding back tears, I was so lonesome."

So she'd stood outside, too, her heart breaking? How many evenings had he done the exact same thing?

Johannes reached over and took her hand. "I was, too. I was miserable. I thought about you constantly—" His voice caught and he stopped. "You should have come home . . ."

"I couldn't." She turned her hand over to twine their fingers together.

While he'd been worrying, hoping, watching his mailbox for a note from her . . . she couldn't come back?

"Why not?" he asked, turning toward her. "What was holding you back? Were you trying to get away from me? Did you not want to get married? I mean—"

"I don't remember everything," she said, her soft voice cutting him off. "But I do remember being lonely—so lonely that my whole chest ached, because I missed you. I missed my family, too, but mostly, it was you."

She'd missed him. This was the first confirmation he had that she'd even thought about him after she left, and tears misted his eyes in spite of his best efforts to blink them back.

"Me, too," he said gruffly.

"And I seem to remember thinking you were better off without me," she said.

"I wasn't," he said fiercely.

"I thought you would be . . ." She sighed. "And I don't know why I thought that. Thinking about it now, all I can assume is that it had to do with my *daet*. My family's reputation is so damaged that my siblings thought it was the best choice to hide my past from me!"

"It was a tough time," Johannes agreed.

"But it would have been hard for you, too. What about being his son-in-law?" she asked. "Wouldn't that affect how people saw *you*?"

Johannes let his eyes roam over a shelf of little figurines, his mind moving back to those early, confusing days.

"When your father was arrested, our whole community was rocked," he said. "Young people started leaving the community because they couldn't trust that what we had was any better than what the Englishers offered. And it was tough for me, too, because there were a few people who started asking if I was involved in the same scam because of my connection to you and my close relationship with your *daet*."

"You must have been furious," she breathed.

Everyone had kept asking each other how a man of Gott could be harboring so much hatred inside of him. And if he wasn't truly a man of Gott, how had they all missed it?

"I was pretty angry," he admitted. "And hurt. And betrayed. I believed in your *daet*, too. I thought he was a good man. I wanted to be *like* him—" His voice shook, and he swallowed.

"Did you change your mind about me?" she asked.

"No," he said quietly.

"Maybe you should have," she replied, and she pulled her hand away from his. "If you had married another woman, like Sovilla, people wouldn't have connected you to all the ugliness. You had a chance to move on."

It had occurred to him, too. He'd been praying that Gott would show him how to move on from his feelings

for Lovina. He'd begged Gott to set him free from
her . . .

"You had no chance to get away from it, though," he
said. "It wouldn't be fair, would it?"

"Maybe this was my chance," she said, and she met
his gaze evenly. "This life here."

Johannes looked around the room at the oh-so-*English*
sitting room. The plush carpet was too pink. The decor
was too busy. The air was even scented with something
cloyingly sweet. And yet he couldn't argue that this home
didn't feel peaceful.

Maybe her leaving had been his chance at moving on,
too. Maybe that had been his opportunity to tear away
from all the ugliness and get back to a quiet, ordered, respectable life.

"And if I left, maybe you could have had a better life
without me," she pressed.

"I didn't want that—" he said.

Johannes and Lovina had been arguing a lot after
her *daet*'s arrest. Lovina was upset, but Abe was still her
daet. And Johannes wanted a clean break from Abe
for the both of them. Abe had been shunned, and in
Johannes's opinion, that was for the best. Johannes had
been thinking about their future together, not just
Lovina's feelings on the matter. He hadn't wanted her to
visit her *daet* in prison, let alone go with her.

"Are you sure you didn't?" she asked, meeting his
eyes frankly. "Because I seemed pretty convinced of it—
I even mentioned it in the letter to my siblings."

Johannes hadn't wanted her to leave, and he hadn't
wanted a fresh start without her. He'd just wanted her to

feel the same way he did about all of it. And that hadn't been realistic.

Footsteps creaked on the stairs, and they fell silent. Lovina pulled her hand free of his and rose to her feet.

"Lovina—" he started.

"Just think about it," she said. "It's possible that my leaving was actually good for you."

Aline appeared at the bottom of the stairs with a pile of blankets and a pillow, and Johannes knew that their time alone was over.

"I should get to bed," she said softly. "Good night, Johannes."

And that was it? She could say something like that and just go up to bed? Not that there was much choice. Aline looked between them—she wouldn't understand the language.

"We have more to talk about," he said.

"Just not tonight," Lovina said.

Their time alone was really over.

"Later, then," he said in Pennsylvania Dutch.

Lovina nodded, then disappeared up the stairs, and Aline came into the sitting room. Her makeup was gone now, and her hair was piled on top of her head with a clip.

"I'm going to make up the couch in the family room for you," Aline said. "It's just more comfortable. Is there anything else we can get for you?"

"No, thank you," he said. "This is very kind. I'll be fine."

* * *

That night, Johannes lay in on the couch that had been covered in a sheet. There were strange sounds in an *English* house—a constant hum that came from the refrigerator in the kitchen, the far-off sound of voices with music in the background that he could only assume was a TV. A clock showing that it was nearly midnight glowed from beneath the darkened TV in the family room where he lay, and strange shadows stretched across the room.

He missed home.

If this was the life Lovina wanted, he couldn't join her in it. He could do many things for the woman he loved, but he couldn't do this.

There were steps on the stairs again, and he pushed himself into a seated position. It felt strangely vulnerable to lie on his back while someone came down the stairs like that. Gordon appeared in the doorway, and he paused.

"Are you awake?" he asked.

"*Yah.*"

"I hope I didn't wake you up," Gordon said. "I was just coming downstairs for a quick snack. You feel like tucking in to my stash of cookies with me?"

"Uh—" What else was Johannes going to do, just watch the man eat? "*Yah*, sure."

Johannes rose to his feet and headed over in the direction of the kitchen with Gordon, and he sat on a stool at the counter while the older man pulled down a couple of different packages of cookies. Then he pulled one open, and they both took a couple of Oreos.

"You're in love with her, aren't you?" Gordon said after a moment of quiet chewing.

"Pardon me?" Johannes was taken aback by the personal question.

"Lovina," Gordon said. "My wife tells me that you're the one she left behind when she came to Erindale."

"*Yah*, that's me," he replied.

"And if I read you right, you're still in love with her," Gordon added.

"We have a long history together," Johannes replied. "Most of which she doesn't remember."

Gordon nodded. "Yeah, I understand that."

"What do you know about me?" Johannes asked. Had Lovina talked about him in her year here? Had she talked about her family at all?

"Not much," Gordon admitted. "We knew she left a fiancé behind. We acknowledged that would be tough. She didn't say much about her family. She didn't want to talk about it."

So she wouldn't even talk about them . . . Was that shame because of her father's crime, or something deeper?

"If she wants to stay here," Gordon said slowly, raising his gaze to meet Johannes's seriously, "will you try to force her to go back with you?"

"You don't know Lovina very well if you think that's even possible!" Johannes said, barking out a bitter laugh. "Lovina is her own woman."

Gordon's gaze didn't waver. "You said you had promised to bring her back, but if she doesn't want to return with you—"

"Will I throw her over my shoulder and stomp back to Bountiful?" Johannes asked dryly.

"That's what I'm asking," Gordon confirmed. "She does have a choice, no matter what you or her family wants."

"Of course she has a choice," Johannes replied, shaking his head. "But did it also cross your mind that she has a family who *loves* her? She didn't just hatch from an egg. Her family found her at the hospital—you didn't! And *they* brought her home."

"If she doesn't want an Amish life, though—" Gordon began.

"If she doesn't want an Amish life, she is free to leave, just like any other person who changes their mind," Johannes replied. "But I'd hope that she'd do me the good turn of coming back with me before she leaves again so that I don't get blamed for her leaving until the end of time. That's my community, too."

"Oh . . ." Gordon nodded. "I hadn't thought of that."

"And it would do her family a lot of good to be able to say goodbye to her this time, if she decides to come back and live *English*," Johannes added. "They were beside themselves with worry for a year. A year! What would you do if your daughter vanished for a year, and then you found her again?'"

Gordon was silent for a moment. "I can appreciate that."

"I'm glad. These are the people who raised her, sacrificed for her."

"If she does decide to come back and be . . . *English*, as you call us . . ." Gordon said, "will they try to stop her?"

"Do you think we're monsters?" Johannes asked.

"No . . ."

"Do you think we lock our women down and don't let

them out?" he asked, shaking his head. "Do you think that a traditional home where a woman is loved and valued means she isn't allowed to choose her own path?"

What did the Englishers think about them, exactly?

"I'm not meaning to offend you," Gordon said. "I'm sorry if I did, but—"

"We hear things about you, too," Johannes cut in. "We hear that Englishers don't love their old people— they put them in hospitals and forget about them. We hear that you don't care about honesty and integrity, and that your watered-down version of Christianity is barely more than an excuse to do whatever you please!"

Johannes's voice stayed low and quiet, but it trembled with the force of his emotions. They heard a whole lot more than that—that the Englishers would take advantage of them if they weren't careful, and that they broke up families as easily as they crumbled clay between their fingers. Gordon didn't answer this time, but the two of them stared at each other in the dim light from the stove, the cookies forgotten between them.

"I'm not saying that's true," Johannes went on. "I can see your life here—I can see that you're kind people, and that you're respectable, and I can see exactly why Lovina was happy here. But if you're going to follow some hearsay about people you don't know, just know that it goes both ways. We both need to open our minds a little further and see the people in front of us, not the rumors about the culture."

Gordon nodded. "You're right. And I'm sorry. I can see why Lovina loved you."

Loved. Past tense. And maybe there was truth in that little semantic detail. Maybe everything Johannes was clinging to was in the past, but he wasn't convinced of that yet. He loved her in the here and now, and without her memory of what they used to be, she was developing feelings for him again, too.

"I'd like the chance to get to know you a little bit," Gordon said. "If that's okay."

"Sure," Johannes replied. Maybe it would be good for both of them. "If she comes back here to work with you, I'll feel better knowing you, too."

Because this just might end up being Lovina's new home. He knew it was a possibility. She'd chosen this life before, hadn't she? She could very well choose it again.

"There's time for that tomorrow. I'll get back to bed," Gordon said, standing up. "Aline will be wondering what became of me."

"*Yah.* I should sleep, too," Johannes said.

"I really don't want to offend you," Gordon said, turning back. "I'm sincere in that. I can see that you're not what I expected, either."

"I feel the same way," Johannes said, softening his tone. "It would be a whole lot easier if we both just lived up to the rumors, wouldn't it?"

"Maybe," Gordon said. "I guess we'll be forced to grow."

Johannes smiled at that. "Good night, Gordon."

"Good night."

The older man headed for the stairs, and Johannes went back to the couch. He'd be up at four whether he slept tonight or not. His body wouldn't sleep beyond that. Whatever part of Lovina had been able to adapt to an *Englisher* life, he wasn't the same. He was Amish to the bone.

Chapter Thirteen

Lovina woke early the next morning, and as she blinked her eyes open, it took her a moment to remember where she was. She reached over to the bedside table without even thinking, and her hand touched the cool leather of a Bible. For a moment, it was like waking up in a dream—familiar, but not quite right. It took her a couple of beats for it to come back to her—the drive in the cab, the day with the Maitlands . . . She turned on a lamp and sat up in bed, pulling the Bible into her lap.

The Bible fell open to a passage that had been underlined in blue pen.

> *Whither shall I go from thy spirit? or whither*
> *shall I flee from thy presence?*
> *If I ascend up into heaven, thou art there: if I*
> *make my bed in hell, behold, thou art there.*
> *If I take the wings of the morning, and dwell in*
> *the uttermost parts of the sea;*
> *Even there shall thy hand lead me, and thy right*
> *hand shall hold me.*

It was from Psalm 139, and the ribbon was holding this place. It must have been a favorite passage, because she'd also written something in the margin, and she turned the Bible to get a better look.

In her own handwriting she saw the word: *Erindale*.

Her heart thudded to a stop. She'd been planning on staying here. She could feel the truth of it sink into her mind. She'd been planning on living *English*, and she'd been making her peace with it!

So why did she have this underlying feeling of deep sadness? Had she still been grieving that decision?

She didn't feel any peace about it right now . . . And wasn't that what she'd come out to Erindale to find out— if she'd suddenly feel the cozy comfort for home to give her some reassurance of the right path to take? It seemed like she'd had it before, if she'd written that in the margin . . .

She put the Bible aside and she spotted the cell phone on her beside table, plugged into the charger. She picked it up and stared at the empty squares where she was supposed to type in her passcode. She had to think for a moment, but she remembered pressing a four first, and when she did that, the rest of the numbers flooded back into her mind. She flipped through the different screens on her phone. She had some social media set up, although she didn't really use it. She only had Carrie and a couple of Carrie's friends on it. She followed the pastor from the local church, and the youth group for the events they had going on. She was starting to remember this!

She'd picked up on the technology rather quickly, ironically enough. It made sense to her. She sighed, putting the phone back down on the bedside table.

If she were in Bountiful, she'd feel guilty for her connection to a device like that. She'd worry that it was a temptation meant to ensnare her. But now . . . Now, it was just mildly comforting—an actual memory.

She shivered in the morning coolness, and she went to the wardrobe and pulled it open. There were *Englisher* clothes in neat piles, and for a moment, her fingertips lingered on a pair of jeans. They'd been comfortable, too, she remembered. But she left the *Englisher* clothes where they were and took out a fresh Amish dress.

She had been an employee here, and she wasn't working on this visit. It didn't seem right to wear the *Englisher* clothes unless she came back properly.

Gott, where do I belong? she prayed in her heart. *Where am I supposed to live my life?*

It appeared she'd made a decision before that accident, but was it some move of Providence to wipe her mind and give her a brand-new start? Did that mean her previous decision had been a wrong one?

Or was the accident just that . . . an accident? The Amish said Gott didn't make mistakes and His hand was in everything. But humans weren't able to always discern why Gott did what He did. There might be some other grand celestial reason for that hit-and-run.

She pulled the dress on and pinned it in place. Then she slowly combed her hair and twisted it into a bun at the back of her head. She touched one of the *Englisher* shirts, feeling the softness of the material. No, she wouldn't wear those clothes. It would only upset Johannes unnecessarily, but she did pick up the cell phone.

This was hers. She'd bought it with her own money, and she'd been paying the monthly service fees out of her earnings, too. Maybe it wouldn't be terrible for Johannes to see a tiny bit of her life here. It was part of who she was, after all.

That day, Lovina and Johannes took a long walk around the subdivision. The houses all looked so similar, but not in an unpleasant way. Amish homes tended to look a lot alike, too. She felt strange here, though, her dress and *kapp* not exactly fitting in. Johannes wore his straw hat and suspenders, and together they drew stares from people passing in cars.

They'd had the choice of attending a Baptist church with Gordon and Carrie that morning, but Lovina hadn't wanted to go. If she'd been wanting church this weekend, she could have stayed in Bountiful. What she'd needed was to just let her heart be still. What would come of that, she didn't know. Johannes seemed happy enough to keep her company that morning, and after breakfast, they went out together for a long walk. She didn't want to see the *English* stores—she just wanted to breathe in the Erindale air and see how she felt.

Johannes was quiet, too. He held her hand as they wandered down half-familiar streets, circling around until they got to the Maitland's street.

"I don't think I could find my way out of here," Johannes said. "It's all the same. You get turned around. And if we just head west, we'll have to go through people's yards."

"There's a map on here," Lovina said, holding up the phone. "See? It's like the kind the taxi driver used. We can just put in the address for the house, and it'll give us directions. I used to use it all the time so I wouldn't get lost. And the Maitlands insisted that I carry it in case I had an emergency."

"What about the accident?" he asked. "You didn't have it with you."

"I guess I didn't take it with me," she replied.

Johannes looked down at the cell phone in her hand, then shook his head.

"We might end up with a cell phone at the farm, you know," he said.

"You could get used to one now," she said, handing it over to him.

He accepted the phone and looked it over. He touched the screen and squinted, then shaded it with his hand to get a better view in the sunlight.

"That's the phone part," she said, leaning over his arm to see the screen. "Touch that picture of a phone and . . . *Yah*, like that. See? That's where you dial the number."

He lifted the phone to his ear.

"You won't hear a dial tone," she said. "You put in the number and then you have to press send."

"Why send?" he asked.

"I don't know. It's just . . . what they call it."

"How do you remember this?" he asked.

"I don't know, but I do," she said. "It's just familiar."

Johannes licked his lips, then handed it back.

"I don't know how anyone makes sense of these things," he said. "I miss the old days, when the businesses would cater to our ways. Changes like this . . . they're dangerous, you know."

Dangerous to the Amish community, to their simple

way of life, to the way people saw the world . . . she knew the arguments, somehow. She tucked the phone back into the waist of her apron.

"What if it just made our lives easier?" she asked.

"What if easier is bad for you?" he asked seriously.

They walked on, and they got rather turned around. Johannes stayed true to his word and refused to look at the map on the phone. Even so, today felt safer with Johannes at her side. If she did choose an *English* life, Johannes wouldn't be here with her. She wouldn't have his stubborn Amish ways to argue with, or his reassuring presence. She'd be on her own, and that thought pricked at a place in her heart that hadn't been touched before.

They finally did stumble upon the right street again, but it took a good hour and a half longer than it needed to.

"That's the Amish way," Johannes said, giving her hand a squeeze. "It might take longer, but I got to hold your hand, didn't I?"

Did he have to be endearing? She leaned into his arm, and they headed toward the big yellow house. The TV was on as Lovina and Johannes came inside. It was a local news station, and the anchor was talking about a local lottery winner, a white-haired old lady with a white, fluffy dog in her arms.

"You're back," Aline said with a smile. "I'm just starting some lunch. Gordon and Carrie are at church still, but they'll be back soon. I'm sorry about the TV. I know it's Sunday, but I just wanted to catch the news. I can turn it off, if you want."

Lovina looked toward the TV again, and there was a reporter on the screen now, walking down a street, and the recognition shot through her like a jolt of electricity.

Why was it that seeing Main Street in Bountiful on a TV screen brought back more memories than seeing it in person? She felt like she could feel every inch of those sidewalks, and her breath caught in her throat.

Aline picked up the remote to flick off the TV, but Lovina stopped her.

"No!" she said. "Just wait—that's my hometown!"

There it was—Glick's Book Bindery, the hardware store, the bakery, a few restaurants . . . Her heart sped up, and she moved toward the screen.

"This is the location of Pennsylvania's biggest fraud case in the last decade," the reporter said. "Abraham Yoder was the Amish face associated with a charity fraud that stole more than three million dollars from the hands of hardworking locals. After spending barely twelve months in prison, Abraham Yoder is now out on parole. We took to the streets in the idyllic town of Bountiful, Pennsylvania, to see how the locals feel about his early release."

"Is this happening now?" Lovina asked. "It's Sunday! No Amish should be in town—"

"It's probably taped," Aline said. "They do a story and edit it, then play it the next day."

So this was from yesterday? Johannes came to where she stood, and they stood side by side, staring mutely at the screen as the reporter—a woman with short-cropped brown hair and an earnest expression on her face— attempted to stop an Amish woman on the sidewalk. The woman looked toward the camera, her expression wary, then shook her head and carried on down the street. The reporter tried again, this time stopping an older man.

"Excuse me," the reporter said. "I'm with CTW News, and we wanted to ask you a few questions about Abraham Yoder."

"Abe?" the older man said, his expression turning cautious.

"Yes," the reporter pushed on. "How do you personally feel about his return to your community after his time in prison?"

"How do I feel? I don't think it matters."

"Do you trust him?" she pressed.

"No, that wouldn't be wise, all considering," the man replied.

"Do you forgive him?" she asked.

The man looked upward thoughtfully, then shrugged his shoulders. "Gott didn't give us much choice there. We forgive others, or we don't get forgiven. So all I can tell you is that we're trying."

"Have you spoken to him?" the reporter asked.

The older man looked straight into the camera, then he sighed.

"I'd better be going," the man replied, and even after the reporter called a couple of questions after him, he continued ambling down the street.

"Excuse me!" the reported called after another man, this one coming out of Glick's Book Bindery, and when he turned, Lovina reached out and grabbed Johannes's shirt.

"It's Isaiah!" she breathed. On the TV screen, Isaiah looked at the reporter, mildly confused.

"Excuse me, how do you feel about the return of

Abraham Yoder to your community after his time in prison?" she asked.

Isaiah stared at the woman, stunned. He swallowed, then rubbed a hand over his short beard.

"Oh, Isaiah . . ." Lovina breathed.

The memory came back as suddenly as a slap, and her breath seeped out of her body. Suddenly she could remember it all—her father's arrest in the middle of Service Sunday. He'd been preaching when the police officers interrupted everything and led him away in handcuffs. The shaken look on her father's face still gave her a shiver, and she remembered the way she'd run after the officers, begging them to let him go—they'd made a terrible mistake!

"Daet, tell them!" she'd pleaded. "Tell them!"

But he'd walked off, his arms pulled behind his back in those shameful metal cuffs that glinted in the sun-light . . . On a Service Sunday . . . And now she knew why she'd wanted to stay away from church—the connection to her father's arrest.

"Do you know Abe Yoder?" the reporter on TV asked.

"*Yah*, I know him." Isaiah's voice was thick with emo-tion. "But we tend to deal with these things privately in our community."

"Do you trust him after what he's done?" the reporter pressed.

Isaiah sighed, his breath sounding heavy with sadness. He looked across the street, and she could see all the anger, the sadness, the old memories battling over her brother's features. Was he remembering it, too?

"I'm sorry, I have to get back to work," Isaiah said gruffly.

It was the right answer, in Lovina's opinion. This wasn't anyone else's business! The reporter beckoned to her cameraman to follow, and Isaiah put out a hand to stop her.

"Please, just leave us alone!" Isaiah barked. "Please!"

The reporter stopped, and Isaiah stalked back into Glick's Book Bindery. The sign in the window flicked to closed.

"This is Talia Davis from CTW News. We'll have more updates to come on this sensational story of fraud and forgiveness in the Amish heartland," she said.

"We'll be hearing from Talia later on, as she attempts to contact Abraham Yoder himself. But for now, let's go to the weather . . ."

There was a news crew in Bountiful, trying to dig up Amish sentiment on the one crime that had wounded them all . . . Tears rose up inside of her, and she battled them back. Now was not the time to succumb to her emotions.

"Johannes," Lovina said, her voice shaking. "We need to get back."

"*Yah.*" He nodded, and when she looked over at him, his face was ashen. "Let's call the taxi."

Aline stood there in the kitchen, watching them in confusion, and Lovina knew this was sudden. She knew Carrie would be disappointed not to have been able to say goodbye. But there was no choice—not right now.

If that reporter arrived at the Sunday service at whatever farm was hosting . . . Lovina's stomach heaved. The last thing any of them needed was another day of worship interrupted by scandal.

"That wasn't in *English*," Aline said tentatively. "What's going on?"

"Oh—" Lovina switched back to English. "I'm sorry, Aline. We have to go. That's my father they're talking about on the news, and my family is going to need me."

And she was going to need them.

The two-hour drive back to Bountiful brought them into the town's limits in the early afternoon. Johannes was relieved to get Lovina back home again—his responsibility would be over. But it also meant his time alone with her was over, too, and he looked over at her in the back seat of the cab. Her attention was trained out the window, but she seemed to feel his gaze on her, because she glanced over at him.

"Do you think the news crew will find my father?" she asked.

"No," he replied. "Not immediately, at least."

"Why so sure?" she asked.

"Because no Amish person is going to give a TV crew directions to Mel Yoder's farm, that's why," he replied. "We might have our issues amongst ourselves, but we don't do that."

She nodded. "I hope so."

"Up here on the left," Johannes said, leaning forward to talk to the cab driver. "The one with the green mailbox."

The cab driver signaled his turn, and Johannes sat back again. They were at the Yoder home, where he'd leave Lovina. The side door opened as they pulled up next to the house, and Elizabeth appeared, drying her hands on a towel. She didn't smile, but she did raise her hand in a wave.

"I'll be back—I just need to say goodbye," Johannes told the driver, and the man nodded.

Johannes hopped out of the back seat, the fresh air a welcome relief after two hours of stuffy driving. He tapped the top of the trunk, and the driver popped it open so he could grab Lovina's bag for her.

"You're back!" Elizabeth said. "Oh, Lovina, thank Gott. I wasn't sure if we'd have to come for you again."

Johannes exchanged a wan smile with Lovina's sister.

"Thank you for bringing her home," Elizabeth said. "Did you want to come in for something to eat, Johannes?"

"I can't," he said. "My *daet* is going to need help I can give him about now. It's almost time for milking. But thank you. I'll be seeing you all soon, I'm sure."

Lovina turned back toward him, and Johannes was suddenly very aware of all the people who were watching them. Bethany had appeared at the door, the baby on her hip and Isaiah behind her. Even the taxi driver leaned out the window, watching him curiously.

"I'll . . ." Johannes swallowed. "I'll see you."

Lovina dropped her gaze, and he caught her hand, giving her fingers a quick squeeze, then releasing her.

Johannes got back into the taxi, and he leaned back in the seat. The taxi driver looked over his shoulder.

"To the second address now?" he asked.

"*Yah*. Please," Johannes replied.

He had more responsibilities than just Lovina, and it

could be argued that she wasn't his responsibility anymore. They weren't a couple, and her memories were coming back much faster now. She'd choose her life, and he'd have to go on with his. She seemed rather convinced that he'd be better off without her, and he wasn't naive enough to think that wasn't a warning.

But Lovina was back in Bountiful, and that would be all Isaiah and Elizabeth could ask of him. He'd brought her home. Gordon's worries that they would try and pressure her into a life she didn't want had hit home for Johannes. He'd never try to strong-arm her into a choice, even if it was the right one. But all the same, he needed to step back. If Lovina stayed, it needed to be because she wanted this life, not because she'd been pressured into it.

If Lovina stayed with *him* . . . Did he even want to let himself hope that she'd want what he had to offer this time around? Or was he courting more heartbreak?

With a few directions, the taxi driver found his address, and Johannes paid him with a moderate tip and got his bag out of the trunk.

"Have a good day," the driver called, then pulled back out again.

Johannes headed up the steps and into the house. He expected to find it empty, and he had full intentions of heading out to find where his father was working this afternoon, but Bernard was standing in the kitchen, his arms crossed and a crumpled bit of fabric in one fist. He looked up as Johannes came in.

"Daet?" Johannes said.

He turned to see Daniel sitting on a chair, his expression morose.

"You're back—" Bernard's frown smoothed, and he sighed. "How are things with Lovina?"

"She saw where she used to work, and . . . uh—" Johanne's gaze fell to the fabric in his father's hands. "Can I see that?"

Bernard handed it over, and Johannes smoothed it out. It was the quilt that Daniel had been working on, but much more than the scraps he'd seen before. It was the size of a pillowcase, and the intricate work painted a scene of sun-splashed countryside with a single Amish buggy on a twisting road of brown cotton. It was phenomenal work, and Johannes's gaze flicked up to his nephew, who sat with a defiant slump to his shoulders on a kitchen chair.

"Did she come home?" Bernard asked.

"*Yah*, she's home," Johannes replied. "I just dropped her off at the Yoder place."

"Good." Bernard nodded a couple of times.

"What's going on here?" Johannes asked, but he had a sinking suspicion that he knew already.

"That"—Bernard pointed at the quilt work in Johannes's hands—"that is something Daniel has been working on secretly. It's . . . it's . . ." Bernard's finger shook.

"It's rather good," Johannes said.

Bernard's finger dropped, and he scrubbed a hand through his salt-and-pepper hair. "It's woman's work, Johannes."

"*Yah*," Johannes agreed. "But better than any woman I know. I have to admit to that."

He held the quilted scene up in front of himself, noting

the way the brown, winding road was chopped up into different textures.

"That isn't helpful," Bernard said dryly.

Maybe not, but it was true, and Johannes was too emotionally exhausted right now to tiptoe around it. The colors Daniel had chosen melded together in a sort of fabric mosaic, the sky moving from blue to golden and the rolling fields having the impression of being sun dappled, although Johannes couldn't see how his nephew had managed it.

Johannes turned toward his nephew. "I thought we talked about this."

Daniel didn't answer.

"Daniel, there are jobs for men, and jobs for women," Bernard said. "We don't cross those lines. Women are the ones who quilt, and we men take care of the outdoor work. You could do woodworking, or leatherworking, or you could even do creative landscaping, Daniel. But this—this isn't acceptable!"

"I'm good at it," Daniel said.

"It doesn't matter!" Bernard retorted.

"I'm not good at very many things—not this good," Daniel said.

"You're good with animals," Bernard countered. "You're good with plants."

"Not *this* good, though."

Johannes looked down at the nearly completed quilt work. It needed to be edged and backed, and probably ironed. He'd watched his *mamm* quilt when he was a boy. He understood the basic idea, but he'd never tried his own hand at it. Of course he hadn't!

"What would your *mamm* think of this?" Johannes asked, looking up.

Daniel's cheeks pinked. "I don't know."

"Yes, you do," Bernard pressed. "Come on, now. Say it."

"She'd probably send me to my *dawdie* and uncle to try and sort me out," he said, raising his chin.

So Linda did know . . . Johannes rubbed a hand over his chin.

"All right," Bernard said, nodding slowly. "All right . . ."

Johannes looked toward his father, and Daniel looked equally curious. Bernard took the fabric from Johannes and looked it over slowly.

"*Yah*, I can see that it's good," Bernard said. "But I'm going to tell you a story about my uncle Nathaniel."

Johannes went into the kitchen and headed for a plastic container of muffins. He pulled one out—blueberry— and peeled back the paper to take a big bite.

"Nathaniel was my father's brother. He wasn't like the other boys, and he was very close to his mother. He loved her very much, and he accompanied her to nearly every outing she went on," Bernard said. "There was a young lady who liked Nathaniel a lot. Where Nathaniel was slight and gentle, she was a stalwart girl, with big personality to match. But my grandmother didn't like the girl much, saying she'd be a bully of a wife, and so Nathaniel never acted on it. He ended up staying a bachelor. He started a watch work business in town, and when his *mamm* passed away, he just continued as he always had, but alone in the house."

Johannes and Daniel were both silent.

"Do you understand?" Bernard said when neither of them had said anything.

"Not really," Daniel replied.

Bernard sighed. "There are some men who never marry, Daniel. It happens, even in our own family. Not everyone *has* to marry. Some men are just different—they have trouble being in those traditional roles, and that can be fine, if the man simply wants to work a job and carry on. Some don't marry because they lost an opportunity—and that is what I believe happened with my uncle. The big girl married a farmer and went on to have fourteen *kinner*, all of whom I went to school with . . ." Bernard sighed. "It's not an easy life, Daniel. It's a lonely one. A man who quilts will just be . . . different. Why choose a life that difficult? You might never marry that way! It does happen."

Daniel swallowed hard. "That's not true. I can get married still. Your uncle could have if he'd married the big girl."

"There might be a chance," Bernard agreed. "There might be some unique young woman who would be a good match for you, but there also might not be. Who is to know that? My boy, this choice is now yours. It's your life, your future. We can lay the consequences before you, but you are the one who must choose the life you want."

Daniel held his hand out for his quilt work. "I want it back."

Bernard handed it over, and Daniel carefully folded it and then turned and headed upstairs. Johannes swallowed his last bite of muffin and crossed his arms.

"Are we going to chase him out of the community, Daet?" he asked seriously.

"What? No, we're telling him the truth," his father retorted.

"Maybe so, but there is a place where he could be a man who quilts and no one would care one way or another. There are men with the Englishers who sew clothes, and they're called tailors. If Daniel really wants to sew, the Englishers will have him. And they have women who'd marry him, too."

Bernard's face turned red. "Don't give that boy ideas!"

"I'm not," Johannes said. "What you say is true—he's not going to be able to succeed here with a needle and thread. But we'd best be careful, because he's thirteen now and he's smart enough to connect the links. Linda wants us to show him what it means to be a man, not to push him out completely."

His father was silent, and then he went to the sink and started to fill up a water bottle. For a minute or two, neither of them spoke, and when the bottle was filled, Bernard twisted the lid on tight and headed for the side door. Just before he opened it, he turned back.

"Then we don't talk about it anymore," Bernard said.

"Really?" Johannes asked.

"We show him what it is to be a man, and then we send him home," Bernard replied. "This decision is his to make. And you know what? If he wants a wife badly enough, he'll do what it takes to get one."

"Uncle Nathaniel didn't," Johannes said.

"There are worse things in the world than celibacy," Bernard replied. "Nathaniel was a solid friend. He was a good Christian. And he was an excellent watchmaker."

Bernard was silent for a beat. "And he was also a very kind uncle."

Then Bernard pulled open the door and headed outside, the screen clattering shut behind him.

There were rules in the Amish world—in the way things ran. Everyone knew what to expect and knew what was required of them. Perhaps Johannes should consider the same lesson as his nephew—if Johannes wanted to get married and have *kinner* of his own, and if he wanted grandchildren at his knees one day, perhaps he'd have to take a different path, as well.

Chapter Fourteen

That evening, Lovina sat at the edge of the quilting frame with Elizabeth and Bethany, the completed top of Elizabeth's wedding quilt stretched across a frame. The layer of wadding had been tacked on top of the patterned fabric blocks, and they were preparing to add the backing. With three women stitching, the work would go much faster tonight, and the next evening, more women were coming to help with the finishing touches.

Vannetta would come tomorrow, and Lovina had started to remember her friend from days past—the way they'd laughed and gossiped together, visited each other, whispered about the boys they were courting . . . And now Vannetta was married and expecting her first baby. She wouldn't be a giggling girl anymore. But neither was Lovina, for that matter. A year had changed a great deal for both of them. Would their friendship be the same? Lovina wasn't sure.

But everyone else was talking about the reporter who'd been in town on Saturday, waylaying good Amish folk as they went about their business and putting a camera in their faces.

"They're trying to make us look bad," Elizabeth said. "Isn't it enough that Daet went to prison? Do they have to follow him around now that he's out?"

"I don't think they're trying to make us look bad," Lovina countered. "They're trying to . . . experience the emotional turmoil we're all going through, maybe. Englishers are different. They think that sharing in the feelings, in the shock and upset, is caring."

"We don't need outsiders trying to feel it for us," Bethany said. "We can do that on our own."

"They mean well . . ." Lovina said. The Maitland family did, at least. They cared about her happiness, about her safety. They genuinely liked her, and it wasn't just because she had worked with their daughter. It went beyond that.

"They said they wanted to find Daet," Elizabeth said. "That's what Isaiah said. They knocked on the door of the book bindery after they finished with their camera, and they asked Isaiah if he could give them directions to where Daet is staying."

Lovina felt her stomach drop.

"They asked him directly?" Lovina asked. "I know Isaiah wouldn't tell them, but would anyone else?"

"No," Bethany interjected. "Not here. They asked old Deacon Adam, too. They stopped him on the street and asked if he'd give them directions, and he told them that gossip was a sin, and what they were doing was no better than idle gossip."

Lovina smiled at that. "That was a good answer."

"*Yah* . . ." Elizabeth smiled. "It was."

"You know that Deacon Adam is leaving us, don't you?" Bethany asked. "He's going to be with his sister in another community. Her husband died, and there's a farm to run. She doesn't want to remarry, and what with Adam's wife having passed away, too, they decided to band together. So he won't be here in a month's time."

Lovina bent over the quilting work, sewing down a corner to begin the work of attaching the backing. The work was soothing, and she realized that at a time like this, she was glad to be back in this house with her family.

"Who do you think will fill his place?" Lovina asked, looking up.

The women shrugged. "Hard to tell."

"I wonder if they'd choose Isaiah," Lovina said.

"No," both women said together, and Lovina eyed them uncertainly.

"No?" she said. "Because of our family's shame?"

"For Isaiah, that's exactly it," Elizabeth said. "Daet ruined any chance of us being trusted in a position like that again for at least this generation. No one will trust Isaiah for that."

Bethany's cheeks pinked, and she didn't look up.

"Bethany, is it hard being part of our family?" Lovina asked.

Bethany smiled wanly. "We all have something, don't we?"

But the Yoders had more shame than most.

"It won't always be this way," Bethany added. "Isaiah and Solomon can prove themselves to be honorable, honest, responsible. They can get the community's respect back with enough time. Maybe our sons will be able to hold leadership positions. Maybe Moses will be a deacon one day."

"Once he's married, of course," Elizabeth said, a smile tickling the corners of her lips.

"And I don't want to rush that," Bethany agreed with a laugh. "Let him be my baby awhile longer."

"A long while longer!" Elizabeth laughed. "He needs all his teeth first."

Lovina smiled at their humor, and for a few minutes, she listened to their banter while they all sewed. She was glad she'd come back, but sitting here in her brother's house, she wasn't sure that it was her home . . . exactly. She was thinking about Carrie, and about Aline, and the peaceful house in Erindale where she'd had her own room and that lovely scene out the window over the front yard . . . Her heart was tugged in two different directions.

She wanted to be the wife a man thanked Gott for, the woman who made his life so much better because she was in it . . . not the woman he stooped to marry. Was it just plain pride that made that thought so distasteful? Was she just so used to being admired that she couldn't let it go?

But when she had gotten that job working with Carrie, she'd discovered that an Amish woman's skills meant something different to the Englishers. They admired her! They were impressed by her abilities. They liked to hear her Amish proverbs, and maybe she *wanted* to be special.

Johannes would never be able to say that because of her, his life had soared. But Carrie might be able to say that. And was it so terrible for a woman to want to contribute joy to those around her instead of tearing their prospects down?

It was another life—one completely different from the

life here. There were fewer people attached to the life she'd led in Erindale, but Carrie had needed her. Memories with Carrie were coming back now—how Lovina had shown her how to plant flowers on some pots on the deck that very spring. How they'd sat together in that floral-patterned sitting room and played games of checkers and Uno. Carrie couldn't do needlework because her fingers refused to do the finer work, but she used to like watching Lovina do a cross-stitch. Lovina would put Carrie in charge of the colored threads, and together they'd decide which color to use next and pore over the paper pattern. They'd completed two projects together— one Bible verse with a flower border, and one smaller Christmas tree decoration. Carrie loved them—she'd been part of the creative process.

It had felt like more than a job. Lovina's skills had been applauded in that *English* home. Not every *English* woman could do the things Amish women had been learning since they were young girls. Here, everyone worked together, but Lovina's skills were really no different than her sister's or Bethany's. The fact that she could put backing on a quilt didn't create any amazement here, and the fact that Lovina had enjoyed impressing the Englishers was prideful. She knew it was wrong, but as an Amish woman in an *English* world she had something bright and special to offer, but as an Amish woman amongst the Amish? Here, she was just a Yoder.

"Lovina?"

Lovina startled and looked up to find Elizabeth and Bethany both staring at her. She hadn't heard what they'd said.

"*Yah?*" she said.

"I asked if we can fit you for the wedding attendant dress," Elizabeth said.

"*Yah*, of course," Lovina said.

Her sister's gaze was locked on her face, and Elizabeth's brow was furrowed. "Will you be here, Lovina? That's what I'm asking."

Were Lovina's thoughts so obvious on the surface?

"I'll be at your wedding, Lizzie," Lovina said. "I can promise you that."

Even if it meant that she had to come back for the event. Even if it meant that she left directly afterward to go back to a job in Erindale, where Lovina's ability to plant a garden or stitch a quilt block meant that she had something to offer, prideful as it was to long for that.

Because in Bountiful, she had nothing left to offer that wouldn't pull Johannes right down from the life he'd hoped for. For Johannes to marry a Yoder would be a step down. She could see that now, plain as day.

That evening, after the chores were complete and the cows were out in the pasture, Johannes came trudging back toward the house. He'd been missing Lovina ever since he dropped her off with her family that afternoon. He'd been thinking about her, wondering what was happening with her family, how she was handling it all . . . wishing he could be there with her.

So while he'd worked—mucking out the milking stalls, disinfecting equipment, taking some milk samples from cows that had finished a course of antibiotics and needed to have their milk certified as antibiotic free before their milk could be sold again—he'd been thinking about Lovina.

"What was it like with the Englishers?" Daniel asked as they trudged together back toward the house.

"It was very different," he said. "It was busy . . . and noisy. There was no quiet."

"They're heathen, aren't they?" Daniel said.

"No, these ones were Christians," he replied. "And they were good, kind people."

Daniel was silent for a few steps, the only sound that of their boots hitting the ground.

"It's very, very different there, though," Johannes went on. "I really missed home while I was there."

"*Yah*, so do I." Daniel took off his hat and scrubbed a hand through his hair. "I miss my *mamm* and my sisters. My sisters might tease me a lot, but . . . you get used to it, you know?"

Johannes chuckled. "Your *mamm is* my sister, and she used to tease me something fierce."

"*Yah*?" Daniel grinned. "She says she was the perfect sister."

"She would say that." Johannes laughed. "Before she got married, when I was small, she used to make me say my memorized verses, and she'd make me stand still. If I didn't do it right, she wouldn't give me a cookie. I used to think she was terribly cruel."

"What did you do?" Daniel asked.

"I said my verses and I stood still," Johannes replied. "And I got my cookie."

"Do you think you'll get married and have *kinner*, Uncle Johannes?" Daniel asked.

"I hope to."

"You won't end up like Uncle Nathaniel?" he asked.

Johannes sighed. The boy had meant it as a joke, but would he? Would he stay in love with a woman whose heart wasn't Amish and end up alone in spite of it all?

"I'm pretty determined not to end up like Uncle Nathaniel," Johannes said. "I'm like you—I have choices to make about what kind of life I want. And I want a family of my own."

Daniel nodded sagely. "Me, too."

"*Yah*?"

"I definitely do. I want a very pretty wife, and a whole bunch of *kinner*," Daniel said.

Maybe they'd made an impact on the boy after all.

As they approached the house, the sun was lowering in the sky, and the smell of corn bread and chili was wafting out of the kitchen windows. There was an extra buggy parked in front of the stables and a horse in the corral. Lovina? His heart gave a little kick, but when he looked closer at the horse, no, it wasn't one of the Yoders'.

"We've got guests," Johannes said.

"Maybe Dawdie has a single widow who wants to cook for him," Daniel said with a grin.

Johannes gave his nephew a nudge. "A real matchmaker, are you?"

"I'm just interested in getting some good cooking," Daniel said.

"We don't do too badly," Johannes said.

"But you don't do great, either."

Johannes chuckled, and they headed up the side steps and into the mudroom. They washed up in the big sink there, sudsing their hands up with a thick bar of soap, and then Johannes was the first one to walk into the kitchen.

Bishop Lapp was sitting at the table, and next to him sat the big, burly Elder Joel. Bernard had just dampened the stove and pulled a golden pan of corn bread out of the oven.

"Hello," Johannes said. The bishop and an elder—this wasn't a social call. Was this about the cell phones for the farmers?

"We were waiting to speak with you, Johannes," the bishop said, pushing himself to his feet. "And we don't want to hold up your dinner. I'm sure the young man here is starving. Am I right?"

Daniel shrugged and smiled uncertainly. "*Yah*, I'm hungry."

"Why don't we step into the other room to talk, then?" the bishop said. "Bernard, you're more than welcome to come with us. If Daniel here would maybe start getting your dinner on the table, we could talk alone?"

This wasn't a conversation for young ears—that much was clear.

"*Yah*, sure," Johannes replied. He exchanged a look with his father, who appeared equally confused about this visit. "Is this about the cell phones for the farmers?"

"Partly," Elder Joel said.

"You have agreed?" Johannes's eyebrows raised.

"That surprises you, I can see," the bishop said. "Other communities have grappled with this issue and come to a similar conclusion."

"But we aren't other communities," Johannes said. "I'm sorry, I don't mean to question what you obviously all discussed and voted on, but this would change things in our community—"

"And considering what we've already been through with Abe Yoder, that's a risk," the bishop agreed.

"*Yah*, that's what I was thinking," Johannes said.

"I'm glad you're thinking about the community, and not just your own convenience," the bishop said with a solemn nod. "That means a great deal, Johannes. Believe me."

Johannes and Bernard led the way into the sitting room, and the two men took a seat on the sofa, while Johannes and Bernard each pulled up a chair. In the other room, Johannes could hear the rattle of silverware.

"But you've voted to accept the cell phones," Johannes said.

"Within certain boundaries," he replied. "One cell phone per household, for farmers only. If others need them for business purposes, it will be decided on a case by case basis. The phone must be kept out in the barn, and it will be used for email and emergency telephone purposes only. The thing is, the cheese factory has a point about fraud and how easy it might be to steal from us. Identity theft has become a rather large problem in the world today, and we are vulnerable, too. There must be a balance between safety and tradition."

It was fair, but it was still a change, and Johannes felt his stomach tighten at the prospect.

"That isn't why we came by, though," Elder Joel added.

"Right." The bishop nodded. "We came by today because the issue with the cell phones is not the only change in our midst. We are losing a deacon, and we need to replace him. We've begun the process of choosing the right man, but we are feeling rather confused as to what Gott's will might be. You see, we did the draw to choose a new deacon."

"Oh?" Johannes looked over at his father. It would be appropriate if Bernard had been chosen this time, but why the uncertainty around the choice?

"Now, please remember that when we originally put the names in the jar, you were going to be married to Sovilla Miller," the bishop went on. "Then we had to stop just before the vote to deal with some of the fallout issues from Abe Yoder's return to our community. We were distracted with that for quite some time, and when we came back to do the draw, we prayed most earnestly for Gott's leading in the name that we chose. We prayed fervently, and I think that Elder Joel can attest, we felt the Spirit move."

"*Yah,*" Joel said soberly. "It's the truth."

"And when I took a name out of the jar"—the bishop met Johannes's gaze—"it was yours, Johannes."

Johannes stared at the bishop for a moment in disbelief, then shook his head. "But I'm not married. A deacon has to be a married man."

"We realize that," Elder Joel interjected. "We had Bernard's name in the jar as well, and we shouldn't have put your name in at all, Johannes, considering that you weren't married *yet*, but . . . we've been watching you these last few years, and you are a young man with strong character. You remind us a lot of your grandfather."

"We also believe that having some younger men in leadership positions would be very good for our community," the bishop added. "Sometimes young blood gives a better perspective on how to meet the needs of young families today. We had believed that you'd be married soon when we put your name into the running, and believe me when I tell you that in all of the other business we were attending to, we overlooked removing your name from the jar."

They all fell silent, and Johannes looked between the elder and the bishop, uncertain of what they wanted.

"My son would have been a very good choice," Bernard said, speaking for the first time. "But like he said, he and Sovilla decided to part ways."

"Are you sure you wouldn't be willing to marry?" the bishop asked. "Perhaps this is a sign from Gott that Sovilla Miller is the woman for you after all."

Johannes shook his head. "Sovilla and I got to know each other a little bit, and while we have great respect for each other, and while I truly believe that the man who marries her will be getting a true jewel, we aren't meant for each other."

The bishop let out a slow breath. "And that should be the end of it. It should."

"But it's not?" Johannes asked hesitantly.

"Gott was in that room with us," the bishop said. "And when we ask Gott to guide our draw, to bring us to the name of the man that Gott Himself wants as a spiritual leader in this community . . . We either believe that Gott is in that choice, or we don't."

"And you believe Gott wants my son to be deacon," Bernard clarified.

"It would be unorthodox for an unmarried man to take the position, but"—the bishop nodded soberly— "we decided that in exceptional times, we were willing to take exceptional steps. You see, Johannes, we watched how you dealt with the whole ugly situation with Abe

Yoder. You were in a very difficult position, your feelings were certainly involved, and you had a close relationship to the Yoder family. It wasn't easy, but you showed maturity beyond your years."

"She left me," Johannes said. What choice had he actually had?

"And you grieved," Elder Joel said. "But you dealt with your grief and sadness in a way that brought credit to your character. You never once spoke badly about Lovina or her family. You simply endured the sadness, and . . . you're moving on."

Was he, though? If that was the impression he was giving, then he wasn't giving an honest one. He was still in love with the woman. He wasn't quite so strong in his resolutions as they might think.

"You told me a few months back," the bishop said slowly. "You told me that you felt like Job in that even if Gott would slay you, yet would you trust in Him. You've been a man of character and you've been someone that the community could look to as an example of a man going through difficult times and still acting like a true Christian. Even after your breakup, you've been helping Lovina to regain some of her memory. That's commendable! How many men would do that for someone after a breakup like the one you went through? You are humble, Johannes, but your character shines through."

His heart hammered in his chest. They wanted to make him a deacon of the community like his grandfather had been before him. They believed in him, respected him—and it was so incredibly tempting to accept their good opinion without question, but that wouldn't be moral.

"Abe Yoder let us believe he was a better man than he

was, and it crushed our community," Johannes said. "I don't want to make the same mistake—acting stronger than I truly am."

"That's a good point," the bishop said slowly. "I have to be frank with you—this community has been through so much that our choice in leadership is incredibly sensitive. When choosing the names to be put into the draw, we discussed all of this very thoroughly. We need a man who is unconnected to the Yoder family—that's imperative. People will be looking to our new deacon for hope and for stability. There can't be a connection to Abe. It was part of the reason we included your name, and your ability to see the subtleties here is encouraging."

Johannes was silent. No connection to Abe Yoder . . .

Johannes rubbed his palms against his knees. They had chosen his name . . . The honor was a deep one. Was it possible that he might step into his grandfather's shoes as a deacon in this community?

"And yet, we chose his name, Bishop," Elder Joel said quietly, the words seeming to be meant for the bishop alone.

"And yet, we chose his name . . ." The bishop leaned his elbows onto his knees. He pursed his lips. "Johannes, Bernard, I do believe we need to pray longer on this decision."

"*Yah*, that sounds like the right path," Bernard agreed.

"And you pray, too," Elder Joel added, turning back toward them. "When Gott helps us to choose a deacon, he works in the hearts of the men drawing the names, as well as in the heart of the one who is meant for the position. It's a good sign that you're taking this step so seriously— it shows that you understand the gravitas of the position.

Let's all pray for the right decision to be made—it doesn't seem we've finished this discussion just yet."

"Shall we pray now, before we leave?" the bishop asked. "You all deserve your supper, and we won't keep you away from it any longer."

The men bowed their heads, and the bishop prayed fervently for guidance and clarity in the choice ahead of them. When he said amen, the two men said their good-byes and left the Miller men to their dinner.

Bernard brought the corn bread to the table, and Johannes dished up big bowls of chili for each of them, his mind heavy with the knowledge that the lot had fallen to him. Him! Was it possible that Gott was guiding his life in a different direction than he'd been considering? Church leadership was both a burden and a gift—not to be taken lightly.

"So, if you marry Lovina, you can't be deacon?" Daniel said, breaking the silence.

Johannes looked up. "Daniel, number one, you shouldn't have been listening in. And number two, it's more delicate than that. People have been severely shaken in this community. Abe Yoder wasn't just a man who went wrong—he was a preacher! He was a spiritual leader, and when he went wrong, he shattered the faith of a lot of people! People arc still healing, and this isn't a simple situation—"

"But for as far as you're concerned," Daniel pressed, "if you marry Lovina, you can't be deacon."

Johannes exchanged a look with his father. "*Yah*, it would seem that's the case."

"Do you want to be deacon?" Daniel asked. "Like Great-Grandpa Menno was?"

To be a deacon like his grandfather before him . . . Yes, he had to admit that the possibility had a certain hopeful glow to it.

"It's not up to me," he said.

Sometimes a man had to let go of something in order to have the kind of life he wanted. But Johannes couldn't be the rock his community needed him to be if he was caught in the current with the Yoders. He couldn't be a deacon and keep Lovina in his heart. It was one or the other.

"Let's eat," Bernard said. "And you, Daniel, shouldn't be listening at doors anymore."

Daniel's face pinked slightly, and they all bowed their heads.

Johannes wasn't so different from his teenage nephew with his love of sewing in a conservative community. He couldn't have everything, either. Welcome to real life.

Chapter Fifteen

The next evening, Johannes and Bernard stood at the counter putting away the washed supper dishes. Johannes had been tempted to go over and see Lovina that day, but he'd held himself back. He'd known from the start that he should be more cautious with his heart, and he'd known just how vulnerable he was when it came to Lovina, and the bishop's visit had sobered him. The narrow path was not an easy one, and it required sacrifice. No one said it was easy, and if he went to see Lovina, he was going to pull her straight into his arms—he wouldn't be able to help it.

The kitchen curtains were open, and outside the evening was dark. A sweep of headlights turned up the drive, catching their attention. Daniel went to the window and shaded his eyes to look out.

"It's a van," the boy said. "Like the one I took to get here."

Johannes headed over to the door and pulled it open. The inside lights of the van illuminated a jovial-looking driver, and the panel door opened. The woman who stepped out brought an immediate smile to Johannes's face—it was his sister Linda.

Linda was middle-aged with some gray streaking her brown hair, which was pulled away from her face. She was slim, and she wore her Sunday best dress and a pair of black running shoes. Her white apron looked wrinkled from the long drive.

"Hey, it's your *mamm*!" Johannes called to his nephew, and he headed outside to help her with the little suitcase that she put down on the gravel next to her.

"Thank you very much," Linda said to the driver. "This is my brother, so I'll be fine."

"Have a good night, Linda!" the driver called back. "You know where to call if you want me to come collect you again."

The minivan pulled out, and Johannes gave his sister a hug.

"It's so good to see you!" Johannes said. She squeezed him back.

"You look like you're eating," she said, patting his stomach, and Johannes laughed and rolled his eyes. "We eat, Linda. We eat!"

"Get married and I won't worry about it, then," she said with a chuckle. She looked up and saw her son. "Daniel! Hello, son. I'm sorry to interrupt your visit."

"I don't mind," Daniel said, and the grin on his face proved that he was glad to see her. They all went inside together.

Bernard hugged his daughter, and Johannes put his sister's traveling bag down beside the stairs. Then they all sat down for some hot coffee and some muffins from the bakery.

"So what brings you over?" Bernard asked. "Is everything okay?"

Linda's expression faltered, and she licked her lips. "I've been proposed to."

"Oh!" Johannes looked over at Daniel, and the boy's expression froze. "By whom?"

"His name is Silas Swarey," she said, and her gaze swung over to her son. "And I know you don't like him, Daniel."

"Silas Swarey . . ." Bernard said quietly. "Is this the same man who was married to a woman named Agnes?"

"*Yah*, that's him," she replied. "She passed away a few years back."

"He's twenty years older than you," Bernard pointed out.

"*Yah*, he is . . ." Linda sucked in a slow breath. "But I can't afford the mortgage on that property by myself anymore. I've renegotiated with the bank as often as they'll let me, and I've just missed the first payment ever. If I miss two more, I lose it."

Johannes looked over at Daniel. The boy's face had turned white, and his lips were trembling.

"Maybe not in front of Daniel . . ." Johannes said.

"It needs to be in front of Daniel," she replied. "Because I think I'm going to have to accept Silas's proposal, and I need my son to understand why."

"He doesn't like us!" Daniel burst out.

"He's more strict than I've ever been with you," she countered, "but of course he likes you!"

"He picks at me constantly," Daniel retorted. "If you

ask him, I never do anything right. He's constantly telling me I have to man up and take care of things, as if I don't help you!"

"It would be different having a man in the house again," she said. "We'd have to all pull ourselves together a little bit more."

"What does that even mean?" Daniel demanded. "Pull ourselves together? Does that include you, Mamm?"

"Maybe a little bit," she said. "It would be an adjustment for me, too."

"Aren't you going to say anything?" Daniel demanded, turning his agonized gaze onto Bernard and then Johannes. "Aren't you?"

"Do you *want* to marry Silas Swarey?" Bernard asked quietly.

Linda shrugged weakly. "I don't exactly have a herd of Amish men lining up for my pie."

"We're fine by ourselves!" Daniel cut in. "I'll take care of you, Mamm. You don't need to worry! I can get a job if you let me drop out of school early."

"You're not old enough for that yet," she said with a tender smile. "You are not dropping out. I'm your mother, and I will figure this out."

"By marrying some old man like that?" Daniel retorted.

"Daniel, mind how you talk to your mother," Bernard said, a warning in his tone, and the boy fell silent.

"How much do you need to get even with the bank?" Johannes asked.

"It's a lot," she said, shaking her head. "I can't ask that of you."

"How much?" Johannes pressed, and when she answered

him, Johannes let out a low whistle. It was more than Johannes had to his own name.

Daniel got up from the table and marched up the stairs, his footsteps thunking overhead. The boy might not like the idea of his mother remarrying, but Linda's life would be a whole lot easier if she did.

"And if you sell the property?" Bernard asked.

"There isn't much available in our area to buy—it's packed with Amish families," she said. "I'd have to move farther out to get anything, and . . . I'd probably have to rent."

A possibility, but it wouldn't leave her *kinner* anything, and she wouldn't have any security when she was old.

"You could move back home," Bernard said. "I'd love to have you and the *kinner* here with me. You always have a home here."

"I considered that already, Daet," Linda said, tears misting her eyes. "But I'd like my *kinner* to be close to their *daet*'s family, too. And . . . it feels like failure."

Bernard pressed his lips together. "I've got savings, Linda. I could empty them for you and get you straight with the bank, but I wouldn't have anything else to help again. Can you make enough income to pay the mortgage every month?"

Daniel's footsteps sounded on the stairs, and Johannes turned to see his nephew return with his quilt work in his hands. He passed it over to his mother without a word, and she took it, looked at the material and spread it on the table in front of her.

Linda was silent. Her fingers moved over the stitches, and she slowly raised her eyes.

"Silas Swarey would stop me from sewing," Daniel said.

"Oh, son . . ." Tears misted her eyes. "*Yah*, he would, but I was hoping you'd stop on your own over time. It's not right for a boy your age to be quilting. You need to be working a farm, building some muscle—"

"I can do all that and quilt, too," he said. "How much do you think I could get for that—if we finished it, I mean. If we made the picture bigger, or maybe did a frame around it to make for a bigger lap quilt. Then with backing and batting . . . how much?"

"Son, this is beautiful work," Linda said, and she looked uncomfortably toward the men, then back to her son. "But you can't sell it."

"Why not?" he demanded.

"Because then people would know!" she said, and a tear slipped down her cheek. "This isn't going to be acceptable, Daniel! You know that!"

"We could say you made it," Daniel said.

"Gott hasn't blessed a lie yet," she replied.

"Well, if you did the rest of it—a border, the backing . . . then we could say it's a family project," he said. "And I think it's good. I saw what sorts of quilts are for sale in the fabric shop, and they aren't half as good as this one."

"That's prideful," Linda said.

"It's just true," Daniel replied. "Mamm, I can help you make money. No one has to know I'm sewing these, and we can finish them together, and then sell them in town. If I didn't have to hide it all the time, I could finish one way faster, and I was just working with some old remnants. Get me some decent cloth!"

Linda's breath was coming quick now, and she licked her lips, passing her hand over the fabric. They all knew that Daniel was right—a quilt like his could fetch a lot of money. But it would also fetch a lot of curiosity about who had made it.

"Daniel, you have to be reasonable," Johannes said. "People will find out who's sewing. All it takes is one person breathing a word to someone else. One sister telling her best friend in confidence—"

"Does no one care about the truth?" Daniel asked. "I'm not doing women's quilting. This is different, and if anyone stopped to look long enough, they'd see that. This one is my memory of watching my *daet* come home in the buggy. And the one I did at home is from Uncle Zechariah's farm—the baling. And I have an idea for one I could do with the scraps I have leftover of a farrier doing horse shoes. I've got almost all the right colors for some horse shoes—the grays and browns. I'm not doing wedding ring patterns, Mamm, or bluebirds. I'm doing manly stuff." Then he shrugged slightly. "With fabric."

Linda sucked in a wavery breath. "Go on upstairs and I'll discuss it with your *dawdie* and uncle."

"I can hear it anyway," Daniel said.

"I said go upstairs!"

Daniel shrugged again and headed for the stairs. He looked over his shoulder. "You want me to learn how to be a man, Mamm. And what's more manly than taking care of your family? I can do that."

When the boy had disappeared, Linda's gaze dropped down to the quilt work in front of her.

"Why does he have to be so good at this?" she asked softly.

"He is good, isn't he?" Johannes replied.

She nodded, then rubbed her hands over her face. "He's right that we could sell these quilts for a good amount. And he works fast. Have you noticed that? At home, he can grab a few fragments and stitch something together when I'm not even looking. But if I marry Silas, he'll put a stop to it."

"Is that why you sent him here?" Bernard asked. "To see if he'd stop sewing with some male influence?"

"*Yah* . . ." Linda's eyes misted. "He's a good boy. He's got a good heart. But to have a *daet* like Silas catch him sewing . . . It would be horrible."

"Let's put aside the idea of marrying Silas," Bernard said. "If I gave you what I have and cleared you with the bank, and if you and Daniel sewed together and made a quilt or two to sell . . ."

"It could work. Financially. But letting my son quilt?" she said. "Who do I say made them?"

"If you sold them here in Bountiful, there'd be no questions to you directly," Johannes said. "You could mail them to us—I'll pay when I pick them up. And then we'll just say that some family members who wanted to stay anonymous were trying their hand at quilting. No names. We'll send you the money as soon as they sell."

"I know it isn't ideal to hide who we are like that," Linda said. "But who knows—Daniel might lose interest in quilting. He's only thirteen. By the time he's sixteen, he might have turned to something else completely."

"It happens often enough," Bernard agreed.

"And I don't want to put his name out there with quilts." Linda looked over at Johannes. "He might change his mind, and . . . you know how challenging this would be for him. You know what people would say."

"I think you're a good *mamm*, Linda," Johannes said. "That's what I think."

Linda put a hand on top of his.

Bernard cleared his throat. "What about Silas Swarey, then?"

"I'll tell him no," Linda replied.

"Good!" Daniel's voice came from the top of the stairs.

Another family secret—but this one would be worth keeping. It was better than putting Daniel's name next to quilt work before he was ready to face the backlash.

And there *would* be backlash if people found out . . .

"And if it doesn't work," Bernard said firmly, "if it doesn't, you come home, Linda. No daughter of mine is going to marry a man twenty years her senior for financial security. If you marry again, I want it to be because you want to. It's not failure to come home. It's what family is for."

But the problem filling Johannes's heart right now wasn't about his sister's financial troubles, or his nephew's love of textiles. He was thinking about the choice that he had in front of him—what he was willing to give up for the respectable Amish life that he longed for.

Or was the love he'd been harboring all this time going to prove to be too much for him, and he'd be swept off to deal with the consequences, whatever they may be?

He pushed his chair back.

"I'll be back in a couple of hours. I need to do something . . ."

Linda looked up at him in surprise, but Bernard just nodded.

"Tell her we say hello," Bernard said with a weak smile.

It seemed that Johannes wasn't fooling anyone anyhow.

Quilting with the other women in the community was almost melancholy that day. Vannetta came, and she and Lovina sat side by side and stitched while they talked.

"I'm just glad you're back," Vannetta kept saying. "That's all that matters. Gott works in mysterious ways, doesn't He?"

Not once did Vannetta ask if Lovina had plans to stay, and Lovina didn't want to bring it up. Vannetta had her own family to focus on now, and she wouldn't be a part of Lovina's decision, anyway. So Lovina enjoyed her friend's company, listened to her stories about keeping house by herself for the first time, about getting the baby's clothes ready, about trying to bake bread in a new woodstove that just didn't seem to heat evenly . . . and for a little while, Lovina felt the gentle rhythms of an Amish life.

After the women left, Bethany and Elizabeth continued to work on the quilt. It needed to be finished, and they were doing the edging as quickly as they could stitch, because there were other things to work on before this wedding, and they weren't nearly ready.

The police came back—a different pair of officers this time. They pulled up and parked right by the side door.

The sun had sunk below the rolling hills, the first few stars pricking through the twilight, and a full moon had risen, softened by some wispy clouds. Isaiah was out doing chores, and the quilt was still on the frame in the sitting room.

The officers knocked on the side door, and when Lovina let them in, they stood next to the kitchen table, notebooks in hand, their expressions stony. They were both men below forty, fit, clean shaven, and about as warm as a cement wall.

"Where was Solomon Lantz on the evening of the fourth?" the first officer asked, his gaze locked on Elizabeth, who was pale.

"What day was that?" she asked feebly.

"Wednesday."

"He came over to see me. We . . . took a walk . . . we're engaged you know." She sounded slightly defensive. "We're getting married in a couple of weeks, and we just want to spend time together. So there was nothing untoward happening—"

"We aren't concerned about the nature of your visit, Miss Yoder," the officer said. "We just need to know when he arrived, and when he left."

"He arrived before dinner," she replied, glancing over at Bethany. "That would have been . . . what . . . six? And we ate . . . then we went for our walk. I was back inside by nine."

Lovina stood there, her heart in her throat. Police . . . would their family never be rid of them?

"He's a good man," Elizabeth added as the officer made some notes. The other officer stood back, just seeming to be watching them, his gaze moving from face to face. Watching for evidence of a lie? Lovina felt the other officer's gaze stop at her, and his brow furrowed.

"Miss, this robbery is local," the officer said. "And we're asking a few questions. Your fiancé has some history, doesn't he?"

"Solomon is not involved in anything, I can assure you," she said earnestly. "He's starting over. Are you a Christian?"

"No."

"Oh . . ." Elizabeth sighed. "Well, he's starting over, and he wants a quiet Amish life. And just so you know, Gott can't bless a thief. We don't *need* extra money—"

"Why not?" the officer asked. "You're getting married soon. A little extra cash right now might be more useful than you think. Your fiancé might want to impress you with his ability to provide."

Lovina felt her stomach clench. It was like these officers wanted to believe that Solomon was involved. And how much evidence against him would be necessary to get them to arrest him and charge him with the crime? Her breath caught in her throat. She didn't know Solomon Lantz very well, but she did know her sister . . . and Elizabeth wasn't a woman who enjoyed danger and intrigue. She liked things calm. She wouldn't be marrying Solomon if she weren't sure that he'd be a good, solid, law-abiding husband.

"More money isn't needed!" Elizabeth insisted. "We make do. We have a community to help us if we need it. It's going to be a small wedding, and Sol is working hard."

"Which brings us to your father," the officer said, flipping the page of his notebook.

The door opened then, and Isaiah came inside. Lovina felt a rush of relief. At least it wasn't just the women alone anymore. Her brother looked around the room quickly, and Lovina caught his uncertain gaze. She could read the worry in his expression—*Englisher* police officers didn't exactly bring comfortable feelings for this family.

"And you are . . . ?" the second officer said, turning to Isaiah abruptly.

"I'm Isaiah Yoder, and this is my home," Isaiah said curtly, and he moved up to Bethany's side, putting a protective arm around her waist. "What's going on here?"

"We're looking into a local robbery," the first officer said. "And I was just about to ask about your father."

"What about him?" Isaiah asked with a sigh.

"How is he settling into life after prison?" the officer asked.

"He's fine," Isaiah said.

"Is he?"

There was an uncomfortable silence, and Lovina looked over at Elizabeth, whose cheeks were still pink.

"Okay, maybe not fine, exactly," Isaiah said. "He's lonely. He's struggling to find a way to fit back in. It's not easy for him. What do you expect? Does anyone bounce back that quickly after prison time?"

"Has he come into money recently?" the officer asked.

"Money?" Isaiah barked out a bitter laugh. "No! Do you see any extravagance around here? Everything was taken after his trial—everything! Our farm, our equipment, our animals . . . The only thing we could keep was our clothing. We don't have any extra! We work hard, we pay our bills, and that's all we do."

"And yet, no one needs any extra money, do they?"

The officer swung a pointed look over at Elizabeth. She looked down at her hands, clenched in front of her black apron.

"Are you suspecting our father of being involved in this robbery?" Isaiah asked.

"He's got a history of it, too," the officer said.

"He's not stupid, though," Lovina said, breaking her silence for the first time. "Our *daet* is out of prison and on parole. Doesn't that mean that if he makes a mistake, he could go back?"

Everyone turned to look at her, and Lovina felt her hands tremble in spite of her best effort to keep them still. The officer made another note.

"Thank you for your time today," the officer said. "We'll be in touch if we need to speak with you again."

Lovina's heart pattered in her chest. What was it about those crisp uniforms and granite faces that made her feel guilty, even though she hadn't done anything wrong?

The officers saw themselves out, and as Isaiah closed the door behind them, Lovina let out a long breath.

"Will it always be like this?" Bethany asked, her voice low.

Isaiah's face fell, and he cast his wife an apologetic look. "It'll get better."

"Will it?" she asked, shaking her head. "I don't know that it will!"

Isaiah took Bethany's hand, they moved together out of the kitchen and into the sitting room—a bid for some privacy, it would seem. The murmur of their voices still made it into the kitchen.

"It's harder for her," Elizabeth said. "She's from a good family, and she married Isaiah because she loved him. Now, because of us, she's got police in her home asking questions and acting like we're somehow connected to any robbery in the area."

"Bethany has a point, though," Lovina said. "Will it always be like this?"

"It might be for me," Elizabeth said, and her eyes misted. "Sol is a good man. He's changing his ways, and he has my deepest respect. But I'm not a fool. I know that no one else sees what I do in him. And I accept that. For a time—maybe for the rest of our lives—people will think he's something he's not."

Lovina went to the window and watched as the police cruiser pulled out of the drive.

And suddenly, a similar day to this one drifted up in her memory. They'd been sitting in a different kitchen— her childhood home—and there were tears in her siblings' eyes. They all felt so lonely, so crushed, and on that Sunday evening after their father's arrest, they'd only had each other.

Lovina looked over at her sister, and Elizabeth paused, seeming to sense that something had happened.

"I remember it," Lovina breathed. "I remember that night after Daet was arrested, and the three of us sat around the kitchen table back at the farm, and we told each other that Daet was innocent, that he needed us to be strong, and that Gott would get us through . . ."

But Daet had not been innocent after all. And nothing had ever been the same again, including their relationships. Their uncle Mel just got angrier and angrier, and their extended family couldn't distance themselves far enough from their disgraced father. Their friends did the same. What used to be friendships between equals turned into something less comfortable. No one could understand what they were going through.

And things had changed with Johannes, too. She felt it start to slide, and she knew she couldn't fix it. *She* hadn't broken it!

But things had been different in every part of her life. Her heart sped up at the memory that was so strong, it felt like it was squeezing her rib cage.

"So you remember . . . ." Elizabeth whispered.

"*Yah*." Lovina swallowed hard. "I remember thinking that eventually it would go away . . . that we'd get over it and go back to normal. But there is no normal anymore. There never will be again."

"But there are a few silver linings," Elizabeth said. "I'd never have given Sol a chance if it weren't for what we went through with Daet. I'd have thought he was too much of a risk."

"And he would have been," Lovina said bluntly, but then she softened her tone. "I know you'll be happy with him, and I'm so glad you found each other! But life would have been very different if it weren't for Daet's crime."

Elizabeth met Lovina's gaze. "You'd be married already."

Her sister was right. She'd already be married to Johannes, settled in some little house together. She might even have her first child already, or be expecting a baby soon, like Vannetta. But more than married, she would have been a woman who was respected in the community. She'd be the daughter of that powerful preacher. Being married wasn't enough if it was done out of pity.

There was one place where this whole scandal wouldn't

change anything, and that was back in Erindale with the Maitland family. In Erindale, Lovina wasn't Abe Yoder's daughter—she was simply that talented Amish girl everyone appreciated so much. She wasn't attached to anyone . . . no one could tarnish her reputation out there like they could here . . .

It was freeing, relieving, and heartbreaking, all at once.

Outside, the sound of horse hooves crunched along the gravel drive, and Lovina spotted Johannes's face in the bobbing light of his buggy lamp. Her heart gave a little leap, and suddenly, all she wanted to do was fall into that man's strong arms.

"Joahnnes is here . . ." she said softly. *Johannes . . .*

"Go on and see him," Elizabeth said. "I'm sure you miss him, too."

Lovina headed for the door, and she looked over her shoulder to find her sister wiping a tear off her cheek. She pushed outside into the cool evening, sweet summer air filling her lungs. The horses pranced as Johannes reined them in, and she looked up into his handsome face, and she realized in a rush that Johannes hadn't lied to her once as her memory had slowly returned.

He was right—they'd been in love with each other. Deeply. Almost madly.

But even love had its limits . . .

Chapter Sixteen

Johannes had expected to go inside the Yoder house for a cup of tea and piece of pie or something at this time of night. He'd expected to chat with her family a little and be grateful for ten or fifteen minutes alone with Lovina before he left, but Lovina came straight out of the house and down the steps and was halfway to the buggy by the time the horses came to a complete stop. The light from the window glowed low and soft, and as the screen door clattered shut behind her, it opened again, revealing Elizabeth in the doorway.

Lovina's sister just stood there in the low light, her expression hard to read.

"Take me for a drive," Lovina said, looking up at him. A tendril of blonde hair had come loose and tumbled down across her cheek. Her eyes looked almost midnight blue against the milky wash of her face.

"*Yah*. Sure." He looked up at Elizabeth, who raised her hand in a wave. "Are you fighting with your sister, or—"

"No, not at all," Lovina said, and she turned back and exchanged a long look with Elizabeth. Then she reached up for his hand like she used to do in days past. It was a gesture she hadn't done in over a year . . . He leaned down, caught her slim hand, and pulled her up, and she settled next to him. She smelled like fragrant cooking, and she leaned back against the seat with a sigh.

"Is everything okay?" he asked.

Elizabeth disappeared back into the house, and he thought he could see the outline of Isaiah and his wife in the sitting room window.

"No," she said simply. "It's not."

As the horses pulled the buggy around, Johannes adjusted the reins into one hand, and he reached over and took her hand. She was shaking—not a tremble, exactly. It was more like a shiver.

"What happened?" he asked, looking over at her, searching her pale face for some clue.

"The police came to our door," she said.

"Why?" he asked.

"There was a robbery around here somewhere," Lovina said, "and they came to ask us about Sol and Daet. They had no other reason but that they were both in prison recently. That's it."

A robbery . . . That thought gave him pause. He knew that Lovina was living with her brother, and technically she was no safer with Johannes than she was with her own family, but he'd still feel better if it was his body between her and danger. Crime was rising in the Amish areas. Criminals had figured out that some Amish families were both well off and vulnerable. Thieves wouldn't meet the business end of a shotgun when robbing the Amish. Their punishment would wait for the afterlife . . . or the police. Vengeance didn't belong to the Amish.

"But you can understand why they'd come by . . ." he said quietly. "I mean, if it weren't family. If this were other people, and there was a robbery, starting with ex-convicts seems like a pretty logical choice."

Lovina pulled her hand out of his. Did she really think that once a man had done time in prison, all was forgotten and the legal system simply wished them well and hoped for the best? Johannes highly doubted that was how it worked. Solomon had a parole officer, and he had to report to him weekly. Sad how many post-incarceration things his family was now familiar with.

"Hey," he said, and he reached over, taking her hand again. "I'm sorry, okay? All I'm saying is that they don't mean to be unfair. They're just trying to do their jobs. They're trying to keep you safe. Maybe in time—"

"Time won't fix this," Lovina said, her voice low. "It won't be like it was before, Johannes."

There was something in her voice that sounded so much like the old Lovina, and he looked over at her.

"I remember," she said, and tears misted her eyes.

"You do?" His heart skipped a beat.

"*Yah*." Her eyes shone in the moonlight, and as they came up to a copse of trees, limbs overhanging the road, he reined the horses in. His mind was spinning ahead— she *remembered*. But how much? And how much had changed?

The horses stamped their feet and nickered. A gentle breeze rustled the leaves overhead, and in the field beyond, he could see the cows grazing, a few lying down and chewing their cud.

A year ago, he'd have taken the chance to kiss her, but tonight—

"You remember . . . everything?" he asked hesitantly.

"I think so." She nodded. "I remember you and me. I remember the first time you asked me home from singing, and the first time you held my hand. I remember agreeing to marry you, and—" She stopped, and he waited, breath bated, for her to go on, but she didn't.

"Do you remember leaving me?" he asked.

She nodded.

His heart squeezed in his chest. When he'd gotten that note from Isaiah, it was like his breath had been knocked from his body.

"Why did you come to see me tonight?" she asked.

"What?" He swallowed hard.

"You came to see me," she said. "How come?"

"Because I love you?" he said, shaking his head.

"It's late, though . . ." She fixed him with a look. She knew him better tonight—this was the whole Lovina now.

He blew out a breath. "I just . . . I had to see you. My sister Linda arrived at our place tonight, and she's going to need some help. But before she arrived, the bishop came by."

"The bishop?" Lovina whispered. "Is everything okay?"

"When they thought I was going to marry Sovilla, they put my name in the draw for the deacon position," he said. "And they . . . drew my name."

"They chose you?"

"It's more complicated than that," he said. "I'm not marrying Sovilla."

Lovina blinked as if his words had physically struck

her, and he felt immediate remorse for not having thought before he spoke.

"I didn't mean it like that," he said quickly. "Lovina, I didn't *want* to marry Sovilla! She's a very nice woman, but she's not you! Okay? And she wanted to marry me even less. It was an idea . . . They thought it would help me get over you, but you aren't exactly replaceable."

Lovina smiled faintly. "I might be."

"Lovina—" What was she doing?

"What did the bishop say?" she asked.

"Just that," he replied. "They felt like Gott had been leading in that draw, and when they drew my name, they didn't want to just throw it out. It felt wrong to them. So they came to talk to me about it."

Lovina put her other hand on the top of his, and her cool, soft touch felt like an embrace. The air between them was almost electric, like just before a storm, and had lightning sizzled between them, it would have been no surprise.

"They think you're the right one for the job," she whispered.

"*Yah.*" Like his grandfather. And it felt wonderful to be considered. It felt like affirmation for them to take him this seriously.

"Will they insist you be married?" she asked.

"I don't know . . ."

She licked her lips and dropped her gaze. He'd need a wife, but they wouldn't accept Lovina. Did he care? Did it even matter if he became deacon, now that he was faced with it? What did matter was Lovina—

"Lovina, I've been waiting and dreading your memory coming back. But I have to know . . . why did you leave?"

he asked. His voice was almost hoarse, his throat felt so tight.

Lovina was so silent, it was almost as if she didn't hear him. But then she swallowed and pulled her hands free of his touch, and he felt like a gulf had opened up between them.

"Because I had to," she whispered.

"Had to?" he demanded. "What are you talking about?"

"Don't you remember what it was like?" she breathed, looking up at him. "Don't you remember how it felt when my *daet* was sent to prison? You asked me to marry you when I was the youngest daughter of a respected preacher. You'd chosen me, but also a particular life! You were choosing a family—and you really liked my *daet*. You and he used to sit and talk for hours on a Sunday afternoon, and . . . And that life was gone, Johannes! Whatever our marriage might have looked like"—her gaze swept the road beyond him—"the community respect, the ability to hold your head up with the other men—that was gone."

"For better or for worse," he said.

"After the vows that would be true, Johannes," she said, her voice trembling. "But not before."

"I promised to marry you!" he said.

"And you would have!" she said, her voice rising. "I know that! Of course you would have, because you're honest and kind and a truly decent man! But not because it was still the life you longed for. How could you? You'd be the son-in-law of a felon, Johannes! What man chooses that?"

"A man in love with you?" Johanne said.

"A man stuck in a promise," she said. "Because you

make a very pretty argument now, but before I left, you were in shock. You were absolutely stunned, and Johannes, you weren't leaning toward me."

"I was trying to make sense of it," he said. "I needed some time to do that."

"So was I," she said. "But the fact remains, you weren't coming to me with your feelings about it. You weren't telling me what you were struggling with. I wasn't enough to comfort you—"

It hadn't been her job to comfort him! She'd been rocked by this, too, and he was supposed to be the one supporting her, not the other way around. To judge his reaction because he'd needed some time to find his balance—

"That isn't fair . . ." he said.

"None of this was fair!" she shot back. "None of it! Our lives got turned upside down, Johannes! And it wasn't fair to me and my siblings, and it wasn't fair to you, either!"

Johanne pulled off his hat and pushed a hand through his hair. "So why did you leave?" he asked. "Because I wasn't quick enough to talk about my feelings? Because I didn't want to add my own fury at your father to your shoulders?"

"Because I wasn't going to hold you to an engagement that you'd resent for the rest of your life," she said.

"I wouldn't resent you," he said.

"If you married me right now," she said, and her shining gaze snapped back to meet his. "Right now! If you took your vows with me and I became your legally wedded wife . . . would they make you deacon?"

The air rushed out of his chest, and Johannes struggled to suck in a new one.

"Would they?" she pressed.

He shook his head. "No."

He didn't have to explain why. She knew it. She knew what her father had done to the community, and she knew how fragile everyone was now that they had to rebuild around a betrayal so close to the heart of their church.

"And that's why I left," she said.

Johannes understood—Lovina could see it shining in his stricken eyes. He knew exactly what marrying her would rob him of, and he couldn't argue that she'd been wrong.

"What about now?" he asked.

"What *about* now?" she demanded, shaking her head. "Has anything changed?"

"I love you," he said, his voice thick, and those words stabbed down underneath all her defenses.

"You don't have to say that," she said, her voice shaking. "It doesn't make you a bad man to move on, Johannes. I left you! Remember that? I'm the bad one."

"Lovina—" His gaze swept over her face. "Do you feel anything now? Anything?"

"Do I love you?" she breathed. "*Yah*! I do. I . . . I didn't remember you, but you were so patient with me, and so kind, and . . . I fell in love with you all over again."

"So did I!" he said, and he slipped an arm around her. "I spent a year trying to get over you, and it didn't work. But having you back—it's different. I'll admit that. Having to put aside our history and just have you without any memories of what we were . . . Doesn't it mean anything that without any of our history, you still ended up feeling this way?"

Lovina looked up at him, silent, and he touched her cheek with the back of one finger and then leaned down and caught her lips with his. His kiss was soft and urgent. She felt him pull in a breath against her face, and then he broke off the kiss and let out a wavering breath.

Lovina blinked her eyes open, and tears blurred her vision. Why did he have to make this seem so simple, when it was anything but?

"Johannes," she whispered, "I loved you before, too—it wasn't like I stopped. Leaving you was the hardest thing I ever did. I cried for weeks. I was a shell of myself. I'm surprised the Maitlands saw so much good in me, considering I was a wreck for the first few months working with Carrie!"

"Then why did you even stay?" he demanded.

"Because it was the right thing to do!" she shot back. "Johannes, you deserve better than what I can give you."

"Isn't that for me to decide?" he asked.

"Then how about this?" Lovina straightened. "*I* deserve better than to be the woman a man has to take pity on and marry her *anyway*. I deserve to be a cherished wife, a woman who makes her husband's life better because she's there. I deserve to be a prize!"

"You are—"

"Don't just say what you think I want to hear!" she said, cutting him off. "Admit the truth, Johannes. At least give me that!"

Johannes was silent for a moment, and she could see the tension along his jawline.

"Your father's crime changed things for everyone," he said quietly. "It rattled this whole community. I'm not saying it didn't. And yes, my life will look different because of it. But that doesn't mean I don't love you."

"I don't even know if my life can go on here in Bountiful," she said miserably. "Here, I'm the one who drags down any man who falls for me. A woman knows what she's brought to the table. If her pie is smashed in, no amount of overlooking it will change facts! And if she makes a strudel of rare perfection, she knows that, too, even if no one tells her. Here in Bountiful, my pie is smashed in, Johannes."

"And with the Englishers—" he said, his voice tight.

"I don't feel like a smashed-in pie," she said. "Can't you understand that?"

Johannes rubbed his hand over his chin, the stubble rasping against his work-roughened hands. He dropped his hand and looked at her miserably.

"Are you staying in Bountiful?" he asked at last.

His dark gaze searched her face, and she felt her broken, battered heart reaching out toward him.

"I don't think so," she whispered. "Hard as it is to keep leaving the ones I love, I need to be the Amish woman with something wonderful to offer . . . I need that."

Because in Bountiful, she'd always be facing the shame of her family and the distrust of her community. She's always be the daughter of the man who'd betrayed them all . . .

She could remember the weight of that realization a year ago when she wrote those letters and packed her bag, and the only thing that had changed was that she now knew what an *English* life offered her. Maybe it was good that she had a chance to come see her family one more time, because she'd missed them terribly. And maybe it was right and proper to get a final goodbye with Johannes and to set him free at last.

Maybe Gott had been in that accident after all—not for her good, but for Johannes's.

The wind had picked up, and there was the smell of rain in the air. Johannes flicked the reins again, and the horses started forward. He turned the buggy around, and they headed back toward her brother's house. She listened to the clopping of the horses' hooves—so calm and rhythmic. Johannes didn't look at her, and she wondered if it was anger or sadness that kept him silent like this.

This was what it had been like after her father's arrest—the silence, his face as expressive as the side of a barn. He locked it down, wouldn't show what he felt . . . and maybe he'd be different with another woman. Maybe he'd be happier.

When they got back to the house, Johannes reined in the horses, and he caught her hand before she could move to get down.

"Lovina," he said, his voice rough.

She looked back at him, and she finally saw some emotion in his gaze, and the agony she saw made her stomach turn. She was torturing him, plain and simple.

"Is this goodbye?" he asked, his voice choked.

"*Yah*." Tears spilled down her cheeks. "This is the goodbye we should have had . . ."

Lovina tugged her hand free and slid down from the buggy seat, her feet hitting the gravel. She wanted to run, to disappear into the fields and moonlight and vent her grief like some wild thing out there in the bush.

But that wasn't an option, so she went to the house and opened the door, and when she looked back over her shoulder, she saw Johannes watching her with that stony look on his face, hiding it all inside once more.

Lovina pulled the door shut behind her, and the tears suddenly burst out. She leaned against the wall, covering her mouth to muffle the sound of her sobs.

"Lovina?" Elizabeth came to the door of the mud-room. "Lovina! What happened?"

But she couldn't talk about it, and she pushed past her sister and went down the hall to bed. She wouldn't have the room to herself for long—her sister would need to come to bed soon, too, but while she could, she lay there, curled up in a ball and sobbing out all the grief, and loss, and regret.

"Lovina?" Elizabeth appeared in the bedroom doorway. "You're scaring me!"

"Leave me alone," she choked out.

Her sister retreated, and she could hear her siblings talking in the kitchen. Johannes's name was mentioned, and so was hers. Undoubtedly, they'd figured it out.

It was all going to happen again, wasn't it? She was going to go back to Erindale with her heart in tatters, and she was going to have to imagine Johannes marrying someone else. Maybe even Sovilla, the sweet woman with the little girls who needed a husband rather badly. And Lovina was going to have to be okay with that.

She was going to have to pray for Gott to provide for both of them, and to help her to be happy with the wife He gave to Johannes. And maybe, if Gott could bless her rebellious heart that kept turning to the Englishers for her answers, He could give her a family of her own, too.

But every time she thought about a man to hold her, and love her, and protect her . . . Every time she shut her eyes and imagined strong arms wrapping around her, she could almost smell the musky scent of Johannes's work shirts, and the voice that murmured in her ear was all too familiar.

Lovina loved him, and there was going to be no easy healing from this goodbye.

Chapter Seventeen

Johannes unhitched the horses, his hands moving through the motions numbly, with no need for his mind to be involved in the chore. His heart ached inside of his chest. He'd done all he could to get over Lovina this last year, and all of that was undone.

Because he loved her—and she was right. She wasn't the woman to give him a good Amish life, was she? He knew what he longed for: the respect of the community that meant so much to him. And with Lovina, they'd both be living in Abe's shadow. Not that she even wanted what he had to offer. He couldn't undo what her *daet* had done, and that was the only thing that would make Bountiful bearable for her.

Maybe Johannes should have tried harder to get over her. He should have found some nice girl and started to court her. He should have taken the community's suggestion and married Sovilla and been a *daet* to her little girls. They were sweet *kinner*, and he'd have been proud to raise them with more of their own. But it didn't matter what woman he chose if she wasn't Lovina, because

Lovina was the one who filled his heart against all his better judgment . . .

He stood there in the quiet, listening to the horses chewing their oats in their stalls, and he felt the incredible emptiness inside of him.

Would he simply get used to it? Would he be able to put his feelings for her aside now that she'd crushed his heart twice?

Johannes headed out of the stable and paused in the moonlight. He didn't want to go inside. His sister had problems of her own, and what was he going to tell his family—that the breakup from a year ago stood? That would be no shock to them.

And they wouldn't understand this fresh pain. He didn't need them to. This was his life, and Lovina was right—if he wanted an Amish life with his community's respect, he had to do what it took to create that life.

But there had been a foolish, hopeful part of him that had thought maybe Lovina could be a part of it this time . . . that her accident might change something, that she'd see that a life here in Bountiful with their community was exactly where she wanted to be.

The house glowed warmly, and he could smell the aroma of baking coming from inside. His sister was contributing in the kitchen, and it was kind of her. They sorely needed a woman's touch around the place. Johannes stood outside in the fragrant breeze, the scent of fall in the air, and he listened to an eruption of laughter from inside. It sounded like they were playing Dutch Blitz, a card game they'd always played when the family got together.

Funny—all he'd ever wanted was the kind of community respect that his Dawdie Menno had had during his lifetime, and now he saw the price. Leadership was a heavy burden—he'd heard that said many times in the past. Leadership meant putting the needs of the community ahead of a man's own heart and hoping against hope that it was worth the sacrifice.

Was it?

He turned away from the house and headed in the direction of the barn.

They may very well make him deacon now. Or perhaps there'd be another veiled attempt to get him married quickly. Not Sovilla this time—some other nice girl who would put her heart in his hands.

And could he finally move on and put together a decent life for himself? Or would he end up like his Uncle Nathaniel? They'd spent a lot of time warning Daniel. It would be bitterly ironic if Johannes became the next warning tale to tell to young teenage boys.

And that is why you choose a girl from a good family. You might want to rescue a girl, but it doesn't work. Look at your Uncle Johannes . . .

That night, Johannes slept poorly. He lay awake for a long time, his throat aching with unshed tears, and when he finally did slip into a fitful slumber, he dreamed about Abe Yoder—that he was standing on one side of a fence and Johannes was on the other.

"She doesn't love you," Abe kept saying. "And she won't see you again."

"She does love me!" he insisted, and he kept trying to

look around Abe, because he knew Lovina was there, but somehow he couldn't quite get a glimpse of her.

He woke up breathless and panicked, and it took him several minutes of sitting on the side of his bed to get his heartbeat under control again.

Johannes got up earlier than necessary to start chores. He tiptoed down the stairs and headed out into the cool, late-summer predawn. When his father came out to the barn to milk, Johannes had done most of the other chores himself.

"Son, are you all right?" Bernard asked.

"*Yah*, Daet."

"You don't seem okay," Bernard said. "What happened with Lovina?"

"The same thing that happened a year ago," Johannes admitted. "It's over."

Bernard put a hand on his shoulder. "I'm sorry, son."

Johannes just nodded.

"I got that cell phone." Bernard pulled out a box and stared down at it. "I should introduce you to a brand-new monthly payment."

"We'll keep it out here?" Johannes asked.

"*Yah*, that's what the bishop says," Bernard replied. "But I don't know how to set it up. The fellow in the store says it's ready to go, but we need it for email."

"*Yah*, email . . ." Johannes took the box and turned it over in his hands. Lovina had a cell in Erindale, and a re-bellious, heartbroken idea entered his head that maybe he could come out here to the barn and call her every once in a while . . . hear her voice, at the very least. "Do we have that?"

"A very kind Englisher working at the shop helped

me set one up. They needed an email address for their purposes, too." Bernard pulled out a piece of paper from inside the box, and there was an address written on it. "I guess I wasted enough of their time, because they didn't get the email put on the phone."

"Oh . . ." Johannes looked down at the address again. "We'll sort it out. Maybe we'll go back to the shop and get more help."

"*Yah*, I suppose we'll have to . . ." Bernard sighed and put the box into a storage cupboard. "There is time enough to figure it out. But for now, the cows need milking."

Johannes and Bernard milked the cows, strained the milk into the metal containers, and then lifted the containers up onto the back of the wagon. Johannes drove the wagon down the winding road that led to the main drive, then up the gravel drive to the end. He waited there with his patient horse until Solomon's wagon appeared over the hill.

Life just kept moving forward. Cows needed milking. Milk needed to be delivered to the cheese factory. People were getting married, having babies, planning daily chores and working to support families. Life—in all its mundane beauty—carried on.

"Good morning!" Solomon called as he reined in his horses.

"Morning," Johannes said. "How are you doing?"

"Pretty good." Solomon tied off his reins and jumped down to the ground. He checked the milk jugs, made a note on his clipboard, and then passed it over for Johannes to initial. Together, they hoisted the first milk container off the back of Johannes's wagon and carried it over to Solomon's.

Solomon grunted as the weight of the next jug leaned back against his broad chest. "I've got this one—"

Johannes watched his cousin carry the milk jug over to his wagon, and when Solomon returned, Johannes jumped down to assist with the next jug.

"Are you okay?" Solomon asked, pushing his hat back on his head. "You look . . . bad."

"Thanks," Johannes replied with a small smile.

"No, I mean—"

"I'm fine," Johannes said. He'd have to get over it. There was no other way.

"I saw your *daet* in town the other day," Sol said. "He was at the electronics store—him and two other farmers."

"*Yah*, he got a cell phone," Johannes said.

Solomon shook his head. "Things are changing around here. We Amish work hard to keep things the same, but it happens here, too. And I know you're going to find this ironic coming from me, but I can't say that I like it."

Johannes watched as Solomon finished securing the milk jugs. "I guess we just have to get used to a new normal."

"New normal . . . *Yah*, that applies to me, too," Solomon said. "No cell phone for me, but . . . the cops came around asking about me the other day."

"I heard about that," Johannes admitted. "Are you okay?"

"I'm fine," Sol said. "I didn't do anything. But it's not going to be like it was, ever again. I'm going to have to remember that when I go out, I might have to account for where I was. And I'll have to think about things differently from now on. Sometimes life changes and there's no going back."

That was the truth, and Johannes sighed. Cell phones were the least of the changes he'd have to deal with, because going forward, he'd have to find a way to carry on without Lovina. He'd have to let go of the love he carried, and his anger at her choices, and his hope that she'd come back. He'd have to stop imagining what she was doing, and he'd have to let go of any rebellious ideas of calling her from that cell phone in the barn, because if he was going to be a man the community could respect, he couldn't have secret sins hidden away.

The narrow path could hurt, but it was worth it in the end. Dawdie Menno had said that a lot.

"Are you sure you're okay?" Solomon asked.

"*Yah.*" Johannes nodded quickly. "I know you're on a schedule. Don't let me keep you."

Solomon gave him a mildly concerned look, and then he hoisted the last container of milk on his own and carried it to the wagon. He wrapped a steadying rope around the front of the containers and then climbed back up into the driver's seat.

"See you!" Solomon called.

Johannes waved, then turned back to his own wagon. There was going to be a new normal . . . and maybe with time, his heart would ache less.

Johannes didn't go back for breakfast, even though he knew his sister would have cooked up a veritable feast. He wouldn't be able to eat it anyway. Instead he headed out to fix fences as far from everyone else as possible.

When he got back at lunchtime, his stomach growling, he spotted Sovilla's daughters playing under an apple tree. They had little dolls with them, and they looked up at him as he walked past.

"Hi, there," he said.

They both waved silently, watching him with wide eyes. He sighed, and when he opened the side door, he was met with the mouthwatering aroma of frying bacon and a cheese cauliflower soup.

"Look who shows himself!" Linda said with a smile. "I was starting to worry. Unless you packed food I don't know about, you're starving."

Sovilla stood at the counter loading fluffy, floury biscuits into a serving bowl. She looked up and smiled hesitantly.

"Hi," he said, suddenly feeling shy at the sight of her.

"Hi," she said. "I stopped by to help out with some cooking, but your sister was already here."

"That's kind," he said.

"I also have some news," she added.

"Oh?"

Linda looked over at Sovilla, too.

"I got the job," Sovilla went on. "It's at the Amish musuem in town. They were looking for tour guides to show Englishers around, and I'm both Amish and available to work their hours, so . . ."

"What about your daughters?" Linda asked.

"That's the best part." A smile broke over Sovilla's face. "They can come with me. They loved the idea of little Amish girls running around the place. They said it would feel more 'authentic.' Whatever that is."

"So your girls can go to work with you," Johannes said. "That's wonderful! I know Becca was worried."

"I know." Sovilla's expression softened. "But they'll

be right by my side, and I'll be able to make enough to keep body and soul together."

"Without the pressure of getting married," Johannes added.

"Exactly." Sovilla's smile fell. "I lost my husband," she added in explanation to Linda. "He passed away almost a year ago."

"I lost mine, too," Linda replied. "I understand the pressure all too well. Were they trying to foist an older man onto you?"

Sovilla smiled faintly. "Not exactly older . . ."

"They were trying to foist *me* onto her," Johannes said, and Linda stared at him in surprise.

"What? Are you serious?" Linda said.

"It wouldn't work," Sovilla interjected quickly. "He's in love with Lovina, and I'm . . . not ready to get married again just yet."

Sovilla was being tactful, and Johannes appreciated that. The women continued talking, a little more animatedly now that they had this bit of common ground, and Johannes snagged a couple of warm biscuits before he headed out into the sitting room. He just wanted some space to himself to think, and he looked out the window at the wind rustling the leaves of the trees with those first few yellow leaves fringing the green.

"It isn't about just a good man and a good woman," Sovilla was saying from the kitchen. "From my experience of marriage, it simply isn't enough, even if we want it to be."

"A good man can make a good woman plenty miserable if they aren't in love with each other," Linda said. "It's not so easy to be married, and there are things that love will cushion."

"Exactly! Love smooths over a lot . . ."

Both women had more experience in these things than he did, but love couldn't smooth over an Amish-born woman wearing blue jeans, her hair hanging loose, and maybe even wearing makeup. It was hard to imagine Lovina dressed like that—but she had. He knew it. What was even worse was imagining some grateful, kind, decent Englisher marrying her.

Johannes was supposed to be the one to make her happy.

Johannes heard the side door open, and the sound of children's voices filled the kitchen. The little girls were chattering about a squirrel in the tree, and something fell, and then everyone laughed. Life was carrying on.

He was an Amish man who just wanted to live an honorable, Plain life. Just as long as no one asked him to marry another woman who wasn't Lovina. He couldn't do it.

Lovina stood next to the buggy, the horses shifting their weight from one hoof to the other, eager to get moving.

"So, you follow Hudson Road all the way down to the big four-way stop," Isaiah was saying. "Then you take a left and you just keep going. You'll pass this big, red *Englisher* barn, and in front there are three or four big, old tractors that are there all the time. So you keep going past there, and you'll pass the school house on the left, and you keep going . . ."

Lovina listened as her brother gave her the directions to Uncle Mel's farm. It wasn't that complicated, really. Two turns, and that was it. She remembered her uncle's farm, just not how to get there from her brother's new home.

"Are you sure you don't want me to take you?" Isaiah asked. "I'd be happy to do it."

He'd asked that twice already, and she could see the worry shining in her older brother's stare. He wanted to help—they all did.

"No, I want to go alone," Lovina said. "I need to talk to *Daet* by myself."

Isaiah nodded. "I think we've all done that—gotten our talk with *Daet*."

The last time she'd seen her father was around the kitchen table when she'd confessed her *Englisher* memories and he'd lied to her. He'd told her that she was remembering some brief defiance, but he'd known it was a whole lot more than that.

"I suppose it's my turn, then," she said. "I have a lot to say."

"I hope you hear him out, too," Isaiah said.

"I'm not interested in excuses," she retorted.

"You've got to make your peace with him," Isaiah replied, his voice still low. "And I daresay he needs to make his peace with you, too."

"What did I do?" she demanded. "I'm not the one who defrauded our own community! I'm not the one who lied to his daughter about her own memories!"

"You *left*," Isaiah said, and she felt her face heat. *Yah*, she'd done that . . . and she was planning on doing it again. "Look, I'm not saying anyone is mad at you, it's just that he might need to understand what you were thinking, too. We might have our problems, but we're still a family, and families owe each other explanations."

Maybe she did owe her father some explanations. And she'd have to offer a few more before she left Bountiful a second time. They wouldn't agree, but at least they'd know why.

"Did talking to Daet about the fraud and all that help you?" Lovina asked.

"*Yah*." Isaiah nodded. "It did. It didn't fix everything, obviously, but it helped. He's still our father, Lovina."

Making peace wasn't why she was so intent on speaking to her father today, though. It was because of him that she couldn't have the man she loved, and the memory of Johannes's tender gaze brought tears to her eyes. Her chance at a proper Amish life was forever tainted because of his mistakes, and she needed to tell him that to his face.

And then she'd go back to her job with the Maitlands, because at least there, she could hold her head up.

Lovina pulled herself up into the buggy and took the reins, swallowing the lump in her throat.

"Lovina—" Isaiah said.

She looked back toward her brother. "*Yah*?"

"You and I can talk, too, you know. If I've made your life harder and you need to let me know about it, or if you just need to vent and figure things out . . ." Isaiah smiled hesitantly. "I'm your brother. That's what I'm here for, right?"

"I'm fine," she said, and she blinked back the tears that kept threatening to fall. "It'll help to talk to Daet, I'm sure."

Her brother nodded and stepped back. "Okay. Drive safely."

Lovina flicked the reins, and the horses started forward.

Mel's farm was recognizable from a distance, and when she turned the buggy into the drive, she had to lean forward when she spotted a white van parked beside the stable. The side of vehicle had the letters "CTW." A man was loading what looked like a handheld video camera into the back of the vehicle, and a woman in a red pantsuit held a hand out toward Abe Yoder to shake. She recognized the woman from TV.

The reporter had found their *daet* . . .

Her heart stuttered as it caught up again. Her father shook the woman's hand, smiled, nodded, and looked up as she reined in the horses. The reporter looked up, too, her eyes shining with new interest at the sight of her.

"No!" Abe's voice carried. "Not her!"

The woman looked disappointed, but she gave a nod and thanked Abe again for his time. Lovina watched as she got into the passenger side of the van, and it backed up, did a three-point turn, and headed up the drive, but the woman leaned forward to get another look at Lovina on their way past. Lovina watched it go, then tied off the reins and jumped down to the ground.

Her emotions had been in turmoil ever since she and Johannes had confessed their feelings for each other, but right now all the rest was buried in a flood of anger.

"You did a TV interview?" she demanded, her voice shaking. She crossed the scrub grass toward her father, stopping front of him.

"*Yah,*" he replied, giving her a funny look. "I didn't see the harm."

Lovina felt the tears prickling her eyes again, and she shook her head in disbelief. "You didn't see the harm? Daet, what were you thinking? I saw the first interview from Erindale—and they're making a spectacle of us!"

"They're making a spectacle of me," he replied quietly.

"You!" Lovina dashed a tear from her cheek. "And your name has nothing to do with the rest of us?"

Uncle Mel stood in the doorway of the farmhouse, his face like a storm cloud, but when he saw Lovina, he softened somewhat.

"You aren't the only one upset about this," Abe said. "Come on. Let's talk."

Her father turned and headed across the yard, and Lovina looked back at the house where her uncle stood, and then toward her father's retreating back. He walked with such confidence—and she remembered that about him. He'd always been so sure of himself, of his way of seeing things. And she'd always believed that was because he was right. But he'd proved himself more than wrong.

"Hello, Lovina," Mel called. "Go on—I'll get Seth to take care of the horses."

"Thanks, Uncle Mel," she said, and without another backward glance, she headed after her *daet.*

Her father stopped at the fence, opened the gate, and waited for her there. When she reached him, he gestured her through and then locked the gate after them both. He continued walking toward the pasture, and she fell into step beside him.

"You drove alone," her father said. "And you know your uncle. You must have some more memory back."

"*Yah*, I do," she said curtly.

Her father slowed, and then stopped. He turned toward her.

"Then what do you want to know?" he asked, his voice low.

"Why did you do it?" she demanded.

"The fraud?" he asked. "Or the interview?"

"Let's start with the fraud," she said.

"Anger. Pettiness. Vengeance." He dropped his gaze. "It was wrong, of course. But I was so angry still. Your *mamm* was sick with cancer, and the community just stopped giving to help with her treatment. And she died, and I . . . I held on to that. So when I was brought into this fraud scheme—at first I had no idea it was fraud. I thought it was legitimate. When I figured out it wasn't, they threatened to blame your brother for it, and . . ." He sighed. "I could have gone to the authorities, but there was the anger inside of me still. These were the people who had turned me down for more money to help your *mamm*." He stopped talking, looking at her sadly. "I'm sorry, Lovina. It was selfish. I was thinking only of my own righteous anger, and I was foolish enough to think that we'd never be caught."

Lovina stared at him mutely. This was the strong, confident Daet who'd taught them that right was right and wrong was wrong? This was the man who'd preached so powerfully about the Plain life and the narrow path?

"*Righteous* anger?" she said. "You were a common thief!"

Her father licked his lips. "One day, you'll get married, and perhaps you'll understand a love like that."

"Get married . . ." Tears misted her eyes. No, she couldn't marry the man who filled her heart. "Do you think that's even possible for me now?"

"Your brother managed it," he replied. "Elizabeth's wedding is coming up, too—"

"I'm not them!" she snapped. "It's a little more complicated for me, Daet! I'm in love with a man whose life will be ruined if I marry him!"

Her father sucked in a slow breath. "I went after you. As soon as I came back, I headed back out to find you. I walked streets, I asked anyone who would listen to me. I know I've made mistakes, Lovina, but I did come after you. And I hope that counts for something in your heart."

It did . . . That was the complicating factor. Her *daet* had ruined their lives, and yet his love still mattered to her.

"You ruined my life, Daet," she said, her voice trembling. "You ruined our good family name. You make it so that anyone who knows us looks at us as different now. Even Johannes! Did you know that? Even *Johannes* saw something different when he looked at me!"

"That boy loves you—" her father replied.

"He does," she said, her voice tight. "He loves me. But if he were to marry me, he'd have to give up the community's good opinion. They want him to be a deacon, but it won't happen if he's with me. Do you see what you've done? You've made me into the liability a man has to take on if he chooses me as his wife!"

"You are not a liability!" her father snapped. "You're a beautiful young woman with a brain and a heart . . . You're like your *mamm*!"

"For all the good it will do me now!" she shot back.

Her father fell silent, and in the distance, Lovina heard

the sound of the goats bleating from the barn. Did any of this matter? Daet wasn't questioning her at all, but somehow she wanted to explain herself all the same.

"I left Bountiful last year because I loved him," Lovina said, her voice trembling. "I loved Johannes with all of my heart, and I will not be the woman who holds him back from the life he deserves. And he loves me still, but nothing has changed, has it? Here you are, giving interviews to *Englisher* TV crews as if what you did hasn't gutted your entire family!"

"You think I don't know that?" her father demanded. "I know what I did! I know what it cost all of you! I have done nothing but beg Gott for forgiveness and plead with him to work even this mess out for good! Do you think I'm trying to draw attention to myself? I've been to jail, Lovina! There is no pride in that, only shame. And when the Englishers come asking questions, it's with judgment, I assure you."

"Then why even talk to them?" she snapped. "Why not just say no and send them away?"

"Because while you say that this last year hasn't changed anything," her father said, reaching out and taking her by the shoulders, "I disagree! This last year has changed a good many things. My sins have been found out—truc. I can't pretend to be any better than I really am! But there are other people out there with hidden sins and secret shame, and the Gott who can forgive a man like me is waiting for them, too. So maybe my story is shameful, my girl. Maybe it's embarrassing! But we're assured in the Bible that Gott works out all things for our good, so maybe Gott sent that reporter to find me for a *reason*. Maybe there are people who need to hear that even the miserable, embarrassing wretches get a second chance with Gott."

Lovina swallowed hard, her arguments drained out of her. Her father dropped his hands, and for a moment, they just looked at each other.

"Maybe," she whispered.

"You want to run away again, don't you?" her father asked softly.

Lovina startled.

"I can see it in your eyes," he added. "It's that spooked look, like when an animal is cornered and it wants to bolt."

Lovina smiled weakly. "Daet, I don't have a future here."

"What about Johannes?" her father asked.

"I already told you—I'm not going to be able to be the wife who makes his life better. I'd be the wife he took on as a charitable gesture! I can't be that woman. At least in Erindale, I have people who need me. I make their lives better for the work I do."

"And you think you don't make Johannes's life better?" her father asked.

She was silent.

"Let me tell you something," he said. "In prison, I was terrified. I had this cloud of guilt that wouldn't lift, and I couldn't hear Gott's voice in there. It was like . . . He just went silent. And I was terrified all the time. The men there are dangerous, and they liked to make fun of the Amish man who ended up with the likes of them."

Lovina's eyes misted, and she held her breath.

"In prison, different things are valuable," he said. "Men use cigarettes instead of dollars. And there's drugs, too, and bootleg liquor, and . . ." He let out a shuddering sigh. "I was given a cell mate, and he was muscular and massive—the type of man who fought hard—and you'd think he didn't have any human feeling at all. He was covered in these blue tattoos that snaked all over his arms and back and chest . . . Even his eyelids had tattoos on them! He was what you'd imagine the devil to look like. But late at night, he would ask me questions, and it turned out that he'd lost the woman he loved, too. And he'd loved her deeply. He had some *kinner* who had written him off completely—wouldn't even acknowledge his existence. He's in prison for the rest of his life. He'll never see freedom."

"What had he done?" she whispered.

"Killed several men," her father replied. "But that isn't what mattered. That big bull of a man gave me something I couldn't put a price on. He was *my friend*. He understood me. And no one else did—they all thought that I was nothing more than a religious hypocrite. I wasn't like any of them, and I daresay I wasn't like my cell mate, either, but somehow we connected on a human level, and our friendship became something incredibly valuable to both of us. I've been sending him letters since I got out. Something as simple as a letter can mean the world to someone in prison."

Lovina didn't know what to say. She just looked at her father, her heart in her throat.

"Now I've shocked you," he said, and he smiled gently. "Lovina, I'm sorry. My point is that what you bring to a man's life isn't measured by dollars or cigarettes, or even influence in the community. It's here." He thumped his chest. "If you understand Johannes, and you love him, and when he lays in bed at night he can open up his heart to you and tell you what he's thinking and feeling"—her father shrugged and let out a long breath—"that's what matters. That's what counts most of all."

"I'm not sure Johannes will see it that way," she said.

"Then you need to find a man who does," her father said somberly. "The wedding vows are for good times and bad, for better or for worse. And the marriages that stay strong through the tough times are the ones where the husband and wife love each other so much that they don't care if they're wealthy or poor, sick or well, accepted or rejected by the community around them, so long as they're together. Your *mamm* was that kind of wife. My cell mate had that kind of woman, too, a long time ago. That's the woman who lodges in your heart, and you never quite get over her . . ."

Lovina's heart pounded in her ears. Was it possible that just loving Johannes and standing by him could be everything he wanted? Was there a possibility that her love was enough, that their love for each other could create a union so strong that they'd never regret a moment of it?

Or had things changed too much for that?

"—Lovina?"

She hadn't been listening, and she looked at her father again to find him watching her with a worried look on his face.

"Sorry, Daet, I was thinking . . ."

"Can I just say this?" her father asked gently. "There is no promise of good times in a marriage. There's just a promise to stick together no matter what. And it really is beautiful, if you give it a chance. Do you love him enough to weather all the storms?"

"*Yah,*" she said, and tears welled in her eyes. "I just don't want to be the reason that he has to weather them!"

"Lovina, storms come." Her father met her gaze earnestly. "Storms don't care about pureness of heart or your best intentions. Storms are bigger than you can ever imagine, and they involve powers of good and evil larger than you can comprehend. You can't stop them, my dear girl. I daresay you can't even run far enough to get out of their way! It's who you want next to you when they hit that's the question."

Lovina was silent, and her heart felt like it was melting into her chest. Johannes . . . She loved him so desperately . . .

"Talk to him," her father said. "I don't know what he's thinking. All I know is that you can't just run off again. You broke a lot of hearts when you did that a year ago."

Lovina nodded. She would have to . . . because a possibility was rising in her mind, and it included a life with Johannes right here in Bountiful. If her love might be enough, after all . . .

Chapter Eighteen

Johannes stopped at the mudroom sink to wash his hands, and he took his time, rubbing the thick bar of soap between his rough hands until he'd achieved a rich lather. The soap turned gray, and he rinsed off, then lathered up again.

It was a regular day of working on the farm, but it had felt like the longest day of his life. His heart wasn't in the work, and all he could think about was Lovina's up-turned face, the sadness in her eyes, the way his heart had torn like a tendon when she'd turned away from him.

The kitchen was busy, and as Johannes came into the room, he nodded at Bernard, who stood at the stove, hovering over the oven. The smell of roasting meat told Johannes that Bernard was pitching in for this meal. The counter was covered with various baked goods—buns, loaves of bread, muffins, even a brown bag apple pie.

Linda sat at the kitchen table next to Daniel, and together they were working on the backing of that quilt.

"Hungry?" Linda asked, looking up.

"Uh—not terribly," he replied.

She rolled her eyes. "I don't believe you. Besides, I've

been baking. When Daniel and I go home, you'll be set up for a couple of weeks."

"You're taking him home?" Johannes asked.

"Well . . . *yah*," Linda smiled. "Are you going to miss your nephew?"

"Of course," Johannes said. "It's been fun getting to know Daniel now as a young man."

Daniel smiled. "It's been fun here. And this is my best quilt work so far . . ." He turned the corner of the quilt to see the front, then continued with his stitching.

Linda pricked her finger with her needle and winced, popping her finger into her mouth.

"Daniel, I'm sorry I put so much pressure on you about these quilts," Johannes said quietly. "You and your *mamm* have found a way to make it work. I was just . . . worried about you, I suppose."

"Because it hurts when a girl doesn't want what you've got to offer," Daniel said quietly, and he looked up to meet Johannes's gaze. Had they been talking about him while he was out? Very likely—that's what family did when they cared.

"*Yah*," Johannes said. "Exactly. Sometimes your family tries to protect you, and we might come across a little more roughly than we meant to . . ."

"It's okay," Daniel replied.

"Good." Johannes nodded. He didn't want his nephew having harsh memories of this stay.

"We'll be back for Sol's wedding, Daniel," Linda said.

"Will we really come for it?" Daniel asked.

Linda looked up. "I think we should. Solomon is getting married and settling in, and I think he could use some family support."

"It'll be a small wedding," Bernard said. "But I'm happy for the two of them."

"What is Sol like now?" Linda asked, turning to Johannes. "I heard that jail time really changed him. He's . . . not the same."

"*Yah*, that's the truth," Johannes agreed. "But he also grew up a lot. He's not the Sol we remember, that's for sure and certain. He's tougher. Harder. But he's a good man under it all. And I'm glad he and Elizabeth found each other, because she's probably the only woman who'll really understand him."

Linda cut her own thread, and then they turned over the quilt. For a moment, they all looked down at it in silence. The colors of the sky, the hills, that winding road with the buggy—it was truly extraordinary.

"That's well done, Daniel," Johannes said, impressed.

"Thank you." Daniel's face reddened. "How much will we make, Mamm?"

"I don't know," she murmured. "We'll have to wait and see."

No one in Bountiful had seen a quilt quite like this one, though—Johannes could almost guarantee it.

"I'm going to be like Uncle Sol," Daniel said, breaking the silence.

Everyone turned to stare at him, and Johannes couldn't help the "What?" that escaped his lips.

"Not the jail part," Daniel said. "Or jumping the fence."

"Thank Gott for small mercies," Linda murmured. "Son, we all love Sol, but he's not exactly the one to imitate."

"You haven't seen him, Mamm," Daniel said. "I'm going to be strong like him. He's got muscles, and he showed me the stuff he lifts to make him strong like that, too. He's . . . Mamm, he's huge!"

"Oh . . ." Linda laughed uncomfortably. "Son, we Amish don't work on our physical appearance like that. We're neat and clean, and we work hard, but that kind of vanity is really—"

"No one will call me girlie if I'm big and tough like Uncle Sol," Daniel interjected. "I've been thinking about it, and everyone is worried what people will think about me if I'm a good quilter. But look at Sol! Even the Englishers step carefully around him. He's tough."

"*Yah*, but—" Linda began.

"I see the point," Bernard said with a knowing nod. "Linda, it's not about vanity, it's about Daniel finding his path to manhood. I think I understand."

"I think the girls would be happy to marry me if I looked like that," Daniel said with a grin.

"It won't be easy to get bulked up like that," Johannes said with a half smile. "And that won't be traditionally Amish."

"I know," Daniel replied, shooting Johannes an arch look. "But no one will be able to say I'm not man enough, will they?"

Johannes shrugged. "No, you're right. They won't."

His nephew had found a third option that Johannes hadn't even thought of, and he was impressed with his nephew for having seen it. Daniel wanted to quilt, and he'd found a rather interesting solution that Johannes had to admit had a possibility of working.

"So you're just going to start lifting stuff?" Johannes asked.

"*Yah*," Daniel replied. "It's about the repetitions, Sol

says. It's not lifting stuff that's too heavy, but doing it over and over again. That's what builds muscle."

Johannes exchanged a look with his sister, and she rolled her eyes. She didn't seem to be taking this too seriously, but Johannes had a feeling Daniel was completely serious. He knew what he wanted.

Was there another option for Johannes, too? He'd been looking at this one way—did *she* want an Amish life with him? But the thing holding her back was her certainty that she'd only make his life worse, and she didn't want to be that woman.

Lovina wanted to bring something to the table . . . He'd handed her his heart, and it hadn't been quite enough. Now he needed to give her some certainty. And there just might be a third way to do that.

Lovina watched as Elizabeth ran a hand over her finished wedding quilt. Elizabeth's eyes glowed with happiness as she fingered the finished edges.

"Thank you for helping me finish it," Elizabeth said.

"Of course we'd help you," Bethany said with a smile. She had Mo on one hip, and she kissed his baby curls tenderly. "Sol wants to display it in the eck, right?"

"*Yah*, that's the plan," Elizabeth said. "I was half afraid it wouldn't be finished in time."

"As if we'd let that happen!" Bethany said with a laugh.

Lovina moved over to the window. The sun was setting, and the shadows were long. Isaiah was in the sitting room with the *Budget*. Her visit with her father had left her with a haunted feeling . . .

When had an *Englisher* life become simpler and safer

than an Amish one? Because in the Maitland household, no one had stories of prison. No one had deep regrets from life-altering mistakes. They were just people, living their lives, doing their best, and the worst that came out of them was a harsh word they might have to apologize for.

The Yoder family had significantly more regrets in their midst. Her gaze trailed after a cat that sauntered across the grass, tail held high.

"Lovina?" Elizabeth said. "Are you okay?"

Lovina looked over to find her sister and Bethany watching her warily.

"*Yah*," Lovina said.

"He's still our father," Elizabeth said.

"I know," Lovina said. But her melancholy tonight wasn't just about her *daet* and the state of their family. It was about Johannes, because she was losing him all over again. Her father had given her some hope that maybe a future with him might be possible, but when she'd gotten home again, she'd felt foolish for even thinking it.

"Lovina, why don't we make some cookies tonight?" Bethany said.

They were trying to distract her from her own thoughts, and they meant well, but baking wasn't going to fix any of this.

"I think I'll go for a walk," Lovina said. Without waiting for a reply, she headed for the door and pushed her way outside before either woman could suggest otherwise.

The evening was warm, and the breeze carried the scent of freshly cut grass. A pile of grass clippings had been left next to the garden, and Lovina sucked in a wavering breath. She bent down to pet the cat that rubbed up against her legs.

What am I supposed to do? she prayed. *If I stay here and love Johannes, am I only making things worse? Was that accident meant to free him from loving me?*

She heard the buggy before it turned into the drive, but when the driver came into view she recognized Johannes right away, and her heart skipped a beat. Would she always love him like this, or would it get easier?

He pulled up the horses a few paces away and tied off the reins. Lovina stood there, watching him.

"Did you come for the eck?" Lovina asked, her throat tight.

"No, I didn't come for the eck," Johannes said, and he crossed the gravel drive and stopped in front of her. "I came for you."

He met her gaze easily enough, but he didn't move to touch her, or to kiss her. Maybe he was already pulling away. He took a smart phone out from under his suspender and passed it to her.

"What's this?" she asked.

"I told you about those receipts that the cheese factory sends," Johannes said. "And I'll need to get at them."

Right. He was here for technical help. Lovina took the phone and pressed the button that brought the screen to life.

"What's the passcode?" she asked.

"We just used one, two, three, four," he replied. "Seemed simplest."

"That's the first thing anyone guesses," she said, and she typed it and got to the main screen. "You'll have to change it."

She pulled up various menus. She'd found that she

enjoyed this part of the *English* life—gadgets. She found the email icon.

"What's your email address?" she asked.

"It's MillerDairy, but no space between the words, like it all runs together," he said. "And then there is this letter A with a curl that goes around it . . ."

Lovina shot him a rueful smile, but she typed it in as he described.

"And the password?" she asked.

"'Welcome,'" he said.

"Your password is the word 'welcome'?" she said. "Really?"

"My *daet* chose it," he said. "Capital 'W,' though."

"You need more than a word, Johannes," she said. "That is a terrible password. You need to change that later, too. Anyway—" She passed the phone back to him. "That's your inbox and your emails."

There were a few emails there from the service provider. Johannes looked down at the phone, then back up at her. What did he want from her now?

"Thank you," he said softly. "Times change, even for us Amish."

"*Yah* . . ." She longed to reach out and touch him, to feel the roughness of his hands on hers . . .

"And you can't go backward," Johannes said quietly. "It's straight ahead, or nothing."

"I know . . ." Her voice caught.

"Lovina, my life isn't going to go backward, either. It's not ever going to be like I never met you, never loved you. There's no going back! And you think that if you leave, I'll return to some innocent state? It won't happen! Even our community is changing—the farmers are getting cell phones, and we're now talking about how to protect our community from various frauds . . . But you've got some skills we need around here, and they aren't the traditional ones—that's true. But at the moment, having someone who knows her way around one of these contraptions is more useful than you'd think."

He held up the cell phone and waggled it between his fingers.

"Also, I love you," Johannes added.

"I love you, too," she breathed.

"Lovina . . ." He caught her hand and tugged her closer. "I've been doing a lot of thinking, and I need you to hear me out before you turn me down. Can you do that?"

Lovina didn't answer, and he seemed to take that for agreement, because he continued, "You're afraid that if you stay with me, you won't bring the same things to the relationship that you did before. But whether or not you stay here, whether or not you stay with me, Bountiful has changed. We'll all have to get used to this new idea of normal that includes cell phones and fraud protections, and . . ." He let out a pent-up breath. "Lovina, you're not going to bring all the traditional things to an Amish relationship anymore."

She winced at the truth of those words.

"But you bring other skills—like your affinity for gadgets," he said with a rueful smile. "Imagine being grateful for an Amish woman who can find your email!"

"Is that enough?" she whispered. For an Amish community, for a man who wanted respect, a wife with a strange skill set and a tarnished family . . .

"Lovina, you'd just be here. Okay?" The smile dropped

from his face and he tugged her closer so that she had to tip her face up toward him. "You'd be with me! You have no idea the kind of wreck I was this last year without you. The community tried to get me married to someone else to try and fix me—I was that bad! But I couldn't forget you, or get over you. So if you'd stay, and you'd be *mine*, I'd be the most grateful man in Bountiful. And if you leave, you'll still be in here." He thumped his chest. "There's no going back. I'm already ruined for anyone else, Lovina. It's too late."

Tears misted Lovina's eyes, and she could feel Johannes's strong grip tighten.

"What about being deacon?" she asked faintly. "That mattered to you."

"I don't need to be deacon, I just need you to love me—"

His voice caught, and she looked up into his pleading eyes. He needed her to love him . . . as if she could stop!

"I do love you!" she whispered.

Johannes's lips came down over hers, and he pulled her in close. She could feel the pounding of his heart through his strong chest, and she melted there in his arms. His lips moved over hers, and his arms tightened around her until she could hardly breathe. She missed this—his touch, his warmth, the smell of him . . . When he pulled back and loosened his hold on her, he touched his forehead against hers.

"What do we do, then?" she asked softly.

"We get married," he said. The words were so matter-of-fact that she almost laughed, and she looked up into his face, trying to read his emotions.

"Just like that?" she asked.

"*Yah*." He looked down at her seriously. "Unless you had a better idea that keeps us together for the rest of our lives, because that's the only thing that's going to make *me* happy."

He brushed a wisp of hair away from her forehead and looked into her face hopefully.

Getting married—promising her life to this man for better or for worse, whatever life might throw at them . . . Waking up to Johannes, cooking his meals, sewing his shirts, helping him with his newfangled cell phone, getting him set up with some proper passwords . . . and loving him with every ounce of her being . . .

"What do you say?" he murmured. "Will you marry me, Lovina?"

Her heart flooded with a love so strong that there was only one answer possible.

"*Yah*," she said. "I will."

Johannes kissed her again, and this time his kiss was slow and deep, and he didn't stop until there was a sound behind them at the house. He pulled back, and Lovina turned to see her sister standing on the porch, Bethany next to her, with Mo in his mother's arms.

"Tell me that's an engagement!" Elizabeth called. Her tone was hopeful, but it also held a hint of warning. They were overstepping every proper boundary.

Lovina looked up at Johannes, and they shared a sparkling smile.

"*Yah*!" Lovina called back. "We're getting married!"

Elizabeth let out a whoop of happiness that was entirely unbecoming to an Amish woman about to be wed herself, and she ran down the steps toward them. Isaiah came outside then, looking confused, and the news was repeated for his benefit.

"Lovina," Elizabeth said. "I know this is a crazy idea, but if Sol was okay with it . . . what would you think about a double wedding next week?"

Lovina looked back at Johannes, and he just shrugged. "Name the date and time to marry you, and I'll vow to be yours. I got what I wanted."

Was she getting her wedding after all? Strange how a hit-and-run accident on a street in Erindale could bring her home to the man she'd done her best to forget. What had her *daet* said about those storms a girl couldn't outrun? Perhaps Gott had been in those details after all.

"If Sol's okay with it," Lovina said, "yah! I'd love a double wedding with my sister!"

There would be no wedding quilt for Lovina—there was no time. There would be very few guests on their side of things, and there would be a good many rumors, but right now she didn't care a bit about any of it. She'd marry Johannes Miller, and she'd sew their quilt later on in the pockets of time between cooking and cleaning and caring for her new home.

It would be a marriage quilt—not a wedding quilt— and maybe that was appropriate. It was about the marriage anyway, wasn't it—the years, the relationship, the dedication? It was about one day after another with the man she loved.

Chapter Nineteen

Johannes stood in the back of the busy little gift shop at the Amish Farmhouse Museum, his arms crossed over his chest. Tomorrow, they'd get married, and while it had only been a week since he'd proposed, it had been over a year that he'd waited for this second chance, and he was anxious to finally take his vows.

He and Lovina had come to town to do some shopping before the wedding. Lovina had already picked up some dishes, a new roasting pan, and two fresh sets of sheets for their bed. She'd wanted to stop in at this little Amish-run tourist shop because she wanted a quilt for their wedding night.

"We have quilts," he'd told her gently. "All sorts of them. Does it matter so much? It's a rushed wedding— we'll have to let some things go."

For himself, he didn't really care about any of the details. He'd wear appropriate clothing, and he'd make sure the house was clean and tidy for when Lovina moved in. The rest he figured they'd sort out as they went along. What did he care about a quilt, as long as his new bride was in his bed next to him?

"It *does* matter!" she'd said earnestly. "I'll sew one myself after the wedding, but for the start of our marriage, we need a new one. Even if we buy it. Please, Johannes."

And how could he refuse her anything? So they'd put their other purchases into the back of the buggy, and they'd come into this shop for Lovina to choose a quilt sewn by the women in this community.

There were a few to choose from, all hung along one wall. They varied in price, and Lovina stood in front of one particular quilt that was a combination of purples and cream. She fingered the edge of the quilt, turned it over to examine the back, and then stood back to look at it again.

Daniel's quilt hung on the wall behind the register. Bernard had brought the quilt to the shop and talked with the owner of the museum, Bernice Sutter, about selling it. It had all stayed very mysterious. The price on the lower corner of the quilt was jaw-dropping, in Johannes's opinion: two thousand dollars. But the quilt itself was stunning, even more impressive hung up on the wall than it had been spread out in his own sitting room.

Three Englishers stood closer to the quilt, a couple and another older woman standing a little bit apart from them. Johannes could overhear their discussion.

"Who made it?" the man asked, leaning closer and adjusting his glasses. The woman next to him—his wife?— stood quietly, her hands folded behind her back.

"I don't even know the answer to that," Bernice said. "I can guarantee it is made by an Amish family, but beyond that, they don't want to be known."

"Why?" the man inquired.

Bernice just shook her head. Bernard hadn't told her much, and that had been on purpose. Right now, the less anyone knew, the better for Daniel. Johannes still felt protective of that boy, too. He might think he knew how to navigate all of life's complexity, but he didn't. That was why Gott provided older relatives.

"It's incredible work," the man said to the quiet woman at his side. "Just incredible. What do you think, dear?"

"It's wonderful," his wife said. "I've never seen anything like it. I can only imagine what the Zimmermans would say. You know Anita . . ."

"I'm definitely interested," the man said to Bernice. "The price is a little high, though."

So the haggling would begin, and Johannes wondered how much money the quilt would fetch at the end of it all.

"I'll buy it," the other English woman interjected.

"Oh!" Bernice smiled. "Well, that's wonderful. We accept cash and credit—no personal checks—"

"I said I was interested," the man said curtly.

"Yes, but I'll pay the full price," the woman said, opening her purse.

"I'll offer twenty-two hundred," the man said, turning to Bernice.

"Twenty-five," the woman retorted.

"Twenty-seven." The man's voice grew terse.

"Three thousand dollars," the woman said curtly. "And not a penny more."

"Good." The man smiled, then glanced down at his wife. "We're agreed, dear?" When his wife nodded, he said, "Three thousand one hundred is my final offer. I'll take the quilt."

The older woman looked deflated, but she did cast the man's wife a conciliatory smile.

"Enjoy it. It's beautiful," she said. "Bernice, dear, tell me if another quilt by this family comes into the shop, would you?"

"Of course," Bernice said. "You can count on it."

Johannes looked around the shop, and his gaze caught Lovina's. She'd obviously seen the same thing he had, because she mouthed, "Wow!" at him, and he grinned back. His sister would be just fine. He couldn't wait to write her a letter telling her exactly what he'd seen. He made his way over to where Lovina stood.

"Three thousand one hundred," Lovina whispered.

Johannes didn't know what to say. It had started out as a few scraps stitched together by a teenage boy in the hayloft . . . and look at it now!

"What about you?" Johannes asked. "Have you chosen yet?"

"This one." She looked up at the quilt she'd been eyeing. "It will be perfect."

Johannes looked down at her and smiled.

"We'll have to wait until Bernice is finished with that sale," Johannes said.

"*Yah,*" Lovina agreed, and she leaned against his arm in a way that made him wish they were alone and he could pull her into his arms . . . One more day, and they'd have plenty of privacy at long last!

At the far side of the store, next to the outside door, there was a sign that read "Tours," and a few Englishers were standing there. The bell over the front door tinkled, and another *Englisher* family came inside and took up their place next to the sign. Johannes heard Becca and Iris chattering before he saw Sovilla, and the little girls came scampering into the shop, smiles on their faces.

"Time to start work!" Becca announced triumphantly in Pennsylvania Dutch, so the Englishers didn't understand her, but they did smile at the little Amish girls dressed in matching pink dresses.

Sovilla emerged after them, and she paused when she saw Johannes and Lovina.

"Hello!" she said, coming over and giving Lovina a squeeze and Johannes a smile. "Congratulations, you two. I'm looking forward to the wedding tomorrow."

"Us, too," Lovina said with a breathy laugh. "I can't believe it's actually happening."

"I can," Sovilla said. "And I couldn't be happier for you both."

"So you've got a tour to give?" Johannes guessed, nodding toward the waiting Englishers, who were now all watching them in open curiosity.

"*Yah*," she said. "It's fun, actually. My girls love it! They take it so seriously. Two tiny professionals."

"What's next for you, Sovilla?" Lovina asked, lowering her voice.

"You mean, will I get married again?" Sovilla asked.

"*Yah* . . ." Lovina shrugged. "We might know some eligible bachelors . . ."

"No, no," Sovilla said. "I've got a job now, and I'm not looking for a husband right away. If Gott wants to send one, He'll have to throw him in my path and make me trip over him."

Johannes chuckled at that. "Don't tempt Gott, Sovilla. You might get what you joked about."

Sovilla laughed. "I'd better go start the tour."

Sovilla headed over toward the Englishers, and at the same time, Bernice handed Daniel's quilt, all wrapped in brown paper, to the *Englisher* couple, their transaction completed. Then Bernice came over to where they stood, wreathed in smiles.

"Johannes! Lovina! Congratulations on your happy news!" Bernice said. "Now, what can I do for you?"

It was just a quilt—made by other hands—but as Johannes watched Bernice climb a stepladder and take it down from where it hung on the wall, he felt in a rush that everything was about to change yet again.

This quilt would be placed on their bed. It would be flung back in the mornings and smoothed down again when they made the bed. It would hold in the warmth as they pulled each other close during cold winter nights, and it would keep their secrets that they whispered to each other in those sacred hours. This quilt would be washed in the wringer washer on Lovina's housework schedule, and it would flutter in the wind on the clothes-line in cool spring breezes.

It was all really starting, wasn't it? Everything was changing all over again, and this time, he was nothing but grateful.

"Johannes?" Lovina said softly.

The quilt was already down, and Bernice looked at him expectantly.

"Thank you, Bernice," Johannes said. "Let me pay for it."

Tomorrow night, Lovina would be in his arms under that very quilt, and he already felt like his heart could burst from sheer happiness. Maybe that quilt mattered after all. He caught Lovina's hand and gave it a squeeze. Tomorrow, she'd be his wife.

Epilogue

The double wedding was being held under a big tent on Isaiah and Bethany's land. Enlarging the wedding to include another couple had sent the women into a flurry of activity, but Lovina didn't once feel like she was a burden. Bethany sewed Lovina's wedding dress herself, since she was incredibly good with a needle and thread, and Lovina worked on a crisp new apron. On the morning of her wedding, Lovina and Elizabeth stood in the kitchen, watching as the men set up the benches under the tarp outside.

Two aunts were busy organizing the food on the counter, counting tubs of potato salad and platters of turkey sandwiches. A large urn of coffee was already on the table, and another young woman was mixing a batch of fruit punch to go into a carafe. This wasn't work for the brides, though. They'd work hard enough later on as married women in the community. Today, they could simply focus on the vows they were about to take.

"Can you believe it's happening?" Lovina asked, casting her sister a grin. The men were working quickly, hoisting benches and calling out to each other as they arranged the tent. Even Bishop Lapp and their father were both carrying benches. There wouldn't be many guests, but they all seemed focused on making sure this wedding moved forward without a hitch.

Johannes and Solomon stood to the side together, and Johannes appeared to be fixing a problem with Sol's suspender.

"It feels like a dream, almost," Elizabeth slipped her arm through Lovina's. "But I love him so much, Lovina . . . In a few hours, you and I will both be wives . . ."

"Thank you for sharing your wedding with me," Lovina said softly.

"Lovina, it's perfect!" Elizabeth said. "I mean that. Getting you and Johannes together at long last is almost as exciting as my own wedding." Elizabeth gave Lovina's arm a squeeze. "Almost."

Outside, the Maitlands' minivan rumbled to a stop, and Lovina felt a rush of happiness.

"Carrie's here!" she said, and she headed for the side door.

Gordon and Aline worked together to get Carrie's chair set up and then to settle her into it. They were all dressed up for the occasion—Gordon in a suit and Aline in a blue lace dress. Carrie, however, was wearing the pink dress that Lovina was supposed to wear as one of her sister's attendants. Lovina had sent it with a courier along with the wedding invitation, just in case the Maitlands could make it.

"You look wonderful, Carrie," Lovina said, leaning down and giving her a hug.

"You won't be coming back, will you?" Carrie asked.

Lovina sobered. "I'm sorry . . . I won't. I'll be married now, and . . . it's different."

Carrie nodded. "The good workers don't last."

"Oh, don't say that!" Lovina said with a laugh. "I'm not dying! And I might not be your support worker anymore, but I am your friend."

Carrie smiled at that. "How good of friends are we?"

"Good enough that you got an invitation to this wedding. Trust me—the guest list is very tight. And right now, Carrie, even if you don't quite feel the same, you're the best friend I've got."

Carrie's eyes misted. "Oh, it's mutual, Lovina."

Across the grass, the last of the benches had been set up, and Bishop Lapp called for the grooms to come speak with him before the ceremony began.

"It's probably time to go get seats," Lovina said. "You'll be in the front row, Carrie. They'll show you where to sit."

Gordon shook Lovina's hand and Aline gave her a quick hug, and then the Maitland family headed toward the house, pushing Carrie's chair through the thick grass, leaving Lovina to have a few moments alone.

A cool breeze with a hint of fall in it whisked through the trees. The leaves had started to change to yellow, and they shivered in the wind. Lovina watched as the bishop spoke quietly with Johannes and Solomon, and then they all bowed their heads.

Thank you for bringing me home, she prayed in her heart. And by "home," she meant all of this—her family, her community, and the one man she'd always love.

Elizabeth came outside then, her own blue wedding dress rippling around her legs as the wind blew her apron strings. Lovina touched her own hair, making sure it was neatly tucked away in spite of the strong breeze, and then went over to her sister's side.

"Ready?" Elizabeth asked.

"Completely," Lovina replied.

And they headed across the grass toward their fiancés. After today, they'd be the Yoder girls no longer.

Everything changed—with seasons, with years, and sometimes with life-changing, miraculous accidents. Gott was in everything—that's what the Amish believed—and today as she fell into step beside Johannes, she couldn't help but feel the truth of those words deep in her heart.

Gott was in everything . . . and Gott had brought her home.